# ABOUT THE AUTHOR

HOWARD LAKIN HAS WRITTEN AND PRODUCED AMERICAN TELEVISION, INCLUDING SUCH ICONIC programs as DALLAS and FALCON CREST, in an entertainment industry career which has spanned three decades. He is also the owner of Lakin & Marley Rare Books, a member of the Antiquarian Booksellers Association of America, which seeks and sells fine Victorian literary first editions and manuscripts. He has a wife, two children, and lives in Northern California.

ISBN-10: 0985908300
EAN-13: 9780985908300
Library of Congress Control Number: 2012944599
DevonBooks, Mill Valley, CA

Cover Art by Robert A. Maguire (kind permission of the Maguire Estate)

First Edition.

Copyright acknowledgement is made to Universal Music Enterprises, owner of Motown Records, for the fair use of partial lyrics from its original compositions "Ain't Nothing Like The Real Thing" (Ashford-Simpson, composers) and "Standing In The Shadows Of Love" (Holland-Dozier-Holland, composers).

# CALIFORNIA NOIR

A NOVEL

HOWARD LAKIN

DevonBooks
San Francisco, California
U.S.A

For Henry M. Lakin

(1926-1961)

*Moi, c'est moralement que j'ai mes élégances*

# PART I

## AUGUST, 2001

*"The past is a foreign country."*

## CHAPTER ONE

WE ARE A SECRET SOCIETY, BUT NOT VERY SECRET AS WE HAVE BEEN MEETING LIKE THIS FOR nineteen years in our noisy and gleeful signature style. But this time it is not just an annual birthday celebration. This year we each turn forty, one by one, all in the same month as always, like tumbling and very crooked dice. Still single, still divorced, still grieving, not an answer among us.

Yet as we gather around this large circular table at a new upscale "East" German waterfront restaurant here in Mill Valley, five miles north of San Francisco, drinks and dinner come undone with the gusto of younger days. The Cold War cuisine is a hit, the servers are well-served by their Soviet Bloc battledress, and lively barbs and banter ricochet rapid-fire. And for a few hours I forget the darkness of my gift and my calling, able to linger with an inner peace which usually lasts no longer than that short silence found in the gap between thunder and lightning.

"C'mon, gang, let's just do it, okay? I'm getting wet from all the excitement!"

Anjuli is revved as usual, her mouth eager with anticipation, her fingers curling and twisting the black ringlets which frame her face. I notice she has accidentally popped the top inch of her zipper, the little zipper on the backside of her favorite size two buttery leather pants. Anjuli, after a White

Russian followed by three or five shots of East German *Schnapps*, is clearly in no hurry to cover up Marin County's most tirelessly advertised derrière.

"First we do dessert. *Then* we do humiliation. Don't mess with the official sacred rules!" Owen's objection is his usual attempt to forestall The Game, because the Secret Society Annual Game is always embarrassing and preposterous, often ending in disaster and chaos. However it also promotes unity, yanks us from complacency, and bonds us even more deeply until our next group birthday so that year after year, although we inevitably continue to disconnect-the-dots when it comes to meaningful and lasting relationships, the Society remains a constant. A family. The Society thrives.

"No. First coffee!" announces Leah. "Kicking butt requires energy." She swivels her gaze, sifting through the throngs of hipsters at similar tables. But caffeine is nowhere to be seen.

"Leah, why do you bother?" Shannon notes matter-of-factly. "You haven't won since, well, the Berlin Wall came down..." Shannon laughs at her little joke, but it's the kind of laugh that automatically doesn't leave laugh lines. She is her usual perfectly groomed self tonight. A former print model before she found her real career, Shannon is our Society's one uptown girl. Her straight-from-work business suit is slim and beautifully tailored but it also draws attention to her too-slender frame; she's obsessive about her weight, a worrisome paradox as she's thin as a rail. Her green eyes have their habitual luster but tonight we can all see Shannon's insomnia is back and that's never good news.

Leah raises an eyebrow. "Hey, this is the brand new millennium. Things are finally going to change. I'm going to be the 2001 champ, bet on it!"

We all exchange glances revealing our serious doubts. Leah's lack of killer instinct, mixed with her strong sense of fair play, makes her the perennial long shot.

Catching the attention of one of the bus boys, easily identified by their "East Berlin Is For Lovers" tee-shirts cheerfully colored black to match the artfully bleak décor and murky if not sinister lighting design, I shout a request.

"Coffee. The real stuff, please…" Then I turn back to Leah, finishing it, "…otherwise there will most definitely be blood on the tracks tonight."

Leah smiles at me, that special dazzling smile which deserves its own Shakespeare sonnet. After all, who else could describe the sudden, blazing sunburst that lights ups her face when she grins? Yes, Leah and I need our coffee. For the night is our hunter. I work the two dangerous hours each side of midnight, she has the grueling midnight to eight shift. Leah handles the gunshots and the car crashes, I get the rest.

"Besides," adds Leah, "I feel lucky tonight."

"You?" Anjuli interjects with icy ridicule. "Not likely. You've got the Midas touch in reverse. *Super* tall, *totally* built, a *genuine-for-real* blonde, *more* money than the Republicans spent winning the election and *still* you couldn't get lucky! Not even on a deserted island filled with men!"

"I didn't say *get* lucky. And if the island's *deserted*, nobody gets lucky."

"Hey, luck is a skill." Anjuli is quick to inform her, ignoring the affront to her vocabulary. "And I've got skills."

Giving Anjuli a weary look, Leah tugs down the creeping hem of her *very* short glittery green retro '80s party dress which, as no one could fail to note, fits her graceful figure like a surgical glove. "So you say…and you say it every fifteen minutes…"

In truth, of all of us, Leah is the one with skills. She directs the late night trauma unit at San Francisco General Hospital. But Leah is not your usual emergency room cutter. She was born soul-drenched and ready to shine. In Boston, where she grew up attending a black church for its gospel choir, she became a regional sensation, a sixteen-year-old white chick with a powerful voice which crossed over into slammin' rhythm and blues. Why she gave up a singing contract in favor of a tray full of scalpels and surgical blades is her deepest secret, one of the few the Society, despite all efforts, still hasn't uprooted.

"You're not gonna win either, Anjuli," snorts Owen. "You couldn't win the lottery even if you were sleeping with the entire state lottery commission."

"And who says I'm not?" Anjuli pouts mischievously, her dramatic red lipstick blatantly calculated for pouting as needed. Anjuli LoPresti, the debatable pride of Sacramento, is fitfully adorable but she is not a girl for the delicate man. Her two rather short marriages left our curly-haired vixen clueless at the shrine of self-knowledge. But the good news is that her "gypsy" palm reader, the one with the thick Brooklyn accent, continues to predict that another hunk of love is just around the corner. So no worries.

"I think it should be pointed out that I've won four of the last five Games," gripes Dylan.

"You cheat, Dylan," replies Shannon calmly. "And we let you cheat to shut you up."

"And you didn't *have* to cheat last year," I add. "Nothing wrong with a three-way tie."

"A three-way? In your dreams!" Dylan's Irish complexion starts to redden on cue. "I won big time and I've got the video to prove it. Special bonus features include Owen throwing his beer cans at me, Anjuli trying to bribe me with sexual favors as if that were something new, Gary switching score pads, and shame on you for recording my harmless little off-color comments and sending everyone a copy!"

We have gotten loud, but this restaurant thrives on noise as evidenced by its endless music loop featuring such coy favorites as "Back In The USSR" mixed with a seamless blend of Soviet Jazz, Soviet Classical, and Soviet May Day marches. The waiter brings the coffee and pours, then takes our dessert orders, chocolate cake and candles all around. Leah uses this brief pause to sharpen her wits as she swaps seats with me and sits next to Dylan with an evil look in her eye.

Last year it was Leah's turn to host the Game, as it is Gary's turn this year. She chose the Game of "Deprivation." Simple rules. Each player announced some experience they'd never had or some item they'd never owned, thereafter receiving a toothpick in return from any player not so deprived. Most toothpicks decided the winner.

In typical Leah fashion, she now goes toe to toe with our beloved cheater. "Dylan, admit it. Last year. Just come clean. You lied at least three times."

"No way!" Dylan is outraged.

"First of all. No sex outdoors, *ever*? You got two toothpicks for that?! C'mon, you've done it behind more redwoods than Anjuli!"

"Hey, Dylan's not even in my league, indoors or out," protests Anjuli. "I buy my condoms at Costco."

Dylan grins. "Sorry, Doctor Foxy. Where's your proof?"

Leah is annoyed, but unwilling to back down. "Okay, you actually swore you'd never driven in a Volkswagen. Yet how is it that Rick co-signed your new car loan after your Bug caught fire back in '92! *And* he's got the papers to prove it. *Four* bogus toothpicks."

Dylan smugly shakes his head. "As I said, correct and for real, my car was made in Mexico! We all know those aren't really Volkswagens, they're knock-offs. So try to live with the disappointment."

Leah, exasperated, finally goes where she doesn't want to go. "Okay, *fine!* And as for claiming you'd never owned a Barry White album, I'd like to know who tried to make me strip to Barry's "It's Ecstasy When You're Laying There Next To Me" during your totally tasteless Hot Tub Game four years ago!"

"You lose. It was *Owen's* scratchy old album. I borrowed it."

"Stole it…" Owen corrects him.

Leah growls. "Dylan, one day your silver tongue is going to get a nasty piercing."

"Hey, you're the cheat. All you stripped off for my fantastically fun Hot Tub Game were your lousy come-kick-me pumps and your little hoop earrings! Admit it, you're pathetic! You deserved to lose that year, too!"

"Bottom line. You got at least six toothpicks by cheating."

"And you deprived the entire Society of the one killer strip tease *everyone* wanted to see!"

"I spotted the video camera you hid above the tub, Dylan. You're lucky to be alive."

"Alive and a three time winner! With a toothpick trophy to prove it!"

Dylan O'Connor, owner and operator of the popular Rubber Duck Pool Supply franchise, is now celebrating his tenth year with the group. With his thick salt-and-pepper hair and vivid blue eyes, his modest height and square build are no impediment as he routinely uses all his fearless charm to win and influence the women he instinctively knows he can bed. Dylan is also the funniest, if least reliable, man I've ever met. He has one switch and it's always on and Leah should know that nothing she says will ever faze him.

Suddenly a dashing, careening shape jolts its way to our table scattering diners and restaurant personnel with equal ferocity. "Okay. I don't want to hear any of the usual crap from you guys…" announces Gary as he finally rejoins us at the table carrying something quite a bit larger than a birthday cake. There are *oohs* and *aahs* as our newest Society member shows off a large two-foot high gold-colored Japanese Pagoda-shaped ornamental box decked out with a number of little red drawers. "…because you're all in for a real good time!"

Instinctively I know hell is about to break loose so I do a quick reconnoiter of the room, finding little evidence of anyone showing interest in us other than a man in his late sixties seated at one of the better water-view tables wearing a flashy silver European-cut suit. He is staring without any attempt to hide his amusement. Well, why not? The circus has come to his town and the clowns are playing the center ring.

"This amazing artifact is a genuine antique Fortune-Telling Box; it's been in my family for generations upon generations," announces Gary, giving his large and striking box-shaped objet d'art a twirl.

"Then what's with the not-so-antique bar-code under here?" Shannon asks. As she stands and points, I observe the way her auburn hair shrouds her face and as usual I'm again reminded of Shannon's slight resemblance to my once-upon-a-time wife Paige, not in build or looks, but in emotional secrecy; Paige kept her feelings buttoned-down in order to gain mastery over life's various hard knocks whereas Shannon's emotional opacity, as now, can never entirely hide her constant neediness to keep all things upsetting and unsettling at arm's length.

"For you disbelievers, this very so-called bar-code…" retorts Gary, putting air quotes around the offending word, "…was placed under this Box as an ingenious form of disguise by my ancestors, the Zen masters of Hiroshima-ken in ancient Japan."

"Mind getting to the point?" Leah asks.

"The point is that this Game is both short and deadly. And it is like nothing you will have experienced before." He turns to favor Leah. "It is not for the impatient skeptic."

Gary abruptly stands taller for effect. His loose Hawaiian shirt and faded blue jeans can't exactly hide his exceptional physique. Dylan originally met Gary at a café across from his gym, a hangout where the soon-to-be forty year old athlete still manages to enjoy the adoring company of women under twenty-five (and lots of them). I like Gary, our resident surfer and skier. He fits in well with our merry band of iconoclasts. And, unlike certain others in our membership, he has clearly given this, his first opportunity to host the official August '61 Secret Society Annual Game, a lot of thought.

Gary begins with a tone of formality. "My Game, and my gift to you, is entirely based on the fact that we're all hopelessly single, all seven of us, on our fortieth birthdays. Yet that dismal statistic is going to change because of this very Game we play tonight."

"Yeah, right." Owen laughs.

"But we love being hopelessly single! It's what we do best," Shannon neatly adds.

However, our Game Master just gives us each a droll individual glare, milking the moment.

"Be foolish. It won't help you. Because, my friends, thanks to *this* Game, one year from this day all seven of us will be married, like it or not…"

# CHAPTER TWO

MARRIAGE SUITED ME. BUT IT ALSO CAUSED ME TERRIBLE INSECURITY, MADE ME QUESTION MY dreams and decisions, led me to feel hollow inside. I was ashamed because everyone around me was making something of themselves. My favorite cousin Gabriel was a rising star in Hollywood, Owen was on the lecture circuit, Shannon was scoring six figures as a print model, and Leah was practicing medicine. But nothing of substance was driving me; there was no direction home, and *every* attempt to figure out who I was and what I was made of left me further from my truth. At thirty years old, I was lost.

My own family was accomplished. Mom was a well-known journalist, Dad was an international lawyer. My older sister was also an attorney, our family tradition. Sure, my parents encouraged me to follow my heart, but they regretted it at the same time and for good reason. I received a degree with honors in Comparative Lit from Cal but stepped off the fast track at Stanford Law School to intern at KHEL radio in Oakland, shocking one and all. There I annoyed everyone by hawking my airchecks incessantly while making a poverty-level wage as one of the Sales Swine. I figured I'd rise through the executive ranks, have my own radio program, be a force in telecommunications. Instead, I had the worst sales list of all the reps, mostly local advertisers who wanted to voice their own spots, which made me unpopular with everyone. Management gave me chance after chance on air. Who knew I wouldn't have the gut instinct, the pipes; who knew I wouldn't have *anything* fresh or meaningful to say?

At that time, Luis Casul was Program Director for our station. He didn't like me much. But at least he was willing to listen to my frustration with moderate compassion unlike the sales manager, the operations manager, or the GM. To be fair, I sucked at what I did; I was an ineffective employee, dead weight kept around only because I was the prodigal son of a potentially litigious family of lawyers. So they simply chose to treat me as if I were invisible. It took me four years of begging but Luis finally gave me one last shot on air, letting me sit in with Righteous Ray Jefferson, our graying blues-fed Oakland home boy who worked the two A.M. slot.

"Try not to give us too much dead air," grunted Luis. We both knew that there was no way I was going to make any kind of measurable impression, especially in the dead zone of late night; that I'd just end up as everyone there saw me: a thirty-year old wannabe stuck in slow rotation going nowhere. Still. This was my chance. My do-or-die four hour shift.

But there was a problem.

My hard-won break coincided with the weekend of the fortieth wedding anniversary of my in-laws, being lavishly celebrated at the Coronado Hotel in San Diego. My father-in-law's private jet had been put at my family's disposal, ready and waiting for me, my parents, my sister, and the twins that night at Oakland Airport. Paige was directed to zoom down to San Diego with her parents in their Aston-Martin. They were a family which just loved speed, in fact her father used to race a Porsche 356 back in the mid-50s and he took great pride in his corporate support of a Formula One team. Paige always did what her Daddy said and so she had packed for the road, entrusting the babies to me.

But I needed my final chance to be somebody, so plans had to change.

I wasn't a liar. All those years with Paige and I never lied once, honesty being my lone if meager point of pride. But I was anxious and so, so hungry for *any* kind of success. Thus I lied with as much conviction as I could muster. I told Paige at the last minute that I had been ordered to work that weekend and that my job was on the line. Of course she saw no value in my job or in my keeping it. Nevertheless I managed to gently guilt her into flying with the twins.

"You really know how to let a girl down…" she responded to the situation dryly, for it wasn't the first time I hadn't matched the bar she set for me. "…I find that *so* extremely attractive in a man." We went for a brief early evening walk in the tall redwoods behind our house and, as I embroidered my apology, I felt small. Paige's response to that was to walk tall. Paige had mastery over disappointment, she had mastery over annoyance; in fact she was above the law in her triumph over runaway feelings of any kind.

I thought of confessing the truth up until the very last second. But as she nosed her car down our languid but precipitous Mill Valley driveway, airport-bound, twins strapped in the back seat, a ruptured mix of self-loathing and fretful urgency kept me silent.

"No big deal," she shouted to me out her car window. But it *was* a big deal as those became her last words to me, irony ever after. She gave me a mock-salute, so much like her father the war-hero, and the three of them disappeared from view.

Later that evening, she took my place on her family jet, settling in her seat beside my mother and father, her witty in-laws. The twins I assume she handed over to my sister as always, my childless sister who loved acting as nanny. My little girls were less than a year old, neither could walk, but they were charming and well-behaved.

KHEL was then a Hot AC (Adult Contemporary) music station and, as I prepared for my late night debut, I still knew I didn't have what it took. At thirty, I was already too old to be starting an on-air career.

The phone call came to me in the middle of the night as I was driving through Richmond on my way to the studio. My father-in-law, normally cool and poised under any circumstance, was out of character as he haltingly confirmed it was me. Then he put on my elitist mother-in-law who, also uncharacteristically, was in pieces.

"You bastard," she howled. "It's your fault, *you useless bastard,*" she keened in her high-pitched, old money accent, this highly rigid and morally upright woman who routinely had herself driven across the Golden Gate Bridge and down Van Ness so she could be seen by all to never miss a night at the Opera. She broke the news to me with fury. Blaming me for not being on the jet where I should have been, for not dying instead of her daughter, this crazed woman seeming to forget my parents, my sister, my twins, in the narcissistic trauma of losing her only child, that forever extension of herself.

Later I came to understand that grief uses language and actions more incomprehensible than any on earth. My own first reaction caused me to rip my car phone from its moorings and crash into the Albany off-ramp.

I drove a heavy Jeep Cherokee at the time or I suppose I couldn't have survived clipping two cars and a pick-up as I reversed back up onto the Interstate. I then plowed forward past Berkeley, not even aware that I thankfully left no injuries in my wake. I don't remember the rest of the drive, just my arrival at the station, a station dead at two A.M. as usual. I ran like a madman to Righteous Ray's studio, except I couldn't find the way to Studio B which I knew like the way to my own kitchen. This was because I was lost at that moment in every way imaginable. And I ran the halls screaming inside like a vigilante armed with the knowledge that the world was ending, the sky was falling, and the sun would never rise again. As I careened from floor to floor, I stripped the walls of schedules and memos, smashed light fixtures by the dozen, making everything as empty and dark as I felt inside until I found the studio and Righteous Ray, saw him through the thick plate glass window which I debated smashing too, except I liked Ray and blinding him with jagged glass was a possibility dreadful enough to be recognized even in my devastation.

We locked eyes. And I saw the puzzled expression on his rugged, black, too-tired face as he reacted to me. Which made me look at my own reflection in the glass, and I saw that, in a brutal split second of soul-smash, I had become a man without a country.

So I began to let it bleed, gushing the whole appalling river of my agony, tearing open the studio door, yanking the cans right off Ray's ears, body-checking him onto the guest couch.

"We're going off-format, Ray!" I barked at him. "Fasten your damn seat belt!"

So that night the station went off-format. So far off-format they never got it back.

The late night listeners were much, much fewer in the early '90s. It was as if no one was tuning in as far as I was concerned. So for the first hour, without commercial interruption or music, I felt uncontrollably free to rant. I was naked, out of control, driven by hurt and loss and the need to hand out bleeding boarding passes to anyone unlucky enough to be listening to this time slot from hell.

Righteous Ray, despite his bewilderment, nevertheless manned the beginning-to-flash phone lines for me like a player riding someone else's erratic streak at a craps table. He was even leaking tears, a man who'd been in this unforgiving business from the start. The listeners were oblivious to some degree about what I was doing until the second hour, when I told them how my two little twin girls died beside my wife. How I lost my Mom and Dad, whom I loved beyond words, along with my precious and sweet big sister. How they were all dead, and how it was my fault and maybe they shouldn't have died, or at least I should have died, and how my little babies weren't even a year old and how they would never walk into my arms or open up their first birthday presents.

"Incoming!" bellowed Righteous Ray. "Incoming!" He meant the phone lines, by now completely lit.

The callers, many callers, fiercely intense callers, demanded to be allowed to speak on air. They were so stricken by my grief and so emotional and so sympathetic and there were so many of them that Righteous Ray was forced into the role of call screener, taking messages, urging one and all to keep the faith. We were in our own little studio jet, without oxygen, diving into an imagined ocean off San Diego in a parabolic arc of lost futures and burnt bridges, unconscious, unknowing, and sinking fast, fast, fast.

The single red light was flashing, someone had alerted the PD. Ray looked at me.

"It's the boss man," he said. "You want me to pick up?"

I shook my head. I had already answered to God that night, why should I answer to anyone else? We both knew the PD would get into his car and quickly be on his way to pull my plug. But I wasn't going to let that happen, not until I addressed the whole issue of unfathomable loss, starting the third hour.

I finally let callers on the air to speak to me. And to speak to each other. They began with empathy, but soon and swiftly they also began to adhere to my anguish, whirling in my tornado, wanting to tell me *their* stories of hell and heartbreak, some of them wanting me to understand that they had been where I was right now, that I must not give up. People asked for the studio address so they could send flowers, cards, donations in my children's names. It went on and on as Ray battled the flashing phone lines like a grizzled Hemingway fighting to land twelve swordfish at a time. And I just talked and talked and talked and talked and I could feel my voice being forged like an instrument, like a baritone sax made of melancholy and loneliness and bone and iron.

I played my first song that night. A long-ago song which wouldn't let go of me because I wanted to hear the one line which spoke to my flooded, drowning heart. When Janis Joplin sang that she'd *"trade all of my tomorrows for one single yesterday,"* I sensed what the rest of my life might hold in store.

I had no idea at the time that as Luis Casul, surly and hot-tempered Program Director of KHEL, listened to me on his car radio, he started to drive more and more slowly. He began to hear the rhythm of my confession, the universality of it. And when he marched into what was now *my* studio, to his own horror I forced him on air, my unwilling guest, and asked him how he was coping with the death of the brother who had died of AIDS that last year. And once I immobilized my boss before he could immobilize me, I went in a different direction and announced to my listeners the small but sad fact that just last week our gruff PD had accidentally backed over his family's pet flop-eared bunny as he left his garage in San Ramon, and his children, then ten and thirteen, still weren't speaking to him. Mine were both cheap shots, but I was red with blood and no one was going to stop me from finishing my shift. Suddenly, proving the existence of miracles, Luis' oldest boy, listening in the dark with his daddy inexplicably gone, called in and we put the dead bunny and dead brother issues on the air, and father and son both started crying and I could almost feel the entire Bay Area itself sobbing, all the way north to Sacramento, all the way south to San Jose. It was a jump start, the likes of which no radio show ever experienced, not that I was aware of. Craggy old Ray fighting tears, tough Luis Casul weeping with his head in his hands, and the phone lines lit up like candles of mourning, candles of solidarity, candles of sympathy, candles offering salvation, candles which were lighting my path, candles which were going to keep me alive.

In a few months, with me at the helm of the ten-to-two slot, KHEL's Arbitron ratings went from worst to first. Luis Casul became my unyielding protector and fended off all attempts by the GM and the parent Corp to force me into reining in what must have seemed to them as insane, dangerous, and ever-increasing on air risk-taking.

Rick Lang, the Midnight Rider.

I blew up nationally, indeed internationally, into a radio phenomenon and why not? I was mainlining the collective unconscious, I was completely authentic, and I was *raw*.

Shannon was the only one of my friends who supported my decision to stay in the house I had shared with Paige in Mill Valley, the house Paige's family had owned for generations, the house her family had given us as a wedding present, the house her angry grieving parents tried to wrench from me but in defense of which I fought them tooth and nail and blood-soaked claw until they realized they'd have to kill me first. All the other Secret Society members, especially Dylan who was the first to join up without having known my wife, urged me to box up her belongings, the twins' belongings, and move someplace new, someplace where I could start living a healthy life again. They were sure Paige would have wanted that for me.

Instead, as mourning people have often done and still do, I changed nothing, touched nothing, let time freeze. I moved into the attic of Paige's ancestral towering manse and let the other three floors serve as my Museum of Hurt.

My listenership has given me many gifts over the years, some amusing, some amazing. But their very first and deeply moving gift was a petition, signed by over a thousand newly minted Midnight Riders, insisting that I play Nat King Cole's "Nature Boy" at the end of every Saturday night's show and dedicate it to myself. Ten years later, it is still the gift that goes on giving. Because every Saturday, without exception, I am forced by their kindness to listen to the verse they somehow collectively agreed they most wanted me to grasp and internalize: that the greatest thing I'd ever learn is just to love and be loved in return.

Deep inside, most people are Midnight Riders. And so I offer everyone who is hurt and lost, desperate or hopeless, a place to gather every night. I've tried to make my show serve as a campfire in the heart of life's brutal and often incomprehensible forest of shadows and darkness. And I will tend that campfire until they stop coming to join me there. I have dedicated this eternal flame to Paige. This is my life's work, nothing can stop me. Nothing and no one.

## CHAPTER THREE

**F**ACED WITH THIS PROPOSED "MARRIAGE GAME," OUR TABLE BEGINS TO ERUPT WITH LOUD AND uneasy anticipation. Even I am uneasy. Gary's Annual Secret Society Game promises barbed wire edginess and moderate emotional danger, traditionally a good combination for an evening of mayhem. But the fact that we are *all* single and without substantive love relationships as we celebrate our communal 40th birthday only serves to remind us that, despite our intelligence and achievement, good looks and desirability (at least on paper), we surely must be the Bay Area's most fascinating tribe of partnership-failures: some of us still running like mad dogs from commitment, others destroying intimacy and marriages, still others never seeing through the daunting camouflage of authentic love. How many times have we danced up to the gates of Oz with brains, heart and courage, only to be turned away by the Wizard for our embarrassing romantic ineptitude?

There are the predictable groans from Owen and Leah, who are most vocal against the siren-songs of matrimony. Expected unsavory jokes from Dylan and Anjuli, unskillfully married seven times between them. Quiet intensity from Shannon, to whom engagement has come easily but who has left three good men at the altar. Of course there's always the man who didn't leave his heart in San Francisco, but rather several hundred feet under the Pacific Ocean, in sight of the Coronado Hotel in San Diego.

"It's a simple Game," intones Gary. "But it will alter our collective destiny. The secret chamber of marital bliss has been electronically guarded from our easy entry, yes, but my Game will help crack the numerical code that keeps us fettered to wretched, feeble solitude."

"Nice speech, well-rehearsed, and I'm sorry to complain, Gary," interjects Leah, "but aren't you really kind of rubbing our noses in it? It makes us sound like a bunch of losers."

"There are no losers at this table," growls Owen. "We're choosers." Despite his doctorate in history, Owen tends to talk like a hostile biker who just lost his tenth straight game of eight-ball.

"Leah, I have to warn you. Keep insulting the magical Box and you will receive a less desirable marriage number." Gary's cosmic tone-of-voice is quickly giving way to exasperation. "*Special* numbers which I'll explain if you all would just *focus* for a change. Besides, The Game has already launched big time. The very moment my enchanted marriage Box was placed among us." He glares at all of us. "Too late to back out now so stop screwing around!"

Dylan chimes in. "Leah, if anyone's gonna win a game with marriage as its theme, it's gonna be me. I've collected more rings than Owen's coffee table. So just chill while I pick up my next trophy."

Leah rolls her eyes. "Come on, Dylan. Did any of your marriages last even five years?" Our doctor is getting feisty, which she does with unbridled verve. This is not good.

"At least *I* left each and every one of my wives, even if it was by mutual decision." He pauses, milking his moment *"Me?* Never been dumped, not once. *You?* Dumped for a cute little teenage fiddle player…"

Owen and I both instinctively, and quickly, grab an upset Leah. She is five foot nine, works out nearly as much as Gary, and has the medical expertise to throttle Dylan without even breaking a mild sweat.

Dylan only manages to regain his smirk once Leah is safely corralled. Sadly, it is indeed true that Leah's ex-husband Ronny (a charismatic but chronically unfaithful jazz drummer) left her many years ago, left her alone with twin boys, left her for a heavily-pierced fiddle-playing street musician, the very kind which the Bay Area breeds like colorful hamsters, a nineteen-year old half-grown girl who drove my playful and trusting friend to become a workaholic who rarely dates, who continues to hide her true radiance and compassionate nature from potentially hurtful partnership.

"Let me explain how the Box works," injects Gary forcefully, forgetting that our simultaneous attention can only be achieved by use of a bullhorn. "The Game takes less than a few minutes to play. But every single one of us must obey the wishes of the Box. And if even one of us refuses, then its super-natural powers will evaporate!"

"Don't mean to be harsh, Gary, I get that it's your first time. But it's a lousy and loaded Annual Game and I'm not into playing it," says Owen quietly. He glances intently at me for moral support. All I can do is shrug, no answers here.

Owen Brucker comes from dairy country just east of Dayton, Ohio. He grew up in the company of an unkempt pasture full of Jersey cows and a pair of alcoholic parents. Owen is tall, blond, and handsome tonight in his best jacket, a vintage Hugo Boss which he found in a thrift shop for a buck, a lucky find as Owen is also poor by local standards; his professor's salary can't cover the cost of life in the Bay Area. He collects and restores old Bakelite radios to make a little cash on the side. He is also a renowned world authority on the mythical Centaur which earns him a small but steady income on the mythical creature lecture circuit. But these things are less odd than the fact that Owen would rather drop dead than marry and have children; he buried all his hopes for normality in Fairborn, Ohio where his father routinely beat him, often at his mother's urging. Twelve-year-old Owen slept in a shed with his one friend, a ragged golden retriever, and when his father shot the dog to death as a punishment Owen compounded the horror by grabbing the rifle and blasting away at his parents then burning their family farmhouse to the ground. His folks both survived though he has never seen them since and he still wears his golden retriever's tag on a chain around his neck. He is to loyalty as I am to mourning. Excessive.

Although he entered neither youth authority nor psychiatric unit due to evidence of his parents' abuse, Owen has been in prison ever since. A prison in which he believes that there is no deadlier institution in America than the American family. Perhaps surprisingly, he is able to love deeply as a friend and to portray his devotion in a profound manner. I am his Butch Cassidy, he is my Sundance Kid. Life drove him to the hole-in-the-wall first; I unfortunately joined him there later. Yet, in a sense, I saved Owen by my tragedies. Because in our Secret Society, there is a not-so-secret ranking of hardship and heartache and trauma. And in this very ziggurat of those whose only luck is bad luck, my ace will always beat his king.

"C'mon, big guy. You can handle anything!" pleads Dylan, who is sensing another easy win. "Just put on a smile..."

"Ain't gonna happen!" snaps Owen. "Right now, I'm feeling no pain and I want to keep it that way..."

Perhaps if Owen resembled short and thick Dylan, he might better avoid the attentions and demands of marriage-minded ladies. But Owen is, by consensus of our women members, "gorgeous," one of those exceptionally alluring Redford-blond men who seem to entrance even women who prefer their paramours swarthy-sexy. Part of his charm and appeal is his lack of guile. Owen doesn't think of himself as strong or magnetic or worthy. But he is all these things, and in a fully masculine understated way.

"Look. Players. The Game is *simple*," Gary goes back into his patter while turning the Box in a 360-degree circle to accentuate its features. "In each of these little drawers is a thin heart made out of bloodstone. Attached to each of these hearts is a gold chain which we'll wear around our wrists for a period of not less than three days. And on each heart is a number from one to seven, one being first to go."

"Oh, nice flourishes, Gary, nice," comments Shannon, mistress of the grace note.

"Sounds almost as bad as Dylan's Hot Tub Game," remarks Leah.

Gary intercedes. "Look. I know my Game has all of your nerves churning at the very thought of holy padlock. But the Secret Society rules are that, unless the Game is obviously malicious or vindictive, it *must* be played."

Leah, hoping against hope to derail this uncomfortable scheme, slides with great theatricality from her tall bistro chair beside me to the lush patterned carpet below. "*Fine.* Wake me up when it's over." Only in Marin County would Leah's swoon to the floor cause nary a ripple. After all, we live in one of the more remarkable counties in America, where odd behavior is indulged and often prized.

"C'mon, Leah! And all the rest of you spinsters," continues Gary, foolishly fighting to retain control. "Sure, marriage is an optional add-on these days. But, hey, this Box may be your only hope for love and security as you rock in your future rocking chairs. So lose the jokes and let's go! Personally, I am predicting that I will end up with a trust-funded supermodel!"

"Very deep, Gary!" A loud, sarcastic postscript from below the table.

I look down. Leah is still sprawled on the carpeted floor, grinning upside down at me, all long legs and heels.

Despite the platonic nature of our friendship, she knows how to tease. She lowers her voice to address only me, innuendo at full throttle. "What's *your* problem, Rick? Don't you want to play this Game with me? I'll let you win. Maybe. But only if you *handle* me just right!"

I blink, amused. "Was that a *giggle*?! Where's your gravitas, Doctor?"

"It's my sparkly green dress talking. Not me. I'm too sensible to flirt."

Gary pounds his fist on the table. "Okay, we're starting! All you whack jobs are about to get a dose of excitement!" I have to admire his enthusiasm. Even though I've only known Gary for eighteen months or so, it's nice that he is as whimsically twisted as the rest of us. But no more twisted than the same older man at the water-view window table, who makes no pretense to disguise his interest in us. He sees me looking at him. Winks and waves.

What the hell, he's having a good time. Dinner theater at no extra cost.

Gary spurs into action. He spins his Marriage Box three times making a clatter. "Okay, okay, I can see you useless Game players can't concentrate unless I hit you over the head, so here we go. Let's get real. First of all, we're all single." He says it ruthlessly. "And, unless you put your trust in me, we'll probably remain single until the second coming…"

"Coming twice is overrated," interjects Anjuli. "I'm usually happy with one really good screamer…"

"Anjuli!" yells Leah, rising from the carpet, her fashionably cut and stylishly hip sandy blonde hair now completely awry. "I'd like to surgically remove your one track mind!"

Gary, to his credit, just pushes past the chaos. "Weep now but rejoice later, dudes and daughters of Marin. For these magic numbers will mystically evaporate all your fears of commitment and true intimacy and make you ready for the ultimate leap of faith!" He starts to open one of the box's little red drawers and then pauses with fairly decent amateur thespian timing. "Oh, beware! I forgot the fine print…"

Gary Inagaki can be nearly as funny as Dylan, if a little more decorous. A third generation Los Angeles-born Japanese-American, he is California tall, exactly my six feet. He and Dylan have become good friends as both own an excellent voice and no karaoke bar is ever safe from their perfect doo-wop pitch. Gary, like Shannon and Owen, has never married. A personal trainer by profession, a ladies' man by predilection, his disinclination to settle down proves he belongs with us. Happy with his work, unconditionally loved by his two Akita dogs, living on a highly coveted houseboat in Sausalito, Gary has an attitude common among men who date often and just for fun. Show him that trust-funded supermodel and, yes, he might get down on one knee. Otherwise, love is just a never-ending buffet.

Gary now shifts into overdrive. "The playing of this Game assures us that we *all* shall be married within one calendar year. In fact, the numbers which we draw will tell us, without error, in which order we will fall. If we marry out of order then all seven marriages will be cursed and our lives forever lost in a tsunami of never-ending, pathetic loneliness." He takes a breath, and then punches it home: "So draw a number to reveal your fate and draw a number to meet your one true love…"

"Gary, that was totally hot," announces Anjuli, breathless as only a voracious speed-reader of romance novels can be.

"I'm ready," announces Dylan.

"Likewise." Anjuli is good to go.

"Forget it! Think of something else!" snarls Owen, nursing his newest Guinness. He is more stubborn and vehement than usual but we all know that, for Owen, old scars can flare up abruptly and glow just like the tubes of his Bakelite radios.

"Your problem is you don't believe in love, Owen," Anjuli counters. "Or money. Or ambition. Or hopes and dreams. Or cruises. Or beach vacations. Or anything meaningful!" Anjuli represents our *vox populi*, although if I told her that, she'd accuse me of calling her an STD.

I am due at the radio station in an hour. "Let's get this over with," I say, casting my vote.

"Where's Shannon?" Gary suddenly shouts, frantic.

"Just blowin' us off as usual," chuckles Owen, "And good for her! I wish I had her quick feet."

"Rick, we can't play without her," yells Gary. "Please go get her back…"

"Yeah, come on, Rick. Get her! You can do it!" Dylan cries out.

They all turn to me, expecting. Am I not America's late night safety net for an entire country? Because we all know that Shannon lives life as if it were a shaky high wire act. So off I go to catch Shannon, awkward and easily embarrassed Shannon, the one who never loses my grip, the one who always hangs on for dear sweet life, the one I'll never drop like I dropped Paige.

# CHAPTER FOUR

$S$HANNON REID IS YOUNGER THAN ME BY A SINGLE DAY. I MET HER WHEN SHE WAS A VIRGINAL reddish-golden-haired eighteen-year old wallflower at a Cal freshman mixer; there we slow-danced that very first dance to Van Morrison's "Into The Mystic," a song which still serves as her theme song, appropriate for a woman whose uncomfortably penetrating wide-set eyes hide much of her true nature just as her sleek appearance and expensive clothing belie her surprising lack of that off-putting sense of entitlement usually found in pretty women.

Shannon's nature indeed had something mystical for me in those early days and it inspired me to seduce her as often and as vigorously as possible during our freshman and sophomore years at Cal. But despite being sexually exclusive and despite having strong if adolescent feelings toward one another, she unwaveringly insisted we never use the label boyfriend-girlfriend. This meant we were "just friends" when Shannon introduced me to Paige, her newly assigned roommate.

Paige, never one to be denied anything she wanted, saw Shannon's uncertainty about love in general and her ambiguity about our relationship in particular as license to aggressively court and spark me away from her. I was impressed by the maturity and wisdom Paige offered in contrast to Shannon, but at the time what *really* sealed the deal for me was Paige's intuitive certitude that we were meant to be together. In spite of the fact Paige wasn't all that sexy or even particularly attractive by the unfair California standard of beauty, I was fiercely drawn to her personality. Paige was brilliant in a street-smart way, sophisticated in an old money way, and she knew how to fully commit to me in an uncompromising way; all of which swept me off my feet.

Shannon took our double betrayal in her own emblematic fashion. She was neither hurt nor surprised; she knew that Paige and I were a better fit and claimed it was really for the best. It was only later that I came to understand that Shannon held (and still holds) the lifelong belief that stability and happiness are impossible dreams for her. She forgave the two of us, kept both of us in her life, with the final outcome that Shannon and I have shared twenty-two years of unshakably-loyal lifelong friendship. She is the only Secret Society member to have really known Paige, to have cared for her unconditionally. And so we still talk the small details of Paige on bad nights, bad desperate late nights when I need someone to remember her with me, despite Paige's death so long ago, so ten years ago.

"Shannon, think about what you're doing…" I call to her as she passes the far end of the crowded chrome and black lacquered bar with its illuminated shelves of bottled booze. The restaurant is naturally too self-involved with its own hubbub to notice our little piece of drama. "You know this isn't the way to go…"

Shannon, soon-to-be forty and never wed, wound up practicing commitment-phobia as her dark art. She has been engaged to be married three times. One can bone up on the extensive details of her thwarted affairs in three pink notebooks chock full of social and sexual details which I know to be kept under her bed. Shannon has jettisoned fiancé after fiancé, each a worthy man, at approximately the three-year mark. To her, perhaps, tonight's Game makes mockery of her unfulfilled life. She spends money as fast as she earns it and lives large, be it ludicrously lavish vacations or preposterously pricy shoes, all to distract from the emptiness of a childhood haunted by men who disappointed. Father, uncles, brothers who gave her nothing, neither love nor hate, not even indifference, just chores and the evil promise of worse, never a gift or a toy on her birthday or Christmas. She tells people she grew up in a backwoods Southern orphanage and this is true in its own way. Raised by men who never forgave her for killing her mother forty years ago in childbirth, who never lay blame on the ignorant midwife who didn't mind dirty sheets and dirty hands, or the doctor who couldn't keep his hands steady without drinking bourbon from a hip flask.

Shannon is like the Tennessee Walker, that exceptional horse with the smoothest gait in the world. She used its classic four-beat running walk as an exemplar; eleven-year-old Shannon silently slipped away from an East Tennessee hell before she could face the same abuse her sisters before her had to endure, and continues to walk through life as carefully as possible, endlessly dodging emotional hazard with effortless pace. She juggles her gentleman callers neatly, like a juggler of chain saws, getting much of the attention she wants but never failing to believe that commitment is sharp and bloody and that the only man she can trust is the one she chose to let get away, the one without sharp teeth, the only one she knows will always protect her and love her for who she is, missing pieces and all.

I catch her just outside the restaurant's ornate double-door entrance. As two couples exit past us, the fog swirls softly and a little summer rain adds texture to a parking lot frilled with upscale cars which seem to be hunkering down in the mist as if humbled by the Ferrari dealership which shows its wares next door. Her perfectly even features are incandescent, lit with a cinematographer's delicate touch by the antique-style parking lot lamps which have put us both in soft focus by the drizzle. I continue: "Shannon, come *on*. You invented the Annual Game! Without you, all our embarrassment and humiliation lacks the flair which gives it meaning!"

"But *this* Game isn't funny. It's too close to home."

"Tomorrow it'll be a memory and a joke. Just like always." I touch her single dimple briefly with my forefinger. It's an old signal, a comfort food, like mashed potatoes.

"It just hurts." There is an ache in her voice. And then there is silence and I wait for her, as I know I must wait. Finally she shrugs a mordant little shrug. "I'll always be like some sad little princess trapped in a tower, won't I?"

"Shannon, you have to show the others, especially Gary, who really wants to host a successful Secret Society Game, that you have faith in them no matter what. You've always been there from start to finish for nineteen years." I soften my voice even further. "Besides, we're family. We're all we got. We have to stick together."

Silence. But it's an evolving silence as the tense expression on her face relaxes.

She crosses one expensive stiletto heel behind the other, parting the slit in her perfectly fitted knee-length skirt and exposing a silky V-shaped glimpse of skin. She then balances her open palm flat against my chest, against my heart.

"Make me stay, Rick. I want to stay. Say the right thing." This sudden but typical Shannon prerequisite is an unexpected tree branch slapped back in my face. Nevertheless, I find myself deliberately brushing her chestnut-colored mane away from her face with my fingers. The summer fog continues to swirl, the light mist almost comforting as it wraps around us.

I take a deep breath. Going from dark to light on command is actually something I've learned to do by virtue of my calling. I put more smile in my voice. "*So what* if something scary pops out of the birthday cake? Gary's Game is just for fun. We're not talking torture; we're just talking a little pain over easy. You can handle it! You know you can. It's not that bad."

Then, without further ado, I slide one hand carefully under her matching tapered jacket and place it gently and as non-provocatively as possible on the left side of her narrow waist. I feel her shudder with pleasure. This is manipulative, I guess, in the sense that I am the only one here who knows that until she met me in college, Shannon had never been held with any kind of love, not as a baby, or a girl, or a teenager. Not once.

Abruptly she uncrosses her heels, rotates her hip toward mine and lingers a chaste kiss on my cheek, her smile now very pronounced. "Hey, I invented the Secret Society Annual Game. Stand out of my way!" She flips her hair to one side, pushes past me, and all is well.

Shannon's return evokes rude cheers from our crowd, four out of five players heavily buzzed, only Leah (on duty at midnight) abstaining as usual.

Gary then bullies us into holding hands as we all sit and/or stand in our circle around the high table with his Japanese-ornamental box placed in the middle. "To conclude without further interruption," says Gary, eyeing us threateningly, "...all seven of us will be married within a year if we do this properly. Custom-made bloodstones designed by me have been randomly inserted into the red-colored drawers of this Marriage Box by my neighbor and his wife. They just celebrated their third anniversary and were the happiest couple I could find on short notice. Each bloodstone has been etched with a number. I will open the drawers in no particular order, you will decisively select your stone in whichever order you choose. Who wants to go first?"

Silence.

"Repeat. Who's going first?"

More silence. We look at each other. Not a promising start.

Finally Anjuli bounces to his rescue. "What a bunch of pussies! I volunteer!"

Gary looks around. "Anyone else like to go first?"

Anjuli bristles. "And what is wrong with *me*? Just *try* to find another woman at this table that is better marriage material!"

"Then we start with Anjuli..." Gary swivels the box toward her as she yips with pleasure, "... and go counter-clockwise. Once all the magical bloodstones have been picked, the magic will take over and you will magically be told the order in which you will magically marry. If anyone refuses, they will magically pay for it big time with the full force of my magical rage."

Gary catches Owen starting to object. "*No* speeches. *Nobody* says a thing. Let's just go. And remember to immediately tie your numbered stone to your wrist using the silver chain. And you *all* had better make absolutely sure you keep it there for three full days! The penalty for taking it off, I *officially* do declare, is the Society gauntlet."

The usual catcalls follow. But our "gauntlet" is another society tradition designed to keep unlike minds in line. It involves enforced public nudity of the most embarrassing kind as well as a financial penalty which is unfairly large and pro-rated to income. It will keep us on course and Gary knows it.

Gary opens the first drawer. "Anjuli?"

Anjuli pulls out a surprisingly pretty heart-shaped bloodstone with the number "2" neatly etched on it. It is attached to a thick and ornate silver chain. We all murmur with respect, Gary deserves praise for his props. Anjuli holds it aloft in triumph. "He better be rich, that's all I can say, and handsome, and well-hung..."

"Jaysus, Anjuli!" blurts out Leah. Leah's beautifully voiced, accurate pronunciation of Anjuli's name always makes our self-styled sex kitten sound far more classy than intended (*On-Zhew-Lee,* emphasis first syllable).

"Oh, yeah, baby." Anjuli continues. "A super sexy Venture Capitalist with *lots* of staying power...that's not asking too much..." Anjuli wraps the heart chain around her wrist. "There. Done deal!"

"Sluts 'R Us opens a new franchise," interjects Owen, not so matter-of-factly.

"Sticks and stones, Owen," chortles Anjuli. "Why don't you just take your number and follow me down the aisle?"

Gary interjects again. "Dudes! C'mon! Lose the chatter! Let's just ride the dream, experience the joy, and get the hell home before I drop from exhaustion."

Leah's turn. She reaches into the drawer Gary offers her, pulls out bloodstone #5. "Back of the pack! Works for me." She swiftly wraps her chain as required.

Owen draws #3, grimaces. "Good news. Now we'll only need two wedding presents." He unsteadily wrist-wraps his heart chain with Shannon's help.

Gary holds a drawer open for me. "Wait a second, wait a second!" yells Dylan. "I've got myself a hunch! Rick, I'll buy that drawer from you for five crisp dollar bills. What do you say?"

"Fine by me," I answer.

"Hey!" Gary barks, upset. "No trading! That's against the rules!"

"Actually, it's not against the rules," Shannon corrects him.

He looks suspicious, so I confirm. "Gary. Bending the rules is part of the Game."

Dylan, feigning outrage: "Yeah, you should know that by now."

"Vote!" yells Leah, finally finding something to enjoy. "Who wants to bend?"

Six hands are raised without hesitation.

"Hell, no! This is *my* Game!" Gary angrily tries to stand his ground.

"Hell yes!" Leah notes. "This is *our* Game."

The table erupts with laughing and gleeful rebellion. Gary looks fit to kill.

So Dylan gives me five crumpled beer-soaked dollar bills and, to Gary's dismay and disgust, reaches in and pulls out a bloodstone.

"BITE ME!" howls Dylan. "I got the big #1! Bad luck, Rick, I win!"

"Here's to your good luck, Rick," interjects Shannon with a small smile. She raises her wine glass and toasts me.

"*Definitely* good luck," slurs Owen, as he and I bang fists like the jocks we aren't.

Gary shakes his head with disbelief and opens one of the other drawers for me. I draw #6. Gary raises his eyes to the ceiling. Poor guy. We've had Society dropouts before. I hope our surfer boy can continue to take the heat in our raucous but never rancorous soul kitchen.

"Bravo, Rick!" trumpets Leah, wrapping the #6 around my wrist, and then holding her wrist-wrapped #5 next to it. "Now we're practically twins," she announces.

Then blanches as the last words catch in her throat.

"Twins" is a word Leah and I avoid saying aloud to each other. Given hers are in middle school and mine are playing in the clouds of heaven.

"It's okay," I say. I am lying of course.

Shannon draws bloodstone #7. Her eyes are glowing green headlights. She high-beams at me, satisfied.

Gary finally pulls open the last drawer and gets #4. Shannon and Gary finish the Game by wrist-wrapping their bloodstone hearts in the manner of all the others. We are done.

"That's it, that's the Game?" asks Owen, surprised, not to mention delighted, not to mention drunk.

Gary is still not in a good mood. "It takes a little time for your marriage partners to step forward. Meanwhile just get ready for the Big Ball and Chain, okay?"

"Sounds kinky. I can't wait!" squeaks Anjuli with pleasure.

"And if your new spouse tanks, there's always a cheap lawyer to annul your butt to safety," chirps #1 on the charts Dylan.

Suddenly I'm aware that a new character in search of an author has entered our passion play. He is the man from the water-view window seat. He inserts himself among us effortlessly.

"Actually I *am* a lawyer. But I'm afraid I'm not very cheap."

All eyes abruptly look to him, as pilgrims to the East.

With the unhurried calm of a pilot used to flying comfortably in the eye of a hurricane he steps completely and strikingly into our midst and puts one hand on Owen's shoulder, then his other hand on mine. His softly commanding demeanor is completely out of place in this chaotic portrait of the "Last Supper" as performed by the August '61 not-so-Secret Society.

"Very unusual game," he continues, "I *enjoyed* what I saw. I *loved* what I heard. And it gave me a rather sudden but inspired idea which I want to briefly share with you."

The others are all frozen with fascination, even Leah who is always our Cynical Playmate of the Month. Amused glances begin to be shared. Anjuli even begins to warm up her infamous and usually ineffective seductive smolder.

Only I'm not buying it.

Not at all.

# CHAPTER FIVE

**T**HE NOT-SO-SECRET SOCIETY CLUSTERS AROUND THIS STRANGER IN ITS MIDST.

Anjuli immediately and baldly eyes his gold Rolex. Gary deferentially offers his chair, one of the few not splashed with Guinness or Chardonnay. The others observe him with attitudes ranging from puzzled curiosity to bleary insouciance. I know it's a set-up, a hired piece of theater by Gary. Gary is definitely inventive enough to have seen the potential for some entertaining drama. Enter the mysterious stranger. His "rather sudden but inspired idea" which suggests more fun to come. Perhaps even now we are being recorded for later laughs by a crack team of high-tech nerds hiding deep within the micro-brewed bowels of this increasingly claustrophobic "East" German eatery.

This distinguished-looking man manages to look at all seven of us at once, a neat bit of trickery. And when he speaks, his phrasing is totally pro, a man accustomed to public speaking and a rapt audience.

"I'd like to make you all a proposition," he continues. "One which I think you'll enjoy."

Oh, this is exceedingly cool! For a brief, thrilling moment I pretend the Devil has actually made a whistle-stop in our very own angst-riddled Marin. I'm sure he would know that I wouldn't hesitate for a split second, that I would gladly sell my soul for just one lousy hour sipping Coronas and lime with my dead bride down at Joe's Taco Lounge on Miller Avenue.

But unfortunately the identity of this well-dressed character unexpectedly clicks for me. It's oddly deflating. "You're Matthew Moss, aren't you?" I ask, knowing the answer, reluctantly letting go of my notion of Gary having been the mad maestro behind this bizarre intrusion.

Matthew Moss smiles at me, a charming smile, but perhaps no less practiced than Anjuli's sexy smolder. "I'm a fan of yours, Mr. Lang. Yes, I know who you are. After my wife passed away eight years ago, I listened for awhile. I still tune in from time to time."

Now the others start to recognize him, one by one, and say so. Anjuli first, because she initially moved from Sacramento to begin her career in sales as a promotion girl (sometimes given the déclassé nickname "record whore") for Pacific Rim Records, a high profile outfit which Moss sold while she was still on the payroll. Then Leah, briefly an NPR intern, who now remembers some of his interviews. Then Shannon who, as part and parcel of her job as a media consultant, also remembers these same interviews. Then Dylan, who has spent enough time in divorce courtrooms to know that Matthew Moss is one of the richest and most successful attorneys in the Bay Area. Finally Owen and Gary, who have both seen his expensive and slick infomercials on cable TV.

Moss' smile is sharp and quick as he immediately takes advantage of his audience's rapidly rippling, if slightly tipsy, respect. "I watched your whole evening unfold. It was a voyeuristic experience of the first water, I must say." He now chooses to swivel in order to favor Leah and Shannon. "Now tell me, ladies. Your provocative game. Was it just for fun or is there some kind of bet attached?"

"Our Games are only for fun, Mr. Moss." Leah explains because no one else seems to want the job. "What you were watching was a yearly ritual played by seven slightly plastered birthday boys and girls."

"Oh, that's a shame. I was willing to *bet* that there was a *bet*," he says, smiling with self-deprecation at his lame *bon mot*.

"You like to gamble, don't you? That's your thing, isn't it?" I ask, as Moss' reputation continues to dawn on me. "On a big scale...."

Gary jumps in. "That's right! That HBO documentary! You're the dude who never loses a crazy bet."

"Me, too! I saw it too!" Dylan enthuses noisily. "Million bucks a hole on some golf game in Singapore or Taiwan or somewhere and you won! Beat a foursome of Arabs or Korean guys or whatever-they-were high roller types! That was *amazing*!"

"Go U.S.A.!" shouts Anjuli, unwilling to be left out of this growing love fest.

"It's true," Moss humbly acknowledges. "I *have* earned a bit of publicity for my wild and crazy winning streak."

"No doubt aided by an equally wild and flashy publicist," suggests Shannon dryly. "Tell me who wouldn't want a lawyer who never loses?"

But Matthew Moss smiles with even more practiced charm, the effect this time almost boyish. "Maybe so. But I also tend to believe the games we play are very much the only real clues to a person's true nature."

"Gimme a serious break," groans Owen, eyeing Moss with a pair of drooping eyes.

But Moss continues cheerfully: "Look. Why waste time? The truth is I just love a good bet and your game is irresistible. So why not let me make you all an offer that will amuse you?"

Dylan, gung-ho: "*My* bet is you're going to pick up our check because we're so ha-ha fascinating!"

Matt Moss, of course, is the doyen of masterful timing. "Actually I *have* paid your tab. I hope you'll forgive me."

Courtroom theatrics continue to rule as our eyes search vainly for the check.

"Sorry," interjects Leah. "We can't accept. We always split the bill using a formula based on previous year's income. It's tradition."

Anjuli breaks in boisterously. "Hey! Who cares about tradition? It's overrated. I say we take Matt's money. He probably needs the tax deduction! Check out that suit, three grand minimum, probably more. The Rolex? Fifteen or twenty grand, I figure. I'll bet he spent more on that tie than he spent on our entire dinner for seven!"

"Anjuli, you're an embarrassment." Shannon shakes her head. I note Moss is straightening his suddenly famous tie, enjoying every second of our cacophonous Society interaction.

I check my watch, sigh. "Mr. Moss, in ten years I've never been late for work. Not once. So could you possibly get to your point? I guarantee that whatever offer or bet or joke you'd like to discuss will be wasted on our group because at the moment they are so-not-sober that you could say you're Batman and they'd ask for your autograph."

"*Au contraire*, Mr. Lang. You underestimate your teammates. You all played your marriage game with compelling energy." He beams. "I think it would be *great* fun to actually play out a real version of your marriage game, don't you? We could stick to your hilarious rules, more or less. And furthermore I'll make it *impossible* for you to turn down my offer to take part."

He pauses to make sure he has us all in his bag, continues. "As I can obviously afford it, what say we make your participation worth two million dollars each? Two million or an equivalent reward for those who are already well off. That feels about right, doesn't it? Not too much, not too little? What do you say?"

He looks at all seven of us again with one gaze, his parlor trick suddenly more effective for we are silent and motionless, a wax museum of the absurd, exchanging varying versions of *"what the hell"* glances.

Then he adds, as if it were an afterthought: "Oh, you *will* have to win the game, of course, to collect. But I think your time frame of twelve full months to accomplish your goal seems fair and reasonable. A *full* year for seven close friends to work together and contrive to become legally married and, *oh* what a *brilliant* twist, in the very order you have chosen tonight! What a fabulous idea for a fabulous bet. All in all, I'm offering an exceedingly exciting opportunity, don't you think? I think so."

Shannon, who has been watching and listening to Moss with quiet concentration, now speaks up. "You know, whoever polished your skill set, Mr. Moss, did a great job. You've trained your facial movements to reveal very little apart from what you want to convey, your tone of voice is pleasant yet entirely unreadable; you don't have a single tell-tale hand movement, your gestures are beautifully scripted. You must have studied with one of my more gifted competitors." She looks at all of us, then back at Moss. "I don't mean to be rude but I really can't tell if you're sincere or full of crap, pardon my lack of manners."

"So much unnecessary flattery! I feel honored." He smiles at Shannon. "Cross my heart, I am sincere to the *very* core!"

Shannon, exasperated, looks to me for help.

"Okay," I say, taking charge. "Let's skip the cake and brandy and get to it. I have to leave, so does Leah, the world will not survive without us tonight, and we all know that." I turn to Leah for confirmation. She moves closer to me, putting her arm around my waist and gluing her hip to my hip.

I continue in the same reasonable tone. "Let's pretend Mr. Moss genuinely would like to bet us some of his major market cash that we can't all get married in a year much less in a specific numerical order. Why not? It's a slam dunk for him. How many commitment-phobics does it take to change a light bulb? Zero. We can't commit to anything. We're a joke."

Leah interrupts, giving my arm an affectionate squeeze. "Whoa! Hang on. At least we're a clever, highly evolved joke!"

Dylan interjects. "On the other hand, Princess Leah, one of us is a broke joke. Business is a disaster. Who wants to buy pool supplies and swim masks and blow-up rafts when they can battle aliens or zombies in the privacy of their gloomy living rooms? Healthy tans are out, sunshine is taking a hit, and I haven't made a decent profit in years!"

"Hey. *Two* of us are broke jokes," slurs Owen without looking up from his slump. "I haven't had a raise in five years, my benefits have been cut in half, and I can't make a dent in my student loans despite the fact I'm nearly forty freakin' years old."

I grab the reins again. "Look, guys. Mr. Moss here knows he can't lose. I'm sure he saw the unbelievable squabbling it took just to agree on our appetizers. Just ordering drinks was more complicated than a moon landing. Let's get real. First clue, he hasn't asked us to bet anything against his overwhelming dollars. How suspicious is that? It makes this reporter think the other hand-made Italian loafer hasn't dropped."

Moss nods pleasantly. "That's very good, Mr. Lang. You're very droll in real life."

I don't let him distract me, but continue to charge onward. "Very interesting, isn't it? To serve up an alleged two million apiece for those who need the money, which is most of us, yet to distinctly specify an offer of other incentives for those to whom cash is less dazzling. I ask you this baffling question. How has he figured out that at least three of us can't be bought for cash?"

Now Moss is loving it. "Well spotted!"

"If this man, who never loses a bet, wants to play a game involving the seven of us on what he claims is a whim, how could a con not be part of the process? And given he wins every single bet he ever makes, he's undoubtedly fond of, well, *cheating*." I give Moss an apologetic look. "We're deep in our cups, not thinking straight, and *my* bet is that we're being set up for a joke or a ride or both."

"But the offer is real." Moss protests with a smile. "The money is real. Think. What's ten million or fifteen million to the bored and jaded law office of Matthew Moss, the man who won, as you accurately remembered, a small fortune on a single round of golf? And the bet won't be fixed. A fact I will prove to you beyond doubt. Every penny of the cash at stake will be put in escrow. How's that? It'll all be in black-and-white." He gives us the seven-way look. "Papers ready to sign by five o'clock Monday afternoon at my office on

Montgomery Street." With that, he starts to hand out his business cards to one and almost all with practiced legerdemain.

Owen swivels to face Gary. "Man, I seriously don't know how you got this big shot to join our party. But he's doin' a great job of getting me outta my bad mood!" Owen attempts to get to his feet and nearly slips, banging his head on the table in the process of righting himself. Shannon, stone cold sober by now, fiercely roots through his pockets, grabs his car keys. Holds them aloft to indicate she'll drive him home.

Gary responds with a grin. "Yeah, give me credit. Not only did I get Mr. Moss here to help me out, I've also got Springsteen, Metallica, and Bon Jovi out in the parking lot waiting to sing us Happy Birthday! I am *so* awesome."

"Yo! All of you! Hush up!" interjects Anjuli, unsteadily attempting to re-zip the zipper on her leather pants at the expense of her bejeweled midriff, now exposed by her hiked-up blouse. "I want to hear more from the man!"

Leah sighs with annoyance. "Do you really think we, all of us, any of us, could get married by next year? My guess is that we couldn't one-and-all get married in *fifty* years even if you hired Marin's finest hypnotherapists and armed them with shotguns."

Dylan snorts. "Hey, I believe what he says! This guy's a legend. We all know he's famous for his funny bets. And he's got more money than Apple and Microsoft put together."

"Thanks for the vote of confidence," chuckles Moss.

Shannon grabs her handbag, clicks her designer heels. "Sorry, you guys. But you all know I live in the land of not-make-believe so I'm leaving." She turns to Owen. "You ready? Your designated driver is waiting."

Owen turns to Moss. "Thanks for the food and the drinks and the show and the two million bucks. All much appreciated."

Moss is pleased. "Does that mean you'll come on Monday to hear my presentation?"

Owen shrugs. "Dunno. Can't think that straight right now. I hate my damn birthday, don't you?"

"Wait just one second!" Dylan interjects. "When have I ever met a marriage I didn't like? I'll be at your office, Mr. Moss. I'm not afraid to see the color of your money."

"Maybe it's legit," adds Gary, looking around the table. "You know how much I have riding on my credit cards. You know my houseboat is financially underwater, pun intended. I like the sound of this. If it's in writing, we can do it. I'll be there too."

The Devil is two for two as Gary and Dylan exchange a high five.

Moss turns to the rest of us. "When you come to my office at five sharp Monday," smiles Matthew Moss, "you can see the contract, confirm that the funds are in escrow, parking is free as we validate, and I am already planning a fantastic surprise for those who feel two million is not worth their time and trouble." Here, he looks at me again. Then he looks at Shannon who is tugging on Owen's arm but is hampered by Owen's current sluggishness. Then he looks at Leah who ignores him. "Matt Moss doesn't disappoint, that's another of my illustrious slogans. What will it cost you to drop by? Nothing. What will you discover? Everything I've promised you and more. Just let me work out some final details over the weekend."

"What's the catch," murmurs Anjuli, now tightly at Moss' side. "Because I never catch anything, you can ask around!" She smolders her best smolder.

"Come on, Anjuli! Don't you ever stop?" Leah glares at her.

"Oh, I'm going to stop. Yeah, I'm going to stop by his office on Monday and let him woo me."

Anjuli slaps ten with Dylan and Gary. The Devil is now three for three.

Moss turns to me. "Any more thoughts, Mr. Lang?"

"Just that you're continuing to mess with the intoxicated minds of my closest friends. So I think it's time for you to say goodnight."

"Mr. Lang. Why deny your comrades a glimpse of a better future because you yourself are skeptical? Does that seem like the *friendly* thing to do?"

"Maybe you're right." I snap. "But if you've listened to my program then you must be aware that nothing could ever get *me* to marry again. *Never* going to happen..."

Just then I feel Leah's hand slip into mine. She presses my fingertips against her thigh so they can brush and linger exactly at the spot where the fabric of her glistening green minidress stops and the dark hose of her long legs begin. Erotic electricity scorches me briefly and startles me enough that I lose my train of thought. I give Leah a sideways look and she flashes me her "lighten up, it'll be over soon" grin. I send back a smile of thanks. Of all my friends, Leah has been the only one over the years whose emotional stability I haven't had to constantly worry about, the only one I could trust to take care of herself. Now I glance at Owen. And he's a different matter. Although he is awash in a Hugo Boss jacket soaked to the elbows in beer and microscopically stained from the splatter of pasta, *and* drunk as a skunk, he is stubbornly refusing to let a very determined Shannon drag him away.

Moss is remarkably indefatigable. "But I'll surely come up with something unique to offer you, Rick. Something you may have been waiting for all these years." As smooth as a perfect jury selection, Moss has put me on a first name basis. "When you assist your friends by coming to our meeting, you yourself may find a persuasive indeed *imperative* reason why you will desperately want to participate in the fun. It certainly isn't impossible."

Seeing my not unexpected reaction, he emits an enormous if insincere sigh. As he changes his tone of voice, he deftly inserts one of his business cards into my jacket pocket. "Look. If money and solutions are not enough to convince you to come to one simple meeting at my office, let me lay a few further cards on the table. It will take some of the merriment out of the game. But I need every one of you. So hear now the rest of the story..."

He subtly moves so that he is standing between the group of us and the door. Such is the exceptional presence of Matthew Moss that this aging man of moderate height and build really appears able to deter us from leaving. "It's really very simple. And I suspect Rick has already worked out that more is at stake than first presented. So here's your explanation. I think you'll appreciate my exquisite angle and the role I am selfishly attempting to bribe you to play. So hear now the truth!"

He pauses, takes a breath, ready for his closing argument. "Okay, I left out all the really marvelous details. So I'll come clean. I'm going to present your Marriage-By-The-Numbers Game to my exclusive short list of gambling friends. They will have the option of betting on your side, believing that you will successfully complete your marriage journey in one year. But I, on the other hand, will bet most heavily that you will fail." With this he beams at us briefly, and then moves on: "I smell a big pot. Maybe I can take them for as much as a hundred million dollars if they bite *and*, as a bittersweet bonus, I also won't have to pay the seven of you. Because if you fail, you get nothing. That's the first rule of a Matt Moss game, all or nothing." He takes a moment to add a spoonful of sugar to help the medicine go down. "No offense intended to your delightful and sharp-witted birthday club. I simply think that no group of friends, however motivated, can triumph against their true natures. But two million dollars each surely isn't a prize worth walking away from. Perhaps you should take one of your special votes?"

And so predictably the Society erupts into one of its civilized discussions. Dylan, Anjuli and Gary all loudly plead the nothing-to-lose advantages of signing on the Devil's dotted line and *winning millions!* Leaving Shannon and Leah to call them names which would make a shock jock blush. Owen puts his hands over his ears.

Moss mutes the Society's escalating vitriol with a friendly wave of one hand. "See you all Monday at my office as agreed, and I do mean *all* of you or please don't bother coming."

But as he starts to exit, Anjuli jumps up and takes his arm. I note that he flinches. "You know, Mr. Moss, if you need a ride back to the city, I've just had my Mazda detailed!" But Gary mercifully sweeps Anjuli away into his athletic arms so the Devil can exit stage left in a more dignified fashion. Moss tightens his overcoat, straightens his tie, gives us a pleasant wave, then exits in such a manner than we can see him through one of the larger restaurant windows, disappearing completely into the pale light and whispery summer evening fog, creating yet another of his never-ending theatrical moments. The restaurant is stunningly empty, the best seats have been vacated, the curtain is down.

And the seven of us look at each other.

Clearly the annual Game isn't quite over yet.

But they all know the Midnight Rider's clock and with quick good-byes, short and loving hugs, and no further commentary, I am able to disappear into the fog much like the Devil did before me. Yet why am I sure my friends will all be calling in on the station's secret family-friendly "warm" line tonight?

I change gears in every way imaginable as I power across the Richmond-San Rafael Bridge toward the station. Moss is quickly put toward the back of my mind, as is my birthday, this 40th birthday I never cared anything about. Because now it's my turn to perform, but for the good of others. Ten to two, six nights a week. But especially after midnight, when demons start dancing the Bossa Nova, and people begin murmuring my name.

# CHAPTER SIX

THIS IS WHERE I STAND VIGILANT AT MY RADIO OUTPOST SIX NIGHTS A WEEK, FITFULLY DIRECTING my call screeners and techs to rotate the spacing and location of my half-dozen gargantuan multi-wick floor candles. Upon my insistence, there is no other lighting in Studio B other than the glow of our technology because I operate more authentically and productively in the shifting shadows of a warrior's life here in the badlands of Hades.

From my lonely bunker, irony indeed, although I could not save my wife and children, I have so far (according to the wire services and the tabloids, documentarians and TV segment producers, online and late night pundits) apparently saved over a thousand teetering lives in my ten years of service. This number is no doubt as inflated and mythologized as is my reputation. But the Rick Lang show is without question a one-of-a-kind focal point where life-saving, life-helping, life-illuminating, and life-advancing is a *group* effort and the occasional miraculous achievement has become a serendipitous by-product of the love and sense of well-being and community I try to generate with music and words.

At the left side of my console, the phone system custom-designed by Telos is immense. It's nothing like the standard two sets of six lines each, not when the show gets more national calls per late night hour than any other in the history of radio. I have six sets of twelve flashing lines, seventy-two constantly pulsing hearts, and they are always on as I am always on.

By necessity, I direct much of my on-air energy to those who live in the darkness at the edge of town as my cousin Gabriel used to call the bleak areas of his own life. He and I share a forlorn gift from depressed and unmedicated uncles and grandfathers of yesteryear whose lethal shotgun blasts and jumps into oblivion created tragic tears which have trickled down here and there upon the next generations of our family tree. So here I am in my candlelit cave, refusing to be seduced by death no matter the devastation, determined to fight and claw for each sunrise despite drinking from a bottomless canteen of woe. And as long as my voice holds out, I will continue trying to talk my way past fire and frost without fear, earning the bonus of extending my life for the purpose of helping others to safety.

My listeners get this, they get me. We struggle together, striving not to catastrophize the loss of a child or a mother or a career or a dream to the point of losing our minds, our soul-balance or, most of all, our will to live.

If there is an afterlife then my family is waiting for me. But right now it is not my time to join them. These same listeners have deeply absorbed my own personal story although perhaps I have conveyed it to them too many times, and I know it makes them think and feel. I suppose my personal endurance, such as it is, has become inspiring in some strange but human way, feeding a collective human spirit which seeks meaning, seeks answers, as we all spin wildly on this ball of confusion.

Ten years ago, the first famous trophy tale of my lonely watch was David the rock-climbing chemist from St. Louis. He called my show from his own prototype satellite phone hoping to share with me, with anyone who would listen, all his reasons for blasting himself to bits while clinging half-way atop that city's famous Gateway Arch which he had actually managed to climb by use of suction cups. He wanted to blow in the wind with the ashes of his younger brother, whose urn he had placed in his backpack, with the troubled notion of creating his own two-man Operation Desert Storm Memorial. No, he wasn't crazy. He was just an example of what grief can look like from the outside in. Within minutes I had summoned several dozen St. Louis Midnight Riders to the scene. A few, to David's shock, attempted to rappel up the monument to join him, others flickered their lighters in that starless night rock-concert style, still others aggressively distracted the potentially counterproductive police. Finally, he came down weeping and everyone wept with him as he dismantled his hopeless home-made explosive which never would have done the job. But David was always cogent, even in the claws of his living nightmare. When I put him immediately on the air he was so articulate in his anguish and loss that my listeners around the nation, as soon as they learned it wasn't Pentagon policy to send letters of condolence for military suicides, rose up as one and sent him thousands of cards and letters of support and respect. Our lawyers pressured Missouri authorities, as only they can do for me, and got his legal charges dismissed. And fully two thousand Midnight Riders filled the streets of St. Louis a few weeks later at six in the morning to help him properly bury his brother's ashes. They also stood by him through a highly thoughtful and touching sunrise memorial service, attended by a full military honor guard made possible by the countrywide attention, a live remote which cost much of my listenership an entire night's sleep.

National drama on that scale happens rarely but Riders around the country continue to turn out every night for smaller crises. And by informal count, the Rick Lang Midnight Riders, I've been told, number four hundred thousand from Arizona to New Hampshire, Alaska to Florida. No wonder that, for nearly a decade, our monthly Arbitron ratings have dwarfed the numbers of most other stations, even their major market A.M. drive time blocks. The CEO of our rarely warm and fuzzy Conglomerate continues to try to clothe me in papal garb whenever I'm introduced at one of our annual conventions. But even in the spotlight, I'm forever the man in black.

I deeply believe in the power and necessity of committed and collective support in the face of every form of life complication. And the greatest proof of it for me came from Shannon, Owen, and Leah.

For two full years after the plane crash, my friends helped me endure and eventually helped me thrive. Shannon, who was hopeless when it came to all things domestic, learned how to cook so she could cook dinner for me Monday and Thursday nights like clockwork. If that wasn't generous enough, she also juggled her schedule so she could assist me as I attempted to take complete care of my house on my own. This was because I stubbornly made it a forbidden shrine which only friends could enter. So, with Owen also pitching in, she helped clean my hapless bathrooms, do my neglected laundry, and dust my babies' stuffed animals, never asking for any emotional coin in return. I nearly drowned over and over; she helped keep my head above water.

Owen spent the first two years after the funerals living with me at my home, getting me out of bed, getting me dressed, watching me during my depressive swings, all despite his own exhausting work schedule. He also tended Paige's enormous garden which would otherwise have gone wild, built a Centaur mailbox as well as an elaborate Centaur fountain which was featured and praised in the Marin Independent Journal.

Leah, because she was raising two children and working a hospital emergency room, had less time to devote to my salvation. But she agreed to be my companion at the myriad charity functions which I had no choice but to attend in order to further my good works and promote my show's healthy agenda. She cleverly absorbed the attentions of the press, for whom tragedy and celebrity were ideal fodder, by forcing herself to wear red carpet gowns and be my vivacious spokesperson. She put herself in the spotlight, which went entirely against her nature, thus keeping me in safe shadow and deluding the world into believing I could function by myself. It appeared to one and all that she was clinging to *my* arm but in actuality I was desperately clinging to *her* arm. Leah McLaren, a serious woman on her way to becoming one of San Francisco's most admired surgeons, disliked every moment of these public appearances but played my social arm charm and did it for me out of kinship and for no other reason.

Their actions taught me all I needed to know about the astounding synergy possible when people unite for a common good, even if it's only for the common good of one individual.

My show is called "Rick Lang, the Midnight Rider" -- although for the sake of big advertising dollars, I actually begin at ten at night and I end at two in the morning with carte blanche to ride on for as long as I choose. This is usually only necessary when I'm on the line with someone whose psychotic boyfriend is trying to microwave her Corgi dog and there she is pointing a .22 purse gun at his head with the SWAT team outside and me barely able to talk her finger off the trigger. Please don't think I'm kidding, it happened only five weeks ago. Here in the borscht belt of bathos, there's a fine line between heartbreak and hilarity.

Like any disc jockey or talk show host, I've got a clock and a format. First Hour is called "Desolation Row" and we talk about a variety of needful things. Listener names, info, and their issues are put on screen for me by my agile in-house tech Kimberly so I can pick and choose. But every Tuesday, we throw out the format in favor of "Snap Out Of It Night" when we pump up the laughs whenever possible and I send free pizza around the country to those callers who proudly report success in fixing their own emotional messes by themselves. My success stories on Tuesday are so legion that my investment advisors had me buy a national deep dish pizza franchise so "Midnight Rider Soul Warrior" pizzas can be delivered to select locations in record time.

Second Hour is the "Temple of Loss." I take song dedications up until midnight. Whether it's the loss of a football game, loss of a pet turtle, loss of a grandfather, loss of virginity, loss of a kidney, it's all grist for the mill and I've got a song for it. I take one call with a brief story, play the dedication, and then take two or three calls that relate supportively or sympathetically to the initial caller. And so on until the witching hour.

After midnight, my third hour on air is called "Ten-One-One" which is for those whose lives seem to be too far gone for 911. This is a difficult part of the show. I usually have very talented call screeners work this hour because a lot of trouble-making flakes try to fly low under radar. I've burnt out twelve screeners in ten years, but Bridget, my current best and brightest, is a super freak, a natural born hit man at her job. Twenty-five year old Bridget wears purple hair with silver streaks (this week), and a sinuous green vine tattooed down her left leg which is always on show because she favors ill-fitting shorts worn with take-no-prisoners army boots. Bridget's murderous instincts are far in advance of her years. She is truly gifted at sniffing out phonies and pranksters, executing them with fervent delight before they can reach me. She was head-hunted and bagged by our General Manager from the most highly-rated radio shrink on the east coast. It was an easy recruitment because Bridget hated her boss, a legendary talk show psychologist who treated her listenership disrespectfully by posing as a mini-goddess sent from the heavens to lecture and judge. Here, Bridget tolerates and almost likes me because she gets that I see myself as no more special than the people we serve.

The last hour, the fourth hour of my show, is known as "No Sympathy For The Devil." Emergencies tend to be attracted to the end of my shift. It seems as if at least twice a week I have to mobilize the Midnight Riders on serious immediate business. They have raced after hit-and-run drivers, helped foil attempts at self-harm, tracked down runaways, comforted the dying.

My Riders are working class, they are professionals, they are young, they are old, they are a rainbow coalition in terms of ethnicity, they have advanced skills, they have no particular skills. But they are all *committed*. They are also not perfect, they make mistakes, and many times they fail despite all efforts. But far more often than not they get the job done.

There is a very long, very large glass window directly behind where I stand most nights. It features the lit-up skyline of San Francisco across the bay, offering me the constant sight of the most stunning cityscape in America with its 43 "official" hills (making it the second hilliest city in the world and La Paz, Bolivia doesn't have a Golden Gate Bridge so there's no real comparison). These illuminated skyscrapers seem to be a glorious magnification of my solitary floor candles, and the unique vibe of this beautiful city of bridges always lifts my spirits a little if not a lot by the end of the night.

My microphone is an old standard Sennheiser, a very forgiving mic because I move around a lot and I can pace to the length of the microphone cord without popping when I'm agitated and working a tough call. My console was custom made for me by Pacific Recorders. Its inputs, switches, sliders, volume control pots, everything is marked in psychedelic color code for my own amusement, plenty retro for this old wooden fire-trap Oakland radio station. Of course, I have a copy stand like any other jock, but I wing everything so it is rarely used.

For comic relief, my studio has a special couch for guests, a couch officially named "The Oakland Stroke" after a song by our honorary in-house Oakland band, Tower Of Power. At one time, the GM surreptitiously delivered to Studio B what must have been the most expensive designer sofa in the world. All because a few of my famous but clearly spoiled guests had complained. But sorry. Our ratty old couch comes from an East Oakland thrift shop, its worn and uncomfortable seat cushions intentionally conspire to maintain all studio visitors on edge in keeping with the often edgy Rick Lang, Midnight Rider show itself.

My listeners also know the names and personalities of my friends. Several times a week, I end my shift with Leah's "last call" song selection which she provides with sensitivity and panache. Her nurses at the E. R. always keep a nearby line open so that in between patching up car crash victims and sewing up knife wounds at San Francisco's House of Carnage, she can call in her nightly closer. Last week, it was Mariah Carey and Alanis Morrisette. As for the others, Gary routinely calls in for Green Day and Aerosmith. Anjuli requests just about anyone who sings with a bare midriff. If Dylan has a sleepover date, it's a double dose of Celine Dion and the Titanic theme. If he's alone, he rarely calls in because he's usually out trolling for his next sleepover. Shannon favors classic love songs on her good days, classic songs about revenge on her bad days.

Owen rarely calls but when he does it's to ask for Tupac Shakur's *California Love* because he and Tupac were Marin City neighbors back in the day.

I'm also partial to playing, as a regular feature every Sunday night, original vinyl cuts from the first album I ever purchased, aged eight: *Wheels Of Fire*, by Cream, that double LP in all its foil-covered glory. From it, I often spin "Crossroads," that questing Robert Johnson cover which craves direction I never seem to have. But I never forget to play "White Room."

A white room with black curtains in the station, as the lyrics go. What better place for the wreckage and residue of Richard Austen Lang, born forty years ago this week? A white room with black curtains in *my* station, that refugee-camp of purpose, a room which keeps fresh the cherished wounds which continue to inspire a boy turned man to live on, to reach out, to be there, to help light up his country with wounded eyes as bright as wheels of fire.

And now I begin the Rick Lang, Midnight Rider Show with its permanent opening tune, blasting off with "Losing My Religion" by R. E. M., alerting all those who follow my not-so-yellow brick road that we're about to get busy.

And as my Theme finally fades to zero, I lean into my microphone and begin, my voice made as deep and warm and restless as a summer lake ready to calmly battle any sudden rainstorm. "It's getting late," I say tonight. "You're still awake. Maybe you're bored. Or sad. Sleeping isn't easy. You're thinking about something. Or someone. Maybe you're lost. Or hurting. Some of you don't get what I'm about. That's cool. Some of you use me as a sleeping pill, also fine with me. Some of you are friends, some of you should be. But we're all together now. It's time to connect with each other. To serve each other. To win some victory for humanity, even if it's just one."

Now I make my voice soft, but soft as soft steel. "This is Rick Lang, the Midnight Rider. I don't have any answers, but you're safe here..."

## CHAPTER SEVEN

**"WHAT SHOULD I DO, RICK?"**
**BOB FROM LAS VEGAS IS IN TROUBLE.**
I can hear the suffering in his shortness of breath, his cracking voice, his stutter and repetition. But it's a no-brainer. My team, such as they are, will have Bob wrapped and in the chute in less than sixty seconds, giving me a sign-off on this call. I am pacing to the length of my microphone cord as usual, a practice that takes credit for my lean frame as I must walk miles each night in this tight circle behind my console.

"You tell me, Bob."

The silence is predictable. My floor candles flicker in tandem with my breath. He wants me to say it, but I want him to say it.

"C'mon, Rick. I gotta fight. I gotta go after her. She took my kid. What would you do?"

"I'd take quick action. Just like you're going to do."

"Yeah. That's right. That's what I'll do. I'll get cops, I'll get lawyers, I'll go after her parents and her brother. I'll get in everyone's face. I'll be the Terminator, right? She won't know what hit her!" There's that voice crack again, he's going down a level, I feel it. Why are they all named Bob? Some nights I get three or four guys named Bob. Is it a Bob curse? Did some Bob rip off a few archangels in a late night game of seven card stud? Did they catch him with a hanging card, spot him dealing off the bottom of the deck?

"Just give me a little help here, okay? Like why did she take him? I mean, sure, she hated living here! But it's a great gig, I'm bringing real money home for the first time! I even opened a savings account for him! Why couldn't she just stick it out another year? I love my son, he loves me! How could she do that to him? Five years old! A boy needs a Dad. My boy needs me! What do I do? What the hell do I do?"

Father-pain, son-loss. I know his wounds; they are deep. I miss my own father and the love he was so quick to share and show.

The hurt never goes away.

My mother. My sister.

The hurt never, never goes away.

Words help. But my little girls?

The hurt never, ever, never, ever goes away.

Ten years of Bob calls. Hurt can smack you flat at any given moment.

Another maxim of the Rick Lang, Midnight Rider show?

Hang tough. Always.

Kimberly, my nineteen-year old part-time assistant from Mills, is near my side, her fingers playing the computer keyboard like a Steinway. On my screen, she has displayed six connections with no degree of separation. Bridget has confirmed that they are all listening. That they have heard Bob's tale of grief. Bridget, whose fingernails this week are Phantom of the Opera Green, is speed-fingering the phones from her glassed-in booth at the far end of Studio B, okaying five of our connections in a matter of seconds, flashing me hand-signals to lose only Kimberly's number four choice. The conference button is flashing. NASA, we've got healers in orbit.

"You listen to the show a lot, Bob?"

"Always. I'm on a late shift."

"Then you know the Ten-One-One motto."

"Yeah, you got no answers. Great motto." He is sarcastic but not really so. My listeners understand.

"This is not something I can talk you through. Hey, what the hell do I know about losing children except it makes you want to blow your brains out. But your kid's out there. There's a boy out there who needs his daddy. We're gonna be active here, Bob. But you're gonna have to trust the people I'm going to make your best friends. You see, I'm going to hand you over to five of our most skilled Riders in the area of child abduction. They're on the line now. Blake's a lawyer in Trenton who will tell you what you can and can't do. Connie from Philadelphia counsels runaway wives; she'll give you insight on how your wife might be thinking and how to treat your family once you catch up to them without making a huge, screwball mess of it. Ben in Des Moines is a bounty hunter, he can find anyone and he gives Rick Lang listeners special deals on a sliding scale. Cheryl in New York City is a rabbi. I don't care what religion you are, Bob. She's a gifted listener, wise as can be, and that's what you need. She'll be on call for you 24/7 until this is over. Finally, Jack in Santa Fe was in the same boat last year, came on the show like you, got his kid back and made it work with a lot of patience and love. He'll tell you how he did it. He's also a cop, which might come in handy in locating your boy. Jack knows the system and we're glad to have him riding with us."

Bob is close to crying. But he stuffs it. "I don't know what to say," he says. "I don't know what to say..."

"Try to keep calm. Be smart. Trust your team. I have faith and you have faith too, okay?"

I signal Bridget to punch in our five volunteers and prepare the conference call, for I am Saint Rick the Closer. "I don't know if the Riders can solve it, Bob. But they'll give you a fighting chance. Ready to talk to them?"

"Yeah, that'd be great." Bob's voice is down to a cracked whisper, par for the course.

Bridget, whose most recent tattoos are barbed wire ankle ornamentation just above her kickass boots, takes my thumbs-up and patches Bob in with our panel of runaway wife and child abduction experts. Sometimes I have these joint trauma discussions on air so I can join in. But mostly,

Ten-One-One leans toward peer counseling. With my listenership at an all time high, I can connect the country in a real web of substance and emotion, give the finger to internet anonymity, and tap into that innate human desire to help face-to-face. I have heard firsthand of strangers giving or nearly giving their lives for other strangers on so many occasions that it seems, at least to me, to prove the existence of God, of a higher power, of something bigger and so much more mysterious.

The studio seems moodier tonight. Candles keep blowing out for no particular reason. The lights of the city are magnificent but subdued by the fog. I signal Bridget to give me someone lighter on the next spin of the wheel. Her smile is devilish which means she's been saving someone special; quickly she signs for me to pick up line twenty-eight. I sigh, expecting the worst. These days I don't have to actually speak to Bridget, instead we sign to each other in our own bizarre and weird version of American Sign Language. She has been much calmer since she took her vow of chastity last year and much more pleasant since she swore to never speak out loud to me again. Kimberly is a hardworking and creative tech with an ever-quicker learning curve. But Bridget, who rides a one-speed bicycle to work, finds it annoying that Kimberly drives a brand new high end Audi, a much nicer car than even our narcissistic new GM can afford. Kimberly is young, her family is well-off and well-connected, and I expect she'll eventually move on to produce some kind of makeover show which would better suit her temperament. Whereas Bridget could be mine forever which would be a mixed blessing at best.

Just then, Owen abruptly enters the studio. He's cleaned himself up, now wearing his genuinely faded and torn jeans (as he can't afford designer faded and torn jeans) and his ratty leather jacket (because he can't afford designer "distressed" leather). I'm surprised. He rarely visits Studio B. His tiny house nestled in the woods halfway up Mount Tamalpais is a long drive in the wrong direction from West Oakland.

Given Gary's marriage game debacle, and attorney Matthew Moss' satanic seven-for-one special, I had predicted communication from several of my

August '61 crew. But not a personal appearance from Owen. And surely not for the reason I dread. He looks anything but drunk or tired now as I wave him to the Oakland Stroke. He sits uncomfortably as the cushions wheeze, tilting him sideways.

"I want to kill someone, Rick. I just need your blessing and a little fire-power." The voice barking into my ears sharply draws my attention. I signal a query to a smirking Bridget, who refuses to signal back.

I then pivot to Kimberly who is already checking our data base, looking to identify our potential murderer as we have technology sufficient to accurately ID most callers.

"Pay phone. Michigan-Ohio border." Kimberly shakes her head. "And no record of someone named Freddie Elmstreet." She rolls her eyes.

I note that Owen has slipped on my guest headphones to listen in; I'm surprised he actually knows the drill.

"Let's start with your real name."

"Hey. You know me. We're old buds!"

As some people never forget a face, I rarely forget a voice. "Jason from Toledo. I thought we agreed that you'd stop calling in."

"Damn, you recognized me," says Jason. "That was my best Tom Cruise imitation too. And hey, I'm not making this up. I want someone whacked. Gimme three or four of your real bad-ass Riders, that's all I need. Once the dirty deed is done, we hit the Midnight Rider Pizza Palace or whatever in Sylvania, and its beer and pepperoni on me."

"Jason, you know the punishment for yanking my chain and wasting my time," I reply, although what kind of punishment can I really offer? Banishment from my kingdom of grief? Gee, everybody line up.

I throw yet another dirty look at Bridget who shrugs and feigns innocence as Jason from Toledo begins his tale of outrage. "Just listen, okay? So my roommate at Bowling Green flunked out. And he took off for Akron with my *entire* collection of Megadeath and Anthrax concert tapes! So all's I want you to do is have your boys cut the somebitch in half, do some major ball sack damage. I want him to feel the Midnight Rider fury! The Midnight Rider wrath!"

There's always the caller's story. And then, often, there's the real story, subtext or the truth. I prepare for the worst. "Why did he do it, Jason? What makes me think you're leaving out the best part?"

"Okay, okay, I did his skanky girlfriend. But only once. What's that compared to being ripped off? It was one dope chunk of listening pleasure, man."

"I'm going to stop you right there, Jason. Say goodnight."

"Wait! You can just cut off a few of his fingers! Like those Yakuza dudes, cut off his pinkies, come on!"

I punch his line dead and load in our number one mix, Greg Allman's long acoustic version of "Midnight Rider" recorded just for us a few years ago from his home in Georgia along with the original cut from his 1973 debut album. Then I hand signal to a silently laughing Bridget that I'd like her to take a flying you-know-what, if her vow of chastity will allow it.

I yank off the cans, walk over to Owen. The mix will provide me with at least fifteen minutes to check in with him.

Owen looks uncomfortable. It's not just the couch.

"What is it?" I ask. "Last time I saw you, Shannon was driving you home and you were wasted beyond redemption."

"I got to thinking. And it sobered me up quick."

"Thinking about what?"

He fidgets. "I want to go for the money."

For a moment, I have a hard time speaking. Then I find myself laughing despite myself. "Owen, it's a scam, not a game show!"

"Moss has the cash," replies Owen. "I Googled him sideways. He's one of the top fifty wealthiest people in San Francisco, not including the east bay or the peninsula, but plenty of bucks to back up his big words. We'll get a lawyer, one just as tricky as he is. We'll lock him in to his promise. All we have to do is marry, sign some papers. It ends at the chapel, no commitment. It's a bet I think we can win!"

I sigh. "Owen, listen…"

"I don't just *want* the money. I *need* it. All my life I've worked for non-profits or I've been underemployed by the private sector or underpaid by the state." He hesitates, but not for long. "Listen carefully to me, Rick. It's important." As I'm standing, he stands. Two inches taller than me but at the moment he seems to tower. He continues: "I sometimes tune in to your show. And it seems that every time I do, I hear people constantly having issues with their self-respect. I hear them talking about losing their self-worth, their pride. I hear them afraid of growing old and being poor. That's me, Rick. How many times am I going to get a chance like this?"

"If you need money, I'll give you money," I say. "You're my best friend, I've got your back, and you'll never fall on hard times. I'm always here for you."

"That's just it. I want something of my own. Something I earn. I appreciate your help, but this may be my only chance to catch a break. There isn't money in Centaurs or restoring machine-age radios or teaching undergraduates. I want to do this." He hesitates again. "And I need you to help me."

It must be noted right now that Owen has never asked me a favor of any size before, whereas he has done a thousand for me. Do I really have a choice?

"What if you're just being used?"

"You're always talking about risks on your show, Rick. How staying in the same place is so much more dangerous than risking. I want to risk this thing. And it's not just *you* I need at five o'clock Monday on Montgomery Street. I need Leah. And you're the only one who can get her."

Leah.

All of a sudden, a suspicious feeling lures me to the studio door. I yank it open. And I am greeted with the three mouseketeers. The three blind mice. The three stooges. In short, our very own Dylan and Anjuli and Gary are all waiting happily as they lean against the hallway wall. They smile as one.

"You'll come to see Moss, won't you, Rick?" asks Dylan.

"And you'll twist Leah's arm, you've got to…" adds Gary.

"Shannon's not the problem," says Dylan. "She'll come. You just have to put your lips together and whistle..."

"Because Shannon *always* does what you do," adds Anjuli.

"Leah's the problem," says Gary.

"Leah's usually the problem," says Anjuli.

"Look. Moss is not just gonna offer you money, Rick," continues Dylan. "He's got something you want. You heard him, didn't you? He's gonna come up with something for you. Something you need. Didn't you see how confident he was? It's gotta be something worth checking out!"

"And he'll have something for Leah too," continues Gary, "Something she's missing. He'll figure out what it is. The dude is *motivated!*"

I take it back. Forget the three stooges. I'm dealing with the three witches in Macbeth. Let fire burn and *trouble* bubble.

"So we get married! That's why God invented divorce!" Dylan is pumped.

"And who says we have to sleep with the person we marry?" interjects Gary.

"Then again, why not!" offers Anjuli.

Dylan circles me subtly and now I'm surrounded. "Leah needs to stop being afraid of dating, even if it's just a set-up! It might help her get over being dumped for a girl that looked like some middle school babysitter."

"Shannon needs to practice commitment with somebody, anybody!" Gary is adamant.

"And Owen..." Dylan adds.

"Poor Owen..." Anjuli adds.

"He needs the money, the experience, the whole package!" Gary insists.

"We keep it simple. All seven of us. At his office." Dylan is Mr. Organized.

"We'll see the cash on the table!" Anjuli enthuses.

"Then we vote. And it's gotta be unanimous, so nothing to lose!" Dylan adds.

"One hour of your time, Rick." Gary is by a narrow hair's width the most reasonable as usual. "It's just a little show and tell. One hour of our lives."

There must have been some give in my expression because Anjuli springs up, wraps her enthusiastic legs around my waist, her arms around my neck, and grinds her petite pelvis against my body with inappropriate zeal.

"You are so great, Rick," simpers Anjuli. "You're my superhero!"

"We know you'll come for Owen's sake," says Gary, as he helps unplug Anjuli from my body. "But Leah doesn't have your same loyalty. Leah's not a team player. I know you guys aren't that close any more. And she gets weird and angry about you sometimes. But she totally trusts you."

On that, much to my horror, Dylan literally drops to his knees, pleading. "Two million plus a possible bonus! Look at me, Midnight Rider. My life's been a bad joke with no punch line. Get Leah and there's a small chance that every crappy thing I've ever done can be undone. Maybe I can get back on track with my kids, show them I care about something besides pool toys. Please! Ten years of friendship has to be worth a lousy hour in a lawyer's office and just one measly light saber attack on Princess Lee-ah! You can do it!"

I grab Dylan by the armpits, drag him upright. I'm annoyed at being played so forcefully yet moved to hear him speak, as he rarely speaks, of his scattered children.

"I have other considerations, Dylan. You know that better than Gary or Anjuli."

"You mean Paige," interrupts Anjuli. "Except she's been *dead* ten years, Rick! We're the living. We're your friends. And we need this! Don't bury us too!"

Gary, far more diplomatic and seeing Anjuli is entering dangerous territory, steps in front of our little hot rocket. "We *all* respect and love Paige, Rick, even if we didn't have the privilege of knowing her. You're not hurting her memory by considering this proposition." He gives me his best smile. "Look. Moss just said seven marriages in order. He didn't mention any other obligation in terms of length or consummation. Just in and out, two million or better. Okay, I won't get down on my knees like Dylan. But I'm living a life I can't afford, credit card debt impossible to pay off, walking away from my houseboat is a real possibility, bankruptcy not out of the question. I don't need a loan, I need a solution. And this is it. It's an out-of-the-blue miracle. We all need it. It's our answer."

61

"Especially Owen," blurts out Anjuli. "His life is so pathetic. Such a cool guy going to waste. And here's your chance to show him some love!"

Fire burn and cauldron bubble, bubble, bubble. There is finally silence in the hallway. Three faces look expectantly at me.

I'm angry. And it's not because of their greed or their ridiculous naiveté. It's because I know how Paige would've handled this. She knew how to chalk boundaries. Her moral compass never wavered. She would *never* have tolerated Anjuli or Dylan's hyperbolic inanity as I do. She would have been kind and firm with Gary, finding him a more sensible solution. She would have found a way to cajole Owen into accepting our financial aid, she would have found a way to defeat his pride.

But Paige isn't here as Anjuli so indelicately pointed out. And what is one meeting compared to the years Owen and the others have spent putting up with *me*?

I yield.

"I'll go and talk to Leah after my shift," I find myself saying to the three amigos, "But no guarantees..."

Before Anjuli can excitedly launch herself at me yet again, I quickly backpedal away from their deliriously joyful faces and re-enter the studio. Their howls of happiness can be heard behind me and the last thing I can see peripherally in the hallway as I close the studio door is my band of iconoclastic friends literally clinking their silver numbered bracelets together, all for one and one for all.

Kimberly informs me that she had to slot in her fave Marc Anthony, Enrique Iglesias mix to cover my longer-than-expected disappearance. Bridget signs me that the phone lines are waning half-full as my absence has been less than engaging.

But first I have to finish up with Owen who sheepishly, guiltily, awaits me.

He sighs. "I told them to keep quiet."

We share a moment of silence. He waits for my reaction. I let him suffer for a moment before I manage a half-smile.

"Leah's going to bite my head off." I say.

Owen nods, relieved. "Probably with one chomp."

# CHAPTER EIGHT

S AN FRANCISCO GENERAL HOSPITAL IS A SPRAWLING
AND INTIMIDATING BRICK CITY WHICH SQUATS,
perched like a gargantuan vulture, upon the long edge of the Mission district.
Its emergency room, always a colorful showcase of hospital culture, is busy
tonight. There is a single row of fifty or so black plastic benches bolted to
one wall, quite a few now occupied by agitated families, one cluster appearing
to be taking turns genuflecting in the hope that Jesus will save their beloved
gangbanger from the bullets he took in the torso. There are also some like-
bolted individual chairs where a ballet chorus of the homeless, sleeping in fifth
position and blissfully snoring in rough unison, make walking to the triage
desk seem like an unasked for performance of Giselle meets The Night of the
Living Dead. Pressed against the opposite wall from the benches and chairs
is a long queue, an endless string it seems, of desperate people in desperate
need of medical attention who form a shuffling, miserable conga line from the
triage desk to the street, prepared to wait up to six hours for basic health care
on this midsummer's night, here in our land of the free and home of the brave.
Yes, it is four-in-the-morning and the only show in this town features a *pas de
deux*: dying and waiting.

At the triage desk, the nurses remember me as I ask for Leah. Their eyes instinctively gauge my threat level. They can't help it, it's a habit. These are combat nurses, baby, with a psychiatric ward to their left and a criminal jail lockdown to their right. My visit is perfectly timed, for Leah has just finished sewing up a teenage girl who tried to commit suicide by driving through the plate glass window of a clothing outlet store, sadly discounting her life.

Leah is paged, and it is only moments before she appears in a bohemian rhapsody of fresh green scrubs. She beams, forcing me yet again to wonder how any smile can be so spontaneously dazzling under even the direst of circumstances.

"That's the great thing about the E. R. You never know who will turn up," she says, dimpling just a little. "I'm short one nurse and we've got a biker coming in with a little drive-by action. How'd you like to help suction?"

"Very tempting," I manage a smile in return. "Got a few minutes to talk?"

She looks at me too closely, intuiting. "Hmm. What could possibly bring you to the Mish in the middle of the night?"

"Owen asked me to come here and twist your arm."

Leah's smile fades. "You're not actually going to meet with that old hustler, are you?"

"It looks like it."

"Please tell me you're kidding." She sees my face. "Oh, perfect! Who else?"

"Gary, Anjuli, Dylan, Owen, and Shannon."

"In other words, everyone but me."

I can see she's not taking this well. Quickly I grab her arm and firmly move her toward the lockdown, out of general earshot except for those zany drug dealers and prostitutes-from-Mensa in the cells behind us who may choose to listen in. "Let me explain…" I begin.

Leah interrupts me. "I'd rather guess. Do you mind? Much more fun that way."

"Fine," I say. This hasn't started well.

Leah surprises me by pushing me backwards, flanking my shoulders with her arms, in effect pinning me against the cinder block wall behind us with lithe forcefulness. It's oddly provocative. Leah is truly something. She can be trusted yet she is unpredictable, a very rare combination of attributes.

"Owen needs money. A well-known fact." She begins, edging a little closer to me. "So, out of character, he convinces himself to buy the con. After all, if he can buy Centaurs, why can't he buy a mythical two million bucks from a man in an Armani suit?" Leah slides a tiny bit closer, using her proximity to make me uncomfortable. It's obvious she plans to make me pay for this favor. "Right so far?"

"Right."

"Shannon follows you out of loyalty, believing she's safe if you tell her so." She raises an eyebrow. "How am I doing?"

"Flawless."

"Great. Then the rest is a throw-down. We've got Anjuli, who's greedy. Gary, who's gullible. Dylan who always leaps without looking." She pauses briefly, her wide and stunning hazel eyes, amber-brown in the center, charcoal-green toward the periphery, and still a little smoky with her birthday party make-up, do not blink as they stare into mine. "What are the odds that they've been falling all over you, appealing to your sense of teamwork and Society solidarity? Am I right?"

I sigh. "Bingo."

"And now I'm the last of the seven dwarves."

With that, she releases me but keeps me pinned to the wall with an eye-lock.

"It's not a shotgun wedding," I say, trying to keep the ball in play. "It's a business meeting and, joke or no joke, Owen wants you to come." Then I lower the now-familiar boom. "When was the last time he asked you for anything?"

She winces. As with all of us, Owen has always given her more than he's taken.

Over Leah's shoulder I can see a policewoman down the hall forcing your basic yelling and screaming meth head into the psychiatric lockdown. Not a pretty sight. I decide to lighten my tone as I continue. "Make it work for you! Throw peanuts. Heckle. But show up for an hour. No big deal and, as promised, plenty of free parking! Try to beat that so close to North Beach!" I throw in the last for a laugh, but she's not laughing. She's not even smiling.

"No deal. No can do. No *want* to do."

"It's an hour of your time. For Owen..."

"You've already played that card."

"Leah. Be fair."

"Why?"

"I don't know. It's the right thing to do. Owen..."

"Oh, come on..." She gives me a look. "This is *not* about *Owen*! What's your problem? It's about *us*."

That sucks the air out of the corridor for a few moments. But it's not rocket science, I get it. "You mean tonight."

"I know you felt it."

"I did. Yes."

"But nothing happened."

"What do you mean by nothing?"

"Hopeless." She shakes her head in dismay. "And sort of brainless, too. Let me help. Where were you a few hours ago? And who was that lying at your feet?"

"Someone who was wearing a green dress that was tighter than a jazz trio."

"And what were you thinking about this woman in the tight green dress?"

"I was thinking a lot of things."

"Name three."

"That she was fun. That she was beautiful. That I missed her...."

"So you must have felt awfully stupid because you haven't spent any real time alone with her in ages."

"I actually didn't think that. Because I see her all the time."

"Alone?"

"Not exactly."

"*That's* why I'm not going to Owen's bake sale. And you can tell him it's *your* fault."

"Because I've been hopeless and brainless."

She glares at me. "No, it's worse than that. Because I was thinking you were here tonight at four A.M. to surprise me because that would have been kind of romantic. Or to dish about the party. Because that would have been sweet. Or to straight out confess that my party dress was *way* too hot for you to handle. Because that would have been the truth." Her tone darkens. "Instead, Rick, you came here to *deliver* me..."

She rests her case.

"You're right." I say. "I'm an idiot."

"You always know how to choose *just* the right word. What else you got?"

"I'm also on the insensitive side. But only with those I care about."

Leah suddenly laughs and rubs one of the booties which cover her shoes over my instep. "I look pretty awful right now, don't I? I was going to keep my frock on while I worked tonight. But who accessorizes with blood splatter?" Her eyes sparkle.

I wish I could fathom this woman, but I know I'll never be that lucky. "No, no. You still have that birthday glow." I peer at her more closely. "It's amazing how sternum splitting can still put that special blush in your cheeks."

"You're probably wondering where this all comes from?"

"I'd like to know. Yes."

"As I was putting on my make-up tonight, getting ready to stroll into Society chaos, I had this thought. The kind of thought that women of a certain age have when they reach a certain age. If you get my drift."

"I'm drifting ... albeit brainlessly..."

She gives me a quick amused look, continues. "Then pay attention. Here I am, getting all pretty for the party, putting mascara on my lower lashes and, given that's when I have all my epiphanies, *boom*, I have the about-to-turn-forty revelation. What is it, you don't ask? Leah McLaren is still moderately damn hot. So that takes me to the next level. What would be so bad to have a man in my life again? Someone to go out with, friendly dates, someone who appreciates me just a bit? And then, by the time I got to my lipstick, I'm thinking, hmmm again, that Rick used to like my remarkably kissable lips just lightly glossed and on the pale side of pink. Which led me to the previously unconscious conclusion that you were always the guy in the back of my head, the one I always put in the picture frame. The happy picture."

She hesitates. But my facial expression does its job, clearly telling her to keep on rolling while the momentum is on her side. So she continues, a little faster this time. "What happened to us? We used to have intimacy, the real kind, not the sex kind, although at the beginning, in our 20s, it was always lurking, the sex thing I mean, though you were with Paige. I'm talking about intimacy, the real kind that began when we were both twenty-three and too cool for school, when we were so perfectly...," she pauses for the right word, "...*calibrated*... that we didn't need language. Remember the way we looked at each other. Like two submarines, side by side, silent but deep and good with each other, no propeller noise."

I look at her. I don't know what to say. But she waits. She waits for me to say something. And I know what she wants. Answers.

"That's a whole lot of poetry," I say softly.

"Sorry. But I gotta keep it fresh."

"I was married. Then you were married."

"Even so, it was always *there*."

"You're saying it's not *there* now."

"I *know* it's not *there* now! But it was still *there* after the plane crash. It was *always* there when I was with Ronny. For ages, no matter what the situation, we were friends who were always *there* for one another." She pauses. "But five years ago that part of you took an emotional hike. I wonder if it's because I'm so much healthier, my life is good, I'm strong. Way past Ronny. Way past the hurt. Getting better all the time." She gives me a look for emphasis. "Maybe you're still not really comfortable with people who are problem-free, is that possible?"

"Okay," I say. "You *do* have a terrible case of *normal*. But it's amazingly great that you've come to that place. It makes me happy to see you like this."

"Then let me be blunt. You hang with Owen all the time, Shannon all the time, Dylan and Gary at least once a week. Even Anjuli sees you more than I do and I live only three miles away from you! Why don't you come to my house? Why don't I come to yours? What did I do wrong?"

"I talk to you almost every night."

"On the air." She replies. "On the air! That's not exactly the same. There are millions of people listening! "I'm just a *segment*!"

In a flash of summer lightning gestalt, I see this past evening with new details coming into focus. She was wearing the Australian opal earrings I was forced to buy her after a famous lost bet. And when I looked down at her, when she swooned on the floor and pointed her heels in my direction, it must have been that she wanted me to see that she was wearing the ankle bracelet I won for her at the Marin County Fair some fifteen years ago when, spouseless for a night, we indulged our fantasy of what we could be like together. That cheap carnival ankle bracelet which came to us on a magical moondance kind of night, which I knelt down to put on her so we could symbolize our special connection.

I look down to her surgical booties. The ankle bracelet is still there.

I take her hand. "Look. You made it to the finish line, you're whole, you're the Society's star graduate. I'm not where you are, Leah. I'll probably never be."

"There's that brainless thing again..."

"I can't help it, I really can't. You're a gem and there's something one in ten million about you. I deserve the others, we're all works in progress. But you...."

I've run out of words.

Abruptly she straightens up to her full five-foot-nine-in-green-booties height. "I love you, Rick. I know you love me. And you're so special to me, so important to my life. How can you dismiss seventeen years of friendship just because I'm not as bruised and hurt as you or Shannon or Owen? There's even the possibility that I can help you now that I've got my act so much together. Ever think about that? Why can't you let *me* be the best friend who holds your hand, who tries with all her heart to help you cross over to the brighter side of the road?" She suddenly softens. "There aren't enough men out there like you. I need your close company. I need your touch and your wisdom. Being a part of my family can help you. Please let my boys help you. They're getting so mature! They've got so many hobbies, so many friends. We hardly need any live-in help anymore. Everybody loves them. *You'd* love them if you gave them more of a chance. I know they remind you of *your* twins, we've been over that, I think we're past that, I hope we're past that. But you haven't been to my house in five years. Why not face your fears and spend some time with my freckles! See what other dresses I might have in my closet. Come to my house for Sunday brunch. Take me to the Boom-Boom Room like old times. John Lee Hooker always wanted me to sing there. Maybe I'll sing for you." She tilts her head in mock self-dismay. "Okay, enough talk. But promise you won't try ever again to protect me with your distance. With you, it's always the closer the better."

I hear the page for Dr. McLaren. I react, start to move, but she gently nudges me back against the wall. "It's just a code two, Rick. No sirens, no lights." She smiles wanly. "Let's not be like that…"

I am a bridge of sighs. "I wasn't aware. Now I'm aware."

And here comes her sonnet smile. "Hey, maybe Gary's Marriage Box is working. Let's make getting back together our birthday gift to one another! How could it hurt?"

She offers her lips very subtly, and I surprise myself by immediately kissing her lightly. Then she grins, closing the brief conduit of attraction between us. "One last thing. Just a small, but important thing." She hesitates. "Rick, all those times I went with you to those banquets and concerts and charity things in your honor? You knew how much I hated all that glamour, the attention, all that red carpet stuff? You knew I was uncomfortable and yet you kept asking me."

"I'm sorry. I was in bad shape. I couldn't have been in worse shape."

"I did twenty-seven public appearances in a row, Rick. Yes, I kept track. Why didn't you ask Shannon to play your companion at these functions? Wouldn't she have been a more logical choice? Loads of media experience. She would've done a much better job at handling the press than I did. Nice legs too, maybe not as thrilling as mine own, but worthy of the paparazzi. How come you always asked me? Why me?"

"You were the one I needed. I'm sorry."

Leah nods. "Stop saying 'I'm Sorry' because *I'm* not sorry...it meant something major to me. Because asking me to play that role over and over again sort of told me that you wanted me by your side as your most trusted babe. And I liked being your most trusted babe. And I really want to be your most trusted babe again."

It's a good thing I'm one tough midnight rider because there is a whole lot of tenderness going on here in this house of mayhem and scalpels.

"Leah, I love you too, in my way, not the greatest way, but in my way and, if you can try to accept that getting to a deeper place of friendship will take time..." Her eyes start to get a little wet. "...what I'm trying to say is that I'll come to your house and see the twins and check out your closet and peer carefully at the only grown woman I know who gives dignity to freckles...but I'll need to take it slow..." I run out of words, wrack my cauterized synapses to find something special to punctuate the moment, to put icing on this last piece of birthday cake, and just grab for the first thing that comes to mind. "I'll even play Twister with you again, never mind I'm inflexible these days, but if you promise not to try those old tricks of yours..."

Leah interrupts excitedly. "Twister! Oh God YES! Great idea!"

"And you won't get mad when I win?"

"I'll never let you win!"

"And we keep it hands on, but hands off, platonic…"

She laughs. "You're so *you*, Rick! I told you. *Any* package you come in. I understand timing, I understand hands off, and it doesn't matter if we never honeymoon on Bali. You are a sweet beautiful man and all I want to do is spend some meaningful time together, that's all I care about."

So I laugh with her and get a glimpse of what, for five dusty years, has been lost in a whirling opaque sandstorm of my design. With clarity tentatively restored, I carefully kiss her again. Like before, lips just parted, but this time it is with a little sweeter and firmer touch of romantic friendship.

"Twister," sighs Dr. Leah McLaren. "Remember when Owen dislocated his shoulder? The time he slipped and Anjuli accidentally landed so hard on top of him?"

"I still have the photo. The one Dylan turned into a Christmas card."

"Anjuli did it on purpose, you know."

"Her favorite Kama Sutra position or so she claimed."

"He was so embarrassed he didn't even yell when I popped his shoulder back in its socket."

Suddenly I find myself saying something to her which I hadn't planned to say. It comes from my unruly auto-pilot and my words actually reek of something very much similar to enthusiasm. "And how about dinner? After this meeting I'm asking you to show up at?"

Leah's radiant expression is my gift in response and her exclamation of pleasure is all thrills and chills. "If my heart could fly, I'd shoot right through the roof, YES! I'd *love* to go out with you! Just the two of us! Just you and me and dinner and a few drinks and we'll laugh about old times, plan new times, it'll be our party time!" But a sudden thought flickers across her face. She hesitates, clearly thinking and re-thinking, before adding: "But would it be okay if you left Paige at home? I know that sounds unforgivably rude. And I have no right to put it that way. But you know what I mean…"

"I'll do my best," I say.

*And I will try, I will.*

Leah's final kiss is all subtle slow dance. The lips are a little wider, the flow of romantic friendship implicit, the hint of sexual promise down the line completely problematic. I don't have the nerve, especially not at this very moment, to tell Leah that Paige is forever in my emotional lockdown. Not much I can do about that.

We stop at the triage desk where she has to take a left turn back into surgery. I let go of her hand not actually realizing I had been holding it all this time. "By the way, please don't wear anything sexy at dinner, okay?"

She laughs at me. "I promise. I don't want to make you uncomfortable. How about my best radiation suit and thickest lumberjack boots?"

"Don't get all fancy just for me."

"Meanwhile, I think a little preparation might come in handy for our ridiculous meeting with this ridiculous scam artist."

"So you'll definitely come, you're a definite yes?"

"You can tell Owen that I'll be ready to roll at his five o'clock farce! But make sure you tell him that he owes me another one of his radios, this time a red one. To match my bloodshot eyes."

Leah exits through the double doors, back to work, happily waving behind her head without looking back at me. I watch her go. After the doors have swung closed and the combat nurses at the triage desk give me their last cautious nods, I slowly start back toward the street.

"Hey, man! You get a good doctor? He fix you up right?" An old and cranky Latino with a badly swollen broken nose has made it toward the front end of the still endless medical waiting line.

"Woman doctor," I reply, "But real good with a knife."

"That's all I need. Don't be fooled, *Mijo* ..." He points to his broken nose. "Women bring you nothin' but trouble..."

# CHAPTER NINE

MATTHEW MOSS' LAW LIBRARY IS ONE OF THE LARGEST I'VE SEEN. THE CONFERENCE TABLE IS made of cherry wood with birch inlay. It is beautiful, as are its eighteen matching armchairs. The building itself is one of the few registered pre-1906 fully restored Victorians to be found downtown. It shows surprising taste, but then it is meant to impress and we are impressed. Currently, the not-so-secret society is being watched by a young technician, perhaps twenty-five years old, who is preparing a computer hook-up at the head of the table. If I were a betting man, which Moss hopes I'll become, I would guess that we are about to receive a PowerPoint presentation of some kind. Given the circumstances, I expect a cornucopia of sophistry and manipulation. Moss is not here, but the Society is present in record numbers. All but one of us is ready and waiting, Owen is still missing. It is ten minutes to five in the afternoon of our discontent.

Leah, always thorough, sent her lawyer ahead, a senior partner in the firm of Barnett, McLaren & Boudreau. McLaren was Leah's father, dead of a sudden heart attack in the seventh row center as he was enjoying the San Francisco Ballet with his daughter. Her best efforts could not revive him; this hardworking self-made man passed away in Leah's arms unfortunately just six months after Ronny left her and only two years after her Dublin-born mother passed away. Tyrone Boudreau, godfather to Leah's twins and one of the most powerful African-American attorneys in the City, whom Leah's father had groomed and brought out from Boston with him, has been examining Moss' proposed contract for nearly an hour, watched by Leah, Shannon and yours truly. We have only recently being joined by the cheerful three-man bobsled team of Anjuli, Gary and Dylan.

Boudreau looks up at Leah. He hasn't said much in this last half hour. Leah has known him most of her life, trusts him completely, his opinion will decide whether the starter's gun even fires. He nods to her. Done.

"Good, bad, or insane, Tyrone?" asks Leah, stepping up beside him. Today she is distinctly underdressed in tight jeans and an uncharacteristically short cropped tee-shirt.

Boudreau clears his throat, gives Leah an amazed shake of his head. "I'll take this copy home and bring it to the office tomorrow. We'll have everyone there take a swing at it. But if you're willing to abide by the conditions as stated in this document… and it is one bizarre contract as far as I'm concerned… I think you'll find it completely legal and… for the infamous Matthew Moss… remarkably straightforward."

We all look at each other, some with that sweet-dangerous glee we are known for, others with dismay. Boudreau begins to pack his briefcase, taking the papers he has been given, adding a few final restrained thoughts. "Moss has asked me not to be specific until he's made his… I suppose you'd call it a sales pitch. And, Leah, you've agreed to this request, so this much I can tell you. The monies are definitely in legitimate escrow, the escrow instructions are a model of clarity. There are some anomalies in the division of the cash, generally in your favor. The amount is significant. Mr. Lang alone will receive no money; instead, he'll be offered a different form of compensation. For some reason known only to Moss, this compensation is to be revealed to me in an addendum, a copy of which will be delivered by messenger to my office after your meeting."

Boudreau continues. "Moss may be a piece of work, Leah, but he's clearly done a lot of expert research on you." Boudreau pauses as if debating his words. "In any case, the contract is dated tomorrow. You have a little time. I wouldn't have any of your friends sign until you've all thought it over carefully."

The Society exchanges glances. Leah hugs her surrogate father. "Thanks, Ty. Thanks for looking after me. You know I'll be careful."

Boudreau nods. "And the firm will be too. We'll go over it just like your father would have wanted. But on first appraisal, this contract is going to hold up in any court of law as long as both sides keep to the letter of the agreement." He gives a small wave, unable once again to keep a slightly incredulous look from rolling over his face. "Good luck, all of you."

As Boudreau exits, Owen strolls in. New haircut. New suit, expensive and well-made. Even an edgy Shannon, who came formally dressed for business and a bad time, checks him out, pleasantly surprised. He looks, well, *fantastic*. Spring in his step, gleam in his eye, and a bright red vintage Detrola radio under his arm which he cheerfully puts in Leah's hands before sauntering over to the table. He notices the place-cards with our names on them then coolly slides into the third chair along the Society side of the table, in between Anjuli and Gary. Anjuli's fingers are all over the fabric of Owen's suit as she coos her approval.

The tech silently leaves. The passenger list is now complete and we are alone.

Leah is the last to walk to her chair, still eyeballing her new radio. She waves her thanks to Owen who had happily acceded to her joking demand. As she sits next to me, placing the radio to one side and giving me a small wink, I notice she has actually had a manicure, not par for her course given her surgeon's requisite short fingernails and non-requisite tendency to gnaw on them when frustrated. She sees that I've noticed and waggles them at me.

We are seated along the same side of the table in this windowless but beautifully lit room in the order of the Marriage Box numbers. We are all in business attire, more or less, except Leah. We also still wear the numbered bracelets on Gary's adamant insistence. Before each of us is an envelope with our name and "number." Numbers One through Four (Dylan, Anjuli, Owen, and Gary) have blue envelopes. Leah has a red envelope. I have a green envelope. Shannon has a black envelope which she has dismissively nudged away from her so it lies just out of reach. All of the envelopes have the instruction not to open until advised.

"Why is Leah getting more money?" asks Anjuli. "Am I not the first woman in this crowd to give my body for the greater good of the Society? And what's with the envelopes?"

"I hope yours has a gag in it," snaps Shannon. She is hiding her agitation well, but not well enough.

"Troops, I think the envelopes are going to have the names of the people we're supposed to marry," notes Owen.

"What's with that?" Dylan frowns. "I've got my own prospects!"

"And I have a major candidate," argues Gary. "Blonde hair to the waist. Little surfer girl. She'll drop in a millisecond. You watch."

"You really think this Matthew Moss is going to make it that easy for us? He wants us to lose, he said so." Owen shakes his head.

Anjuli pouts her disapproval. "No way! I'm set too. I've got a half-dozen Mister Rights in love with my paint job and my reclining seats. I'll be married within five minutes of Dylan."

Owen turns to face her; they're almost nose to nose. "Anjuli, we're playing for two million each, he says he's playing for fifty times that. You really think he'll let us pick our own ringers?"

Anjuli's pout deepens. "Hey, I'm the hardest working date in the Bay Area. Even if you're right, say you're right, I can still make myself irresistible to any man. My beauty routine is second to none and, believe me, fifteen years of Yoga has left me as flexible as any college cheerleader!" Anjuli punctuates by fiercely twisting her black ringlets.

Leah speaks up. "We should *not* be assuming this is going to work out."

Owen responds quickly. "Leah, your own lawyer said it was legit."

Leah shakes her head at Owen's sudden sureness and yanks down her creeping tee-shirt, exasperated. "Well, no matter what kind of infomercial we get here today, I'm not marrying anybody for money, no matter how I feel about you guys."

Shannon quickly joins in. "That's true for me too. I can't change that, I'm sorry. So don't get excited. And please don't blame me if I'm the one who ruins your plans."

Suddenly Owen stands; I can't remember the last time he looked so ferocious. "Look, the whole point of the Game is that it's not about marriage. It's about *getting* married. Just getting someone to sign the marriage certificate. Period. Then we're done with it! Depending on the time line, we don't have to sleep with them, live with them, spend a life with them. Repeat. Just get them to sign on the dotted line! Even if we have to lie a lot and do wrong things, we can settle our karma later. We won't be bad guys." He comes around the table to address us from the other side and continues. "Look. After our party last night I came home to find my General Electric F-51 had slipped off its shelf. Totally smashed, tubes shattered, Bakelite cracked, disaster. I mean there are only a handful of totally restored models in the world. One's even in the Rock 'n Roll Hall of Fame! And guess what? I don't have enough money in my bank account right now to pay for *radio parts*! I'm poor, gang. Poor. And I'm sick of being poor. You know I don't take handouts, but I will work my butt off for this ticket out. Like my suit? Now my last credit card is officially maxed. Hey, gotta look good for my new girlfriend, because this chick is going to punch that ticket. But I've got a problem because I suck with women. Most of the time I say the wrong thing, and I *always* seem to *do* the wrong thing. And I won't be able to do this job without you. All of you. I need your input. Teach me how to do this. Help me out of my crap finances." He walks over to our end of the table. "I hope the rich Society guys will put aside their independence and consider how easy it is getting these things annulled. Shannon, what do you really have to lose? Leah, there's no emotional involvement; it won't be another Ronny, just a quick gift to me. Rick, be a Midnight Rider for your best friend. It's nothing to do with Paige."

Owen steps back from us all, spent. Now he lets a little self-conscious discomfiture show with a blush.

Anjuli, Gary, and Dylan clap! The rest of us sit in stunned silence. Owen, a man of few words, a researcher more than a lecturer, has just made his maiden speech in our very own Parliament of the unreal. He returns to his seat.

Just then the ever-impeccable Matthew Moss enters the room looking chipper and pleased with himself, the computer tech right behind him. And finally, in walks a Third Man. He is just the opposite of jovial. Late 60s, probably early 70s, gaunt and silver-haired, coal-black suit with a white shirt and a dark regimental tie, he looks like a wealthy undertaker who scored with a chain of theme-park graveyards.

Moss takes a moment to look at our anticipatory line-up of apprehensive nearly-forty year olds. Not an answer among us.

"All seven, neatly in a row," Moss smiles at us. "And I had a little side bet with Mr. Brock here that you wouldn't get it together! Looks like I lost." Moss walks directly over to Leah. She gives him a false smile which would freeze a lesser man. But he just smiles back. "Now that you know the contract is legitimate and the millions are right there waiting for you ...," he turns to the rest of us, "I expect you'd like to hear all the juicy details. Am I right?"

## CHAPTER TEN

**T**HE THIRD MAN TAKES A SEAT AT THE HEAD OF THE TABLE. HE APPRAISES US ONE BY ONE, A CALM, measured intelligence in his expression. This guy is not here just for the peep show, that's for sure.

Matthew Moss opens his briefcase and starts passing out a single sheet of paper to each of us. "I'd like to be more direct today, given what's at stake." Nevertheless, the Devil takes one of his increasingly tedious dramatic pauses. Then indicates. "This is Mr. Roger Brock, who represents the premier gambling cartel in America, many of whose members are heavy hitters in banking, natural resources, and technology. They are a visionary group of exciting players with a taste for unusual bets. You might also recognize Mr. Brock himself, although he does tend to keep a low profile. CFO of New Helicon Corporation, one of New England's most profitable software companies."

"Shannon Reid. Let's see if she remembers me," says Brock. As one, we all swing our disbelieving eyes to Shannon.

Shannon, startled, stares at Brock, who is at the farthest end of the room from her. Out of the blue, her expression alters. "Roger Brock. BBC-2 interview. 1997. You were with Brown Technology in Providence then." She continues to recite. "Oh, yes. You were a real challenge. Lip compression under stress. A serious head-tilt. Eyes to the left when the questions got tough. Restless hands. And those terrible suits! We had to go for much darker colors, didn't we Roger, to enhance your credibility."

"You did a good job, Shannon. I hope you spent your bonus wisely."

"It's hard to believe I didn't recognize you right away."

She's on a first name basis with our newest Mystery Man? What next?

"These are strange circumstances." Brock smiles. "But I believe in you, Shannon. *And* your companions. By the way, I'm throwing an extra million into the pot just for you. You have quite an expensive lifestyle, if I recall. Consider it a personal incentive because you're the key player on your team, the closer. It's no surprise to me that you have such intelligent and creative friends. So we happily expect to fleece Matthew Moss yet again."

Moss breaks in irritably. "Well that pretty much says it, doesn't it? Roger here represents my competition. He and the other members of his alliance are betting on you to succeed. In fact, they are confident of it. Would everyone please examine the page you are holding?"

We all dutifully do so.

"These are some of the other members of Roger's betting cartel. Many of them are very well-known; all are legitimate as you see. This list, which may not leave this room, is shown to you for one reason only. To prove to you conclusively that, as the host of this bet, if I attempt to interfere with your due process in any way, these men would clearly have the power to destroy me financially with a single phone call. Also it clearly shows you that the rather large sums of money we're speaking of represent, as a shared risk for these players, a drop in their ocean."

We again look at Shannon, who has devoured the list. She nods her confirmation.

Moss continues. "Nevertheless, a bet this large requires safeguards to ensure a quality game and a fair outcome. The penalties for, as we discussed, *cheating*, on anyone's part are stiff, to say the least."

Anjuli abruptly speaks out. "Are we in any danger? I like rich people just fine. But not when they get pissed off."

Brock is reassuring. "There's no risk for you at all. Trust me, if you fail, whoever loses will walk away with no hard feelings and no comebacks."

"This is ludicrous," interrupts Leah. "Why *this* kind of game? Can't you race your polo ponies and yachts and such? Why involve ordinary people?"

Brock answers. "We're trying to have fun, Dr. McLaren. Or may I call you Leah? Please call me Roger." He shrugs. "Golf gets boring. Life gets boring if you have everything you want." His enthusiasm returns. "But there are always ten or twelve highly imaginative bets taking place around the world at any given time so ennui is a thing of the past. San Francisco is one of our usual venues because Matthew is a longtime player. For this bet, he's both host and broker; much like Mr. Inagaki...may I call you Gary?" Brock looks at Gary, Gary gives him a thumbs up. "... was the host of *your* clever version. It's just downright amusing to put interesting people in a difficult situation; in this case Matt offers us a real tickler. Seven single people with what we'll call marriage issues, who must marry within the span of twelve months. Trendy! Punchy! Different! All the best elements. In six months, if you're doing well, maybe three or so marriages to your credit, we'll probably have twenty or thirty more punters to add to the action. We'll have all the big boys in the cartel lining up to bet for or against you."

"So we're sort of like pawns?" Gary asks.

"Well-paid chess pieces," corrects Moss, "with a fortune to gain by triumph in this venture." Moss eyes us one by one. "And Roger is absolutely right. Here we have the potential for a *record* pay-out!"

"Please give us a moment, Matthew. We're almost ready." Brock signals to the tech who now steps behind his laptop. I realize the tech works for Brock not Moss. We are about to see *Brock's* presentation. I get it.

Moss nods his assent. "Let the fun begin!"

Then Moss conjures up his old look-all-seven-of-us-in-the-eye-at-once trick.

"One last thing before you view this upcoming presentation. I've always been a successful gambler on a large scale. But Roger's cartel is the only adversary to thoroughly humiliate me on a regular basis. So believe me, I *live* for payback... and you seven will be the weapon for my revenge."

As he draws breath for another lengthy sentence, I find myself beginning to pity those poor jurors who must been driven comatose by closing arguments from the law firm of Moss, Moss, and more Moss.

Moss now zones in on me, so my friends do the same. "Rick, Roger's researchers particularly believe in *you*. They're sure you can work miracles with your skittish friends as you have done with so many of your listeners around the country. Given their expertise in behavioral science, I cannot fault their conclusions. They give credence to your financial and emotional needs. They give weight to your long term allegiance to one another. They see you as the ultimate lineup. But I know the truth. I see this test as one which cannot be won by people who don't have the right stuff. I don't think all seven of you can convince seven strangers that you're marriage material. The cartel is sure you can rise to the challenge. I'm sure you will self-destruct. Therefore this is the perfect bet. It works because each side truly expects to win."

Moss goes to take a seat beside Brock. The tech steps behind his laptop. Final preparations.

Leah whispers to me. "Why is everyone treating this as if it's really going to happen?!"

I shrug, whisper back very softly. "No idea."

"Well, *I've* got an idea..." Leah squeezes my knee. Underneath the conference table, I feel a key being slipped into my pants pocket. I nearly jump. Her fingers have a "yikes" factor which my pocket wasn't expecting.

She whispers again. "Since we're downtown, let's have dinner downtown. We can meet at the company suite first. And you'll need the key to get to the penthouse level. Seven thirty? You won't flake out, right?"

The company suite, at the top of the Pan-Pacific Hotel, belongs to her father's law firm, a perk for out of town clients. Leah uses it as a pied-à-terre, keeping clothes there, sleeping there on rare occasions when she's too exhausted from work to safely drive back to Larkspur.

"I will not flake. I promise."

"That's the spirit!"

"You're dressing casual tonight, right?" I try not to sound uncool, but I have to be a little wary.

Leah answers, still *sotto voce*. "Hey, give me some credit for subtlety. I said I'd play by the rules. I won't wear fishnets or leopard skin. Okay?" Then she playfully kicks my shin to seal the deal.

The room begins fading to dark.

Abruptly, the entire wall of books at the far end of the conference room closest to Shannon is suddenly converted into a huge floor-to-ceiling projection screen.

And in the dark, Roger Brock speaks. "Matthew picked the game and the players. Our side thus had the right to choose the men and women you'll be required to marry."

"Told you," Owen can be heard to say.

Brock continues. "Because we had only three days to prepare, we put our best people to work. Despite the time pressure, we feel confident in our decisions. After all, our research staff has been doing this since the Reagan era so they know their stuff. The people you're about to meet, so to speak, were chosen for their desire to marry. They were chosen for their... let's call it *ease of capture*. Do not necessarily look for beauty or intelligence. Keep in mind; *you* are their dream life partner, *not vice versa*. Ethically, we are crossing many boundaries. Be assured that each of your counterparts will be given recompense in one form or another, that will be our problem not yours. And, if you treat your chosen counterpart with respect and kindness, you may feel better about the whole process."

The Presentation begins. And it's not what I expect. Not at all.

The entire large screen fills up with a deft display of animation. A cartoon tomcat struts across an animated Golden Gate bridge to the tune of Louie Prima's "Just a Gigolo." Its face is a cartoon Dylan. No doubt about it. The tomcat is checking out passing girl cats and winking. Theater of the disturbed strikes again.

Dylan speaks up in the darkness. "Uh…that's meant to be me…?"

"Correct." Brock replies.

"Well, so you say." Dylan announces. "But I'll have you know my tail is a hell of a lot *bigger* than that!"

Delighted laughter from the cheap seats.

Superimposed over the animated Dylan tomcat swagger are the rules of the "bet" and the letters move from big to small, front to back, exactly like Star Wars credits.

**You have one year for all seven of you**
**To become legally married**
**To the people we choose.**
**You must marry in the correct order.**
**Or forfeit.**
**Your proposed spouse can know nothing.**
**Or forfeit.**
**Absolutely no discussion of the prize money.**
**Or forfeit.**
**Upon the marriage of number seven,**
**payment is immediate.**

In actuality, the only thing seemingly being forfeited at this moment is my definition of insanity. You'd think a batch of "billionaires gone wild" could do this with a little more dignity and savoir faire.

"No popcorn?" I ask.

Well, *someone* had to ask, right?

I look around at the Secret Society fellowship. Trust them to stare into the funhouse mirrors with such rapt attention. Only Shannon is determined not to be drawn in at any cost. She is freshening her lipstick in the dark like a forties femme fatale.

Onscreen, the Tomcat meets a hot Latina cat and they begin to salsa. With that, the animated image fades into live action film footage featuring a petite, dark-haired woman in a bathing suit as she dives into a pool. The camera goes in for a close-up of her face as she emerges from the water. Freeze frame. Cue some more Star Wars graphics:

### Dylan Meet Tina
### 35 Years Old
### 5'1" 105#
### Brown/ Brown
### Never Married/No Children
### Owns Lingerie Shop/ Sausalito
### Loves To Swim/Loves The Beach

Dylan speaks from the shadows. "You guys are turning out to be lots of fun."

"Yeah, it's like a foreign film with subtitles!" Anjuli enthuses.

"Her salsa is spicy hot, dude." Gary is impressed.

"Yeah, but I hate sand in my shorts," states Dylan. "So lose the beach. Other than that, this chick is pretty, she sells garters and probably wears them too. I'm in."

"You're hard to please," interjects Shannon, sarcastically.

"Eat me, Shannon," replies Dylan. "Bite my big one."

Leah erupts. "You're disgusting, Dylan!"

"Yeah, right, Leah. Who'd want to marry me? Well, ask the last five women who said yes when I proposed." He takes a more reasonable tone. "Look, I've got the toughest job. I have to stay involved the longest. So cut me some slack. Picky Little Shannon can get hitched on the last day of the year. She doesn't have to play fiancée for more than five minutes. But I have to tread water until every one of you gets it together. So who's the hero going to be? That would be me. *I'm* going to be the hero!" Dylan settles back in his chair, a model of faintly wounded self-righteousness.

Louie Prima fades out only to be replaced by Hall and Oates' "Maneater." An animated lioness, with black ringlets serving as her mane, drives a red Mazda Miata so fast the rubber burns off the tires. The lioness, of course, has Anjuli's face. Suddenly an animated lion on a motorcycle pulls up next to her. He indicates he wants to drag.

Anjuli interjects from her shadow. "Check out the lion's tail, Dylan. Now that's *my* idea of *big*!"

As before, live action follows, revealing a heavyset man with reddish-gray hair and a rugged face. He looks like an overweight Marlboro Man as he rides his 1930's Indian motorcycle. He's dressed in vintage leathers. Freeze frame.

### Anjuli Meet Rusty
### 52 Years Old
### 5'11" 240#
### Red/ Hazel
### Divorced/ Two Children (Not At Home)
### Soils Engineer/San Francisco
### Restores Vintage Motorcycles

"He's road kill!" raves Gary. "Anjuli eats his type for breakfast!"

"She always did go for leather," I observe for the hell-bent of it.

Anjuli is exultant. "Where's the damn contract? I'll sign it in the dark!"

"How hard can it be to score James Dean's grandpa?" drawls Leah.

As further proof that our pilots of Con Air have done their research, we now all view an animated Centaur with Owen's cartoon face. "Maneater" fades into, of all things, "The Sound of Music." The centaur gallops after a female unicorn. In live action, an outdoorsy woman hikes on Mt. Tam, singing as she hikes. She is short-haired, big-boned, and reasonably nice-looking in a healthy unadorned way. But an unbelievably cheesy moment follows as the camera attempts but fails to duplicate the famous Julie Andrews "hills are alive" singing moment leaving only a sadly out of focus freeze frame.

## Owen Meet Justine
## 41 Years Old
## 5'7" 156#
## Brown/Brown
## Never Married/No Children
## Biologist / San Francisco
## Performs In Amateur Musicals

"Not exactly your type, Owen." I say.

Anjuli pipes up. "So she's a three and Owen's a ten. Don't be so *shallow*, Rick!"

"Actually I meant the singing and the hiking."

"*Sure* you did," retorts Anjuli caustically. "Men are all alike. Look at me. I'm a ten and I'm gonna be just fine with a three!"

Leah makes a strangled noise.

Owen is less confident now than before. "Worst case scenario, what happens if I really *do* end up liking her?"

"Just *don't*...," interjects Shannon forcefully. "If you really want to go through with this, then *please* keep your emotions out of it."

"Shannon, don't be such a pain." Gary retorts. "It's a legitimate question."

I glance at Owen through the shadows. He's looking a touch more conflicted. But he is definitely eyeing the woman on the screen with a pensive attentiveness.

Gary, calmer, adds. "Come on, guys, I want to see who they've got for me."

Right on cue, the screen fills up with an animated Akita sporting Gary's face. The Gary Akita is mushing a sled of fellow Akita dogs across a beach. "The Sound of Music" segues menacingly into the theme music from "Jaws." The Gary Akita spots a girl poodle swimming away in panic from a cartoonish Shark. The Akita rescues her, turning the Shark into sushi with his teeth. The poodle shakes her wet fur, gold coins clank out. Live action brings us a blonde woman in a white tank top and shorts walking along the Embarcadero. Eyebrow piercing, a tattoo sleeve down one arm, a healthy tan on a nice older surfer girl chassis. Freeze frame:

## Gary Meet Callista
## 37 Years Old
## 5′5′ 135#
## Blonde/ Blue
## Divorced/No Children
## Aromatherapist/ Berkeley
## Windsurfer/Bicyclist

"Can you handle a woman over thirty, Gary? I thought twenty was your speed limit." Leah is losing patience.

"Can you even remember *being* twenty, Leah?" Anjuli retorts. "Let me refresh your memory, it was *two decades* ago."

"Nobel prize for maturity, ladies." Gary is distracted. "I like her tattoo. Bold."

"You'll have Miss Tattoo nailed in about ten seconds," responds Dylan.

"Is that yet another sexual remark of a sexist nature, Dylan?" asks Leah.

"Turn of phrase, Princess Leah."

"I think it's a very tasteful tattoo," Gary says thoughtfully. "Okay, I'm good to go."

"The Jaws Theme" becomes "Someone To Watch Over Me," a song Leah often requests on KHEL's "Last Dance." Jeez. What research! An animated girl fox with oversized fox freckle-whiskers is wearing a doctor's white coat and stethoscope. This Leah-faced fox is proudly leaning on a sign which says *James McLaren Trauma Unit, Marin General Hospital.*

## Leah, Make A Difference
## Restoration Of Marin General's Trauma Center
## Twenty-Five Million Dollars Initial Funding
## In Your Father's Name

Silence. The Secret Society stops in its proverbial animal tracks. Huh?

Leah can't speak. So she punches me lightly in the shoulder. Thus I speak for her. "I think Leah would like me to tell you that this is a dirty trick."

Leah manages a nod.

Brock's voice rings out. "What do you give the woman who claims she has everything? We want to offer you a genuinely nice carrot, Leah. One which will *inspire* you to chase after it."

"You can't be serious..." Leah's voice is raspy, far from normal.

"Think of the lives you'd save... and yes we are serious..." observes Brock. "Now let's check out your bachelor."

Onscreen, an animated male fox speeds by the Leah fox, riding a gurney like a skateboard. Live action reveals him to be a very good-looking Richard Gere meets George Clooney type, with a full head of gray hair which flies in the wind as he skateboards with three teenagers in a park.

### Leah Meet Jay
### 45 Years Old
### 5'10" 184#
### Gray/ Blue
### Widower/ Three Children (At Home)
### Pediatrician/San Rafael
### Trains Guide Dogs For The Blind

Gary snorts with disgust. "Look at that! What a set-up! Giving you the dream dude! He's a widower so you don't have to deal with an ex-wife, he's got kids the same age as yours, he's a doctor just like you, he's got movie star looks *and* he's a candidate for sainthood....trains guide dogs for the blind... come *on*..."

"I'll trade you," cries Anjuli. "I mean, your guy really *is* a fox!"

"Twenty-five million for a building full of medical stuff and a guy out of GQ," gripes Dylan. "I guess the squeakiest wheel got *all* the grease..."

"Twenty-five million to start," interjects Brock. "There is a codicil which will provide for cost overruns."

"In my father's name," repeats Leah.

"We aim to please," Brock quickly replies.

I exchange a look with Leah and put my arm around her in a gesture of support and encouragement. Her armor pierced, she is giving me a *get me out of here* look.

But not until Matthew Moss ensures they serve me some devil's food cake.

"Someone To Watch Over Me" turns into Springsteen's "Dancing In The Dark." An animated coyote with my cartoon face is chasing a female cartoon roadrunner.

"Beep Beep," trumpets Anjuli.

"Beep Beep," throws in Dylan.

The coyote paints a fake tunnel on the side of KHEL's Oakland radio station with a paint can labeled "Acme Temple Of Loss Paint." The girl road-runner goes through. And, of course, my coyote-double smacks into his deceptive handiwork and flattens. The roadrunner stops, chortling, outside a cartoon version of San Francisco's Symphony Hall and all of a sudden I'm faced with a live action presentation of a younger woman, slightly disheveled, her sensational long red gown worn carelessly and awry, her long hair dreadlocked with thick silver-blonde plaits. She plays the Symphony's grand piano with performance intensity despite the fact that the concert hall is entirely and eerily empty. The Springsteen version of the song fades into this woman's own highly idiosyncratic vocal of the same "Dancing In The Dark" but she sings it with clever and sophisticated jazz styling. Paige was an extremely competent classical pianist, a fact of which I am very proud. But this woman is many cuts above, singing and playing with breathtaking innovation.

### Rick Meet Vicki
### 29 Years Old
### 5'5" 115#
### Blonde/ Blue
### Never Married/No Children
### In Between Jobs/ Pacific Heights
### Expert Calligrapher

"What the hell, Rick. She looks a lot like Paige, just like Paige used to look when you first met her!" Owen is right.

"Her hair, Rick. Almost the exact same color…" Shannon mutters. Paige was proud of her premature wavy gray hair, blending it skillfully to a silvery-blonde effect.

"Blue eyes, too." Owen adds. "Just like Paige."

"Plays piano like Paige. And red was Paige's favorite color, right?" Leah circles a comforting hand around my wrist and squeezes. "These hustlers are shameless, huh?"

I am riveted. Paige had a nice, firm build while this woman is far more slight and ethereal. Paige was outgoing and dynamic, this woman looks seriously depressed. But there is *something* so similar in her posture. The movement of her hands on the keys, something else… something unmistakably *familiar* in her facial expression.

Brock's "In Between Jobs" seems a false card. Calligraphy, a mathematician's art form, requires rigorous exactitude. This woman has both a free-spirited danger about her and yet a sense of confident control, both very Paige-like. I look down at the green envelope in front of me. They probably think I can be manipulated by comparisons to my dead wife; that's one piece of research they got wrong.

"Dancing In The Dark" turns into Sting's "If you Love Somebody, Set Them Free." An animated, very feminine zebra with strawberry colored stripes and wearing blinkers is trotting along a deserted Tiburon waterfront. The zebra continues to trot until it is out of view.

Suddenly the image freezes on the San Francisco skyline. And all of us in the room also freeze as we read:

**Shannon, you are the wild card**
**Choose any partner you wish**
**Just wait for the other six**
**Find your comfort zone**
**Make this work for your friends**

"Brilliant," says a yet-again-stunned Leah.

"Hey, she got the best deal! What's the story?" Anjuli is miffed.

Brock answers in the dark. "Shannon, our analyses don't lie. You have the highest probability of losing this bet for your comrades. Every researcher we have on staff agreed. Only by giving you this freedom is there any probability of success."

Moss interrupts, buoyant. "Bless you, Shannon. And thanks *millions*! Because of this last minute alteration in the bet, I've negotiated even better odds!" His voice shifts in Brock's direction. "Roger, have you been listening to all this bickering? This is going to be priceless! You *must* be sorry you gave me the extra vigorish." He repeats, back in our direction, a man apparently born and raised to always have the last word: *"Priceless!"*

All we need now is a maniacal laugh.

The lights begin a steady glow to full illumination. The screen recedes, evolving back into a bookcase. As we blink, some of us pocketing needed eyewear, Brock, playing good cop to Moss' bad cop, speaks up reassuringly. "Shannon, you get to make this easy on yourself. You can marry anyone you please, as long as you don't divulge anything about the bet. I know you'll do the right thing for your friends."

As Shannon is refusing to look in his direction, Brock turns to address the rest of us. His tech begins to pack the laptop and its associated gear.

"So there you have it. Eleven million in cash. A further twenty-five million to charity. Although to be a little churlish, *we'll* be taking the tax deduction…" With that Brock tips an imaginary cap to Leah. Then he catches my eye. "And Rick, forgive me for being robustly self-satisfied, but what we have put together as your reward is truly a case of saving the best for tomorrow."

Brock taps his tech's shoulder. An exchange of nods. And unexpectedly they disappear without any further ceremony. No puff of smoke. But nearly as quick.

So I turn to Moss. "You're presuming there will be a tomorrow."

"Same place, same time. The contract will be sitting right where Shannon is sitting now."

I may be the only one in the room close enough to Shannon to sense she is on the very precipice of running yet again. She already has her purse and jacket in one hand.

Moss strolls in front of his first set of players as if he were making a closing courtroom summation. "Dylan, Anjuli, Owen, and Gary. You're playing for two million each." They exchange energized looks. Owen shoots me a courtesy glance then slaps Gary a high five. So my good buddy has chosen to stay on board the Hogwarts Express, magically en route to Matt Moss' millions.

He strolls further down the line of chairs. "Leah, you're playing for twenty-five million or more to restore the Marin General Trauma Center in your father's name." Leah glances at her watch. She picks up the red Detrola radio Owen gifted her, fiddles with its dials. "Ty Boudreau is going to check in with me tomorrow morning. I'll let you know then."

"Fair enough. But you heard what he had to say. Our contract is a model of clarity and a fount of profitability!"

Moss executes a theatrical shrug, takes yet another step down the line to me. "Rick, you are playing for what's in the envelope, sorry to sound like Let's Make A Deal. But once you look inside, once you realize what Brock has come up with, you will see he is not exaggerating. You will be the first to sign."

"I doubt that very much." I reply.

"Don't!" Moss' response is sharp enough to startle. "Because I'd stake my *life* on it."

"That sounds risky, don't you think?" I ask.

"I've seen what's in your envelope."

"Can we call it a night?" I've got two very quiet, and thus potentially lethal women, on either side of me.

"Absolutely…" But his hand tickles the green envelope closer in my direction. "But prepare for the fact that your world will never be the same. Roger is serious. In an effort to get your participation, he has come up with something for you which defies imagination…"

"Regrettably, my imagination has blown a fuse."

"Droll to the last!"

He finally walks over to Shannon. She looks him straight in the eye. Shannon has chosen to mirror Moss' trained affect. She shows nothing but calm matter-of-factness. She's become a cipher, exuding a lightness of being which suggests that she's just had a refreshing visit to her spa. She is, even for me, unreadable.

"Shannon, you're playing to help your friends." He begins. "Also three million, which includes Roger's sentimental bonus." He probes Shannon's face. And then figures it out with a grin. This woman who helps media darlings be darling is showing him how an expert does it. "Pardon the black envelope," Moss continues. "A little joke. Full of blank paper."

Shannon gets to her feet with efficient femininity. She actually shakes Moss' hand and murmurs a polite thank you. She shoulders her purse, picks up her black envelope, hands it to Moss. "Then shred it. And don't forget to recycle…"

"See you tomorrow?"

"I'll have my assistant call your assistant."

Shannon focuses primarily on Gary, Dylan, Owen, and Anjuli. Her tone is neutral and has a whiff of amiability to it. "How many of you feel good about me being named the emotional cripple of our group?" She doesn't give them time to react. "Not a problem. Don't sweat it and off I go."

With that, the Tennessee Walker breezes out the door, flipping her red-gold hair out of the way as she puts her jacket on. She opens the door to the reception room and closes it behind her with ladylike precision.

A brief moment of quiet. But Dylan's not a fan of quiet.

"Relax! She'll get over it," says Dylan.

"She's won't let us down." Gary adds.

"She'll be here tomorrow. I'm sure of it." Anjuli does seem sure of it. "We're her only true friends. Her only friends, really."

"Rick…" Owen begins.

"Don't look at me. Why don't you chase after her this time?" I say. "I've got dinner plans."

"And so do I…" adds Leah.

I'll say this much. Our long day's journey into night did offer us an impressive and entertaining piece of film-making. But if I were assigned the task of superimposing final credits over the betting cartel's home movie, they would have to go like this:

**Ignore the men behind the curtain**
**We're the secret society**
**We don't turn to the dark side**
**Yeah, it sucks to be forty**
**But the party is over**
**Deal with it**

And tomorrow we will deal with it.

But tonight's another matter.

# CHAPTER ELEVEN

THE PAN-PACIFIC HOTEL IS A 21-STORY TALL GLASS TURRET IN THE HEART OF DOWNTOWN, A FIVE-STAR hotel which is part of a chain primarily serving clientele from East and Southeast Asia. This gives it a special feel different from most of our local equivalents. Adjacent to the St. Francis Hotel and Union Square, it is understated only in comparison to its surroundings. Tonight, the hotel lobby is busy with the August tourist trade and it pulses with foreign colors.

My souvenir of filthy rich Suits Gone Mad, the not so mysterious green envelope with its allegedly fascinating marital desiderata, has been left in my car, to be opened tomorrow with not very trembling fingers. An ersatz, near anorexic Paige-lookalike is hardly the thing to inspire a potential groom despite all hyperbole to the contrary.

In an elevator sardined like a Tokyo subway train, I am on my way skyward to pick up Leah for dinner. And as the elevator empties floor by floor, leaving me increasingly alone, I realize I'm on what could be called my first date since the Society's unsuccessful attempts to revive my love life five years ago.

Five years after Paige's death, my friends finally decided it was time for me to dip my toes in the non-grieving world. Up until that time they made sure

I still had family, family almost as good as blood. But I was neither changing nor growing, just grieving. So they decided, after a unanimous vote, that I must find new love. The plan was that each of them should choose a champion, guided by the spirit of illuminating the joy of partnership (never mind their own Society shortcomings). And so it was decreed I would date no Toxic Chicks. Just healthy fully-vetted long-term prospects.

Owen thought he should start. So for my first date he hand-picked a colleague, a professor from nearby Stanford named Kennedy. Kennedy was rapidly becoming the world authority on mermaids just as Owen had already achieved that pinnacle with Centaurs. She was as quick-witted as Owen had promised. We dined at an Indonesian restaurant in Noe Valley and I was delighted that she hadn't even heard of the Rick Lang, Midnight Rider Show (her bedtime, ten sharp). Alas, after chit-chat about the arcane subtleties and stringent ground rules which were required knowledge for the dating man, I subsequently embarrassed myself (and later Owen) by excusing myself to the rest room, thereafter squeezing out a narrow bathroom window into a restaurant dumpster. From there, covered in Indonesian food, I sprinted to the nearest cab, anxiously catching the last ferry to Larkspur where my celibate car was waiting.

Shannon and Leah worked together to arrange a blind date for me. After painstaking deliberation they chose Kate, a physical therapist whom they both knew through a mutual acquaintance. Our lunch date took place at a Greek restaurant on Polk Street. Shannon and Leah informed me that Kate was famous in the world of physical therapy where specialties ruled. She was the queen of hands, she did only hands, and she healed hands better than anybody on the West Coast. Kate said all the right things, almost as if she'd been coached, which I suspect she had. I learned, in alphabetical order, the names of every bone and tendon and muscle in the human hand, which made me laugh, and I agreed to let her look at my own hands. Between coffee and dessert she ran her fingers over and around them with a probing grace and a teasing sensuality, all of which was increasingly unbearable. I wasn't ready to be touched even in such an innocent way. Despite the fact that Kate was clearly gentle and kind and suitable and earthy, upon being over-aroused by her relatively innocent digital skills, I abruptly announced a toothache, and then politely inserted her into her valet-parked Volvo. I was told later that she waited weeks for me to call again. Leah was quietly angry at me; Shannon called me out for not trying. But I was clearly not fit to endure the emotional colors of a woman I didn't know. I was not fit for anything but the black romance of my candlelit cave.

Dylan was not a man one could easily escape. He blamed my first two failures on the fact that I hadn't gone to an expert (him). Who in fact was the King of Dating? What did Leah, Shannon, or Owen know about women? He was the resident expert. He would find someone casual and fun and distracting. His little black book was chock full of names and secret markings. I noisily and adamantly declined. But at long last I gave in and agreed to a date with Darielle, a woman he swore he hadn't slept with, whom he insisted was a former girl scout, teacher-of-the-year, and soup kitchen volunteer. He even showed me her page in his little black book. She was a birth-control practicing ("e/z") bottle blonde ("b/b"), with brains ("I/q") and an especially affectionate nature ("24/7").

I met Darielle at a little hotel bar on Sutter. She was a true Dylan girl; her libido oozed out of her repartee like a shoulder strap slipping off a bare shoulder. Initially, I was amused by her monochromatic three shades of yellow outfit which was skintight, partially reptilian, and enhanced by shocking yellow pumps with gold stiletto heels. She thought my radio show was fabulous but totally gloomy which won her points. But to my surprise, for what did I know of dating, she had already reserved us a room in that very hotel. She told me Dylan had advised her that I was grieving and that she should be ladylike and treat me with care. So she only brought simple velvet restraints and just one special change of clothing which she felt might do the trick. I was gone in sixty seconds.

These dates were so demoralizing that I declared my love life to be off limits and I let Shannon, Leah, and later Anjuli serve as the women in my life.

As I insert Leah's key in the elevator panel, and the elevator rises to the Penthouse level, I am paying attention to my feelings. And this "date" feels very, very different. I don't know what it will offer. But Leah was born to surprise a man like me, so I brace myself.

Leah yanks open the door to the Barnett, McLaren and Boudreau company penthouse suite. The heavier curtains are open, but the others remain drawn and gauzed, making muted city lights seem celestial. The inner door to the bedroom is open, its coverlet nap-rumpled, still holding her impression. The living room has a candlelit dinner table by the window. Leah's smile is bright, but the smile in her eyes is brighter. And as she grabs my arm and playfully pulls me inside, kicking the door shut behind me, I immediately notice two things, both disturbing.

She has spread out the game of Twister right in the middle of the floor, plastic sheet and spinner at the ready. And she is wearing a short pleated skirt, black and white plaid. The lightweight cotton clings to her slim hips as she leads me in.

Tonight there's a more carefree musical rhythm to her walk. Leah always looks ten years younger than her age but tonight I can almost catch a glimpse of the girl I met when we were twenty-three and it gives me a soul-shudder of unexpected pleasure. White ankle socks, no shoes, along with the infamous counterfeit-silver anklet I won for her during our alternate universe fairground excursion. Above her equator, a cream cashmere sweater graces her graceful silhouette. I am still absorbing the whole of this tender trap as she hugs me, takes off my jacket.

She grins. "I decided we'd eat in."

"You promised. Twice."

"Promised what?"

"Seriously. You *did* promise. Nothing sexy."

"Are you saying I'm sexy?" She twinkles.

I am already in trouble. "You said casual. You said dinner out."

"Can't go out. Couldn't find shoes to match my skirt."

She indicates the candlelit cuisine. "Besides, look! Garlic Chicken without the garlic! Garlic mashed potatoes without the garlic! Vegetables sautéed in garlic without the garlic! I cooked it all myself, she lied. And for dessert? A tough game of *Twister*!"

She tilts her head at the Twister game, ominously spread out on one of the suite's lush Asian carpets.

"And you're going to wear that skirt?"

"It's my Twister Skirt. What's wrong with that?"

"It's cheating."

"You mean it's a dangerous weapon in the wrong hands."

"So to speak."

"Well, maybe it'll end up in *your* hands."

"Leah..."

"Oh, yeah, sure. Like I can really seduce the famous Rick Lang. You could win a Grammy for best self-control. So what chance does *this* girl have? I have no illusions. Besides, why are you so scared? You're the defending champ...you won Anjuli's Secret Society Twister Game of '98 without a single defeat."

"So why should I risk my perfect record for you? You're obviously planning to bend the rules."

"What rules?" She can see where my eyes keep getting stuck. "You mean my *skirt*? Twister has no dress code." She pauses to think. "Maybe an *undress* code. Don't remember...."

"Leah..."

"Not every sports event requires *full* coverage!"

Leah can be funny. But this is flirt-mania. "We'll probably break an arm or a leg..."

"I can't believe you said that! You are playing, player. And keep in mind that this is my home court, my rules. I kick butt here." She pauses. "And you've got a nice butt." She twinkles again. "Um, to kick, I mean."

"You've had a few glasses of wine. I can tell."

"So? Wine is the breakfast of champions." She gently pushes me backwards into the folds of a stylish, richly patterned chair and yanks my shoes off. "Hmm. Big feet. Bad for Twister. But generally a good omen for everything else."

Then Leah's hand moves to my hand and her index finger touches my wedding ring. She says it softly. She says it with just the right tone of voice. "Mind taking it off? Just for tonight?"

Old habits die very hard. I give her a reassuring smile. "I take it off to arm wrestle. I take it off for softball. And I take it off for Twister." And so I stand, slip off my wedding band and place it on top of my jacket which she has folded over a lacquered hallway chair by the front door. Then I join her at her candlelit table where we sit.

I don't know how she kept the food hot but she did. I don't know how many bottles of wine she has on hand because there seems to be an endless supply. But I do know that for a woman who stopped dating long ago, she's awfully adept with her universal remote control. With a sweep of her arm and the press of a button, the curtains' inner layer of gauzy material parts to reveal the penthouse view.

"Spectacular," I say.

"I am, aren't I?" She replies. "How about a toast?"

She pours us both a glass of wine. Then she salutes me with her glass. "To Rick," she continues. "You fight in darkness. Now fight in daylight. Fight with those who love you."

Her sincerity after all the joking catches me by surprise. We drink to her toast, eyes locked. Then I raise a glass to her. "To Leah. Who must be an extra-terrestrial because no human being can possibly be so beautiful inside and out. Please take me to your home planet."

Leah grins happily and hits her remote control one more time and the sound of Luther Vandross surrounds us from a dozen softly murmuring speakers. Perhaps I drink my wine too quickly, perhaps she does too. I start to lose focus as I watch the reflection of the neighboring skyscrapers carom the moonlight behind Leah's sandy blonde hair as it crests over her dead straight shoulders; it creates a halo effect. I begin to handle my fork and knife with nifty insobriety.

Leah eats quickly, that's what ER cutters do; she is a legendary speed-diner. "I'm sorry I didn't cook for you myself," she says. "But I couldn't find any macaroni and cheese in time."

I look down at the gourmet cuisine. "Big time shame." I say. "I like macaroni."

"Like hot dogs? Maybe you'd like to come to the house? See the boys again? They cook, did you know? Hot Dogs. They've been written up in the Zagat Guide. Six stars."

This is a big moment for her. I can make or break her heart with my reply.

"I'm not really into hot dogs." She reacts, but I continue, smiling. "But I *do* like pizza. Especially frozen pizza, the more it tastes like burnt cardboard, the better. Can they overcook pizza? I think in Italian that would be *Pizza Morto*."

There is such love light in her eyes. If only she knew I was tipsy.

"For you, they will burn it to a crisp, you watch."

"Okay, I'll come by. Could be in a few months or so. You know. Gotta finally get some therapy, work it through, confront my fears, plumb my unconscious. Then again, maybe only a few weeks. Let's play it by ear."

"That's good enough for me," her smile is relieved, radiant, and getting very randy.

I guess I'm on a roll. "Do they like sports?" I ask.

"They're fourteen, they're boys." Leah hasn't stopped smiling.

"As you know, they give me season tickets to everything. You think they'd like some tickets to a few ball games?"

"Maybe when you'd want to go with us. No hurry."

Leah is happy, happy, happy. On the other hand, I find the wine is playing havoc with my senses. Her All-American freckles seem to spray farther across her nose. The alchemy of alcohol strikes again.

Then I feel a little cotton sock on my ankle.

"You're playing footsie."

"I'm warming up for Twister. It's a warm-up routine. Don't read too much into it." She rubs this same foot against my thigh. "Why don't you warm up too? Don't you want to score big time?"

Trash talk meets double-entendre.

I move on to wine glass number five, knowing that, despite clearly recalling Paige's caveats vis-a-vis the danger alcohol poses to a radio exec's best efforts for success and achievement in the highly competitive field of communications, I have checked my inhibitions at the penthouse door.

Then Leah matter-of-factly changes the subject.

"By the way, I read my red envelope," she says. Her probing foot de-probes. "Did you read yours?"

"After all their mystery and fanfare and promise of life-changing information?" I ask. "Actually, no."

"The guy they set me up with is dating service perfect for me. If this is a sting, they've really stung pretty good."

"Do tell," I say. Preferring in fact that she doesn't tell. I have had my fill of envelopes. Why can't they use folders instead, just to keep it interesting? Somebody in Matt Moss' gambling empire must be envelope-obsessed.

"They gave me lots of pictures. Jay at work. Jay at play. Nice-looking, bright, artistic. He's a watercolorist, has gallery exhibitions all around the Bay Area. If there is any truth to what I'm being offered, Jay is a wet dream for this lonely chest-cutting girl."

"Trying to make me jealous?"

"Can't you at least pretend? And don't forget, as a bonus, I get my very own trauma center."

"You'd actually consider it?"

"Depends."

"They'd never deliver."

"Tyrone says they'd have to if we win the bet." She gives me a sly look. "Although I'm willing to trade a wet dream for a wet reality right now, this minute, a one-time offer, you ready to pull the trigger on the deal?"

"You know," I say, "I can put this marriage bet thing on the air. The Riders will unravel the whole scam in a few hours. National listenership. Six degrees of separation. Just like that."

"Then you'd be the villain."

"Because…?"

"If this whatever-it-is scam comes apart on your show, your friends take a big embarrassing *public* hit. Illusions are one thing, dreams are another. Right now, our friends are dreaming the dream. If you crush their dreams, I guarantee Gary will walk. There's every possibility that Anjuli and Dylan might quit the Secret Society out of sheer petulance. Owen won't walk, but you know what he's like. He probably won't speak to you for six months. Remember how he reacted when you talked about his parents' cruelty on the air? Without telling him first? I know you meant it as a kind of public service. But after that, he didn't talk to you for ages!"

True enough. It was hell.

"Leah, you're not going to sign. It's Ethics 101. Their game is dependent on us lying for a year. Lying non-stop. That would doom the Society even more profoundly."

"I agree, I totally agree."

"Then we've got to talk sense to them tomorrow."

"By now, they've read their envelopes. Hope in their hearts. Dollar bills in their eyes."

"It's up to us."

"You can't make decisions for them."

"Then what? Are you willing to play along? Date your wet dream until our friends recover their sanity?"

"Maybe you should open your envelope. Maybe they have your number too? Maybe they've brought Paige back to life."

Just like that. Hammer time.

I see her staring at me, stricken.

"Jaysus, Rick. I'm sorry. I meant the woman who looks like her. I'm a little, lotta, drunk. Sorry, sorry, sorry."

She suddenly starts to sob. Really sob. It's heartbreaking.

"Leah, don't."

She looks at me, naked in that other way.

And, in this most awkward moment, I feel utterly loved by her.

And, at this most awkward juncture, I want to tell her that I get it, I get her. Because I love her too.

Love is a variable, restless thing. I've learned this after ten years of listening to people try to describe it. Love is fond of changing with circumstance; it can morph like mercury, swift like mercury. But this doesn't feel like mercury, it feels like home.

"Leah, Leah, stop. I know what you meant. It's okay. Cool it!"

If radio has taught me anything, it's that what we say matters far less than what we do. That's why I send my Riders around the country. That's why I reach across the table to comfort her.

Except after too many glasses of wine, I have lost most of my fine motor skills. With a truly timely loss of panache, I knock over the entire table, which is only the size of a card table after all, sending dishes and candles and cutlery and glasses flying. Leah dives to catch me, for I am falling. She misses and the table rolls over on me. As she blows out the now dangerous candles, I squirm out from under, covered in food. She is no longer crying. She is laughing. It is a Rick Lang, Midnight Rider, infamous moment. Forget the rest of dinner. I am the rest of dinner.

"You're a Garlic Chicken." Leah says, doing her best to stifle her snuffles. "Without the garlic." She is standing; I am flat on my back.

"I can only imagine."

"I can't Twister with you like that!"

"Rain check."

"Better take off your shirt. It's a mess."

"Forget it."

"And definitely take off those pants..."

"Definitely forget it."

"Rick, they're covered in food. I'll help you get them off."

Resistance is futile. She yanks my shirt off over my head, bikini-waxing my chest hairs. I yelp. My socks disappear into the vortex. She undoes my pants clasp with surgical precision. My pants come off with a yank.

"Black boxers!" She reacts. "Even your underwear is in mourning." She drops to the floor next to me, clambers on top of me, kisses me. It's a real kiss. My hand gently rolls over the pleasantly taut curve of her derriere. Her skirt is cotton thin. My fingers can tell, but just barely, that some paean to minimalism waits underneath.

"No feeling up the opponent before Twister has even started!" Leah remarks.

"I'll stop if you get off me."

"I like it on top of you. It could become a habit."

"Keep in mind you're drunk."

"So are you. Big deal. Does that mean you can't make love to me?"

This time she looks at me unapologetically.

I look at her as she lies on top of me, in my arms, atop my heart. This is too fast. I should have known. I should have been more specific with her. I try to deflect with humor.

"How many guys have you slept with on a first date?"

"Counting tonight? If I get lucky? One."

"This is sudden, Leah."

"Oh, come on! I've known you seventeen *years*. Who knows? I've probably been in love with you for seventeen *years*... so make *very* passionate love to me, okay? Let's start with your hands. I want to feel your hands *everywhere*."

"Do you believe I want you?"

"I can *feel* it."

"Do you realize what it would mean if we made love?"

"Yes, I *do*."

"Actually I don't think you do."

Her laughter fades away and quickly. "Rick. Stop it! I don't believe you. Why are you like this?! You're *always* like this."

"If we make love tonight, all emotional hell will break loose tomorrow. It'll suddenly be all or nothing. Because that's how we are. It'll be total commitment or it'll fall apart. We need a plan. And if we want something real, it's not going to happen by just hoping it falls into place. We have to *grow* it."

She looks at me. And looks. And looks. And looks. Finally:

"Well, why not? I can't say you're not worth waiting for, can I?"

She rolls off me, although I don't want her to roll off me, not really. We both stand. In my case I am clad only in my boxers of mourning. On the other hand, through some trick of smoke and mirrors, she looks as she looked when she opened the door onto this unsuspecting dinner date. She brushes food out of my hair. "Twister?"

I reply. "Twister."

We are now at the Twister mat. "You do know those ankle socks are a disadvantage. No traction."

"Then it'll be okay if I go first."

Leah puts the spinner in the middle of the mat where we both can reach. She spins right leg blue. I spin right leg red. She spins right hand yellow. I spin left leg green.

She speaks first. "Never could hold your booze. Feeling dizzy yet?"

"Not even," I reply.

Left leg blue. Right hand green. Right hand red. Right leg red. We are unmercifully tangled already. The spinner spins.

"Rick?"

"You're planning some mischief, aren't you? It's in your voice."

"Give me a break! Just wanted to ask how you feel about oral sex. Personally, I think it sucks!"

I nearly fall. She hoots with pleasure.

"That's just *wrong*. You should be eliminated!"

"Almost. Almost. Almost got you."

Leah spins. Right hand yellow. She is now bent over across the mat, her tiny black-and-white skirt hiking up.

"How's the view?"

"Two millimeters short of pornographic."

"Excellent."

The spinning is faster, right and left legs, right and left hands, red and green and blue and yellow.

"You're about two minutes away from losing," I say.

"Just look straight up. You'll stop gloating."

My cheek is jammed against her upper thigh so I can't look up. I can tilt my eyes however. I'm looking right up her skirt.

"See, I'm in mourning too. Please don't be mad. But the only thing I had available in black today was a thong. With two kids, it's really hard to get around to all the laundry."

I close my eyes again. I have about one second of willpower left. I know I have to leave very soon or I will never leave.

"I'm sorry, Leah. Gotta beat you." I spin, left leg red and I curl it behind her. She can't move leg or arm without falling, the Twister equivalent of checkmate.

She realizes the end is inevitable. So she laughs. "Was I a fun date? Will you ask me out again?"

"I dunno," I raise my body a little to look at her. "Depends."

She spins right leg yellow. And she falls, but as she falls, she contrives to fall under me, pulling me on top of her.

"You beat me. So much for you being a gentleman…" She smiles, a smile right out of *All's Well That Ends Well*.

"I need a cold shower." I say.

"Funny. So do I. Let's take one together."

I look at this fusion of soul and beauty and humor and harmony.

"Why not?" I find myself saying.

"Undress me." She says. "Please."

And so with stupidly tremulous hands, I undress her. No one could look more elegant and classy without clothing than Leah McLaren.

"Keep the anklet on, though." Leah beams. "Cold shower? Or very cold shower?"

"Very, very cold shower." I reply.

We soap each other in a massive elevator-sized, two-nozzle, compartment of pleasure. We compare tan lines. I lose. She is unfairly sweet as she serenades me with a gospel-tinged medley of "Let's Twist Again" and "Do The Twist" and, of course, "Twistin' The Night Away." It occurs to me gingerly that if she can learn to be so happy-playful from the wreckage of her marriage then perhaps some day I too might learn to better thrive, to wake up without the quicksand of hurt lining the bottom of my mind.

Dressed as well as I can manage, two cups of strong coffee in me, food stains everywhere on me, I kiss her goodnight by the door. The kiss lasts three years.

She closes the door behind me, her hair all wet blonde straw, her eyes giving me a last amber-olive blink-blink of contentment. And as that door closes behind me, I find myself in an inner hallway I don't recognize, a place which looks like all my door keys might finally, magically, unlock something important.

It's not until I'm in my car and driving to work that I realize I left my wedding ring behind. It remains in Leah's suite, most likely on her rug, perhaps brooding in a dark corner. This presents a dilemma which I push from my mind. I must have it back. But calling Leah about it now is something I won't do. So I decide to call the hotel and deal with it tomorrow and it's just at that moment that I glance over at the green envelope on my passenger seat. I purposely left it face down, but currently it lies face up.

So I flip it over and see that someone has penned, in excellent calligraphy, in classic old-style invitation copperplate, a six-word message on the back side of this envelope allegedly full of mystery and answers. It reads:

LOVE ME
And on the next line:
I AM HER SECRET

# CHAPTER TWELVE

**B**RIDGET AND KIMBERLY ARE IN HOT ROTATION AS THE PHONE LINES BLAZE AS BRIGHTLY AS OUR huge floor candles. It's been a lively night and time has been zooming along. My only real distraction has been the fact that Kimberly is wearing a plaid scarf with her best finishing school ensemble as she sits with the computers, the better to remind me of Leah's soft plaid skirt and Leah's plans for my newly less hopeless soul.

*Love me, I am her secret.*

My mood is so elevated, Leah Leah Leah, that I actually don't feel offended that the billionaire boys club has broken into my car to scrawl all over their precious green envelope. I even find myself impressed. The pitch meeting is over yet here they are, still duty-bound to intrigue. The car was locked but the envelope was in plain sight; perhaps Moss himself broke in using one of his own promotional ballpoint pens in order to add this postscript in calligraphy, making sure that I continue to believe that silver dreadlocked Vicki, my proposed Paige-lookalike bride, the expert calligrapher between jobs, is stalking me even as I am meant to stalk her.

Right now we are in the middle of Desolation Row, the dedication hour.

"How about 'My Whole World Ended The Moment You Left Me'?" Denise from Wichita Falls has been persistent in her quest for just the right song dedication for her husband who has stormed off and moved into a motel. This is her third suggestion. She has already been shot down twice.

"I'm sorry. It's just against Desolation Row policy."

"I don't get it. What do I keep doing wrong?"

I wave to Bridget for the next call so I can move on. Bridget signs me from her booth that she's lined up a top dog. I sign her back; let's get the new caller ready to rock. I turn my attention back to unhappy Denise.

"Let me go over the Desolation Row dedication rules, given you're a new listener. Sorry to everyone out there who has them memorized."

"What kind of rules do you need for a song dedication?"

"Just a few simple ones. For example, we don't play songs with titles like "I'll Kill Myself If You Leave Me" or "Beat Me Up But Please Don't Go."

"Why not?" interrupts Denise. "They're just songs. Who really listens to the words anyway? It's all mumble, mumble, mumble."

"You do. You may not realize it, but you do." I find myself replaying in my mind the lyrics of the Luther Vandross love ballads which Leah subliminally played for me at low volume during dinner.

"Then why don't you just pick one for me? Something that tells him I love him, I'm sorry, and that he should come back home and quick."

"I'd be glad to."

I signal Bridget. Is the next caller ready? She gives me a third finger waggle which means *you betcha.*

"This song goes out to Joe in Wichita Falls from his loving Denise..." I prepare to play Boz Skaggs' "Come On Home." *No matter's who's right, no matter who's wrong, come on home cuz that's where you belong.*

I cue Kimberly. She punches in the song. The studio speakers begin to throb.

Peripherally, I have spotted Owen slipping into Studio B. He's still wearing his new suit, remarkably (for him) unwrinkled. I have also spotted that he continues to clutch his blue envelope as though it holds a treasure map. He waves to me, I nod back.

Kimberly perks up. "Wow. He looks so much happier than the other night!"

"You think?"

"Oh, yes!" replies my young sidekick. "It's like he's like sugar coated!" Kimberly pours him a quick cup of coffee. Of course she knows Owen takes milk and sugar. Bless her; she knows all our guest beverages by heart. The only time she really got it wrong was when Justin Timberlake came on the show and she mixed up his drink order five times until it became obvious. Bridget is better versed in our strict policy against hitting on our celebrities. She did handcuff Gene Simmons to the Oakland Stroke last year. But that was to keep him, she claimed, from exposing himself every time he passed her booth.

As Kimberly demurely slides next to Owen, stirring his coffee and giving him a friendly greeting, Bridget is unexpectedly there too, plopping on Owen's other side with ninja stealth, blowing in his ear and rubbing her army boots on his ankle just to provoke our resident debutante. Owen motions to me for help, but I have more immediate work to do.

"Now let's go over tonight's most talked-about dedications. André in Brooklyn dedicated a Jay-Z set to his girl, swearing he'll never forget that special anniversary again. No man should forget the first anniversary of their first hook-up, isn't that right? Michelle from Baton Rouge went down a similar road with a pair of great Whitney Houston cuts for that man of hers who *will not* be flirting with her stepmother any more, isn't that so? Thank you, Michelle for letting me exclude *Saving All My Love For You*, unbelievably great vocals and I have no problem with the married man thing because life rolls out like that sometimes. But I'm not good with celebrating a woman who sits home all self-destructive and co-dependent, until she gets the booty call. Yeah I know my crusade seems to a lot of you as self-righteous but my show is my truth, hope you can respect that."

Bridget signs me, annoyed. In the old days, she'd be hollering at me. Her vow of silence limits her ability to express her temper although, as Eskimos apparently have dozens of words to describe snow, she can give me the finger with such nuance that I know exactly what she means. But clearly the top dog she's got on hold is going to split unless we get moving. "Okay, Riders. Since I'm still on the Desolation Row soapbox, let's see if our next caller sticks us with another I'll Die If You Leave Me song." I look down. Neither Kimberly nor I have any data on our screens. Bridget's got us flying blind again. I really should fire my ill-pierced and ill-tempered call screener. But Bridget's no worse than a loving cat who delivers half-eaten mice as gifts of love. I punch line thirty-two, top dog central.

"Rick Lang, the Midnight Rider. Welcome to Desolation Row."

"It's Emma from the city of lost angels. How's it going, Rick?"

Usually I just throw out something like *hanging in there* just to get past the polite bit. But tonight I'm still in Leah-land. "I'm doing just great, Emma, feeling great. What's up?"

"Good for you! Hey, I was going to request one of my usual gloomy favorites but you sound so upbeat that I think we should rock the casbah instead."

This call is not what it seems. My cousin-by-marriage Emma, checks in every few months. Not only is she one hardcore midnight rider, veteran of dozens of tough interventions around the LA area, but her success rate is outstanding. She says her secret is a box of tissues in one hand, and a baseball bat in the other. She also keeps in better touch with me than my cousins do. She won't acknowledge our family connection when she calls; I wouldn't mind if she did, but that's how she wants to play it. She'll also never call me on my warm line which she, as part of the friends and family plan, is encouraged to do. But she *will* tackle any and all sorts of heavy problems and she has a special interest in defending the underdog; she's been arrested more than once in defense of the downtrodden. Emma owns an intensity that takes a back seat to no one and she has a dark side which isn't for everyone. But she got Gabriel through the worst years of his mental tribulations when nobody else had the skills.

"Been thinking of you," she continues. "Someone left a very strange message for me yesterday and it reminded me that I hadn't called in awhile."

"Whatever the reason, strange or not, it's always great to have you ride with us."

"I have a great idea."

"Let's talk about it."

"Standing In The Shadows Of Love."

"You mean the original version? Four Tops?"

"Yeah, let's go *there*."

"And dedicated to...?"

"It's for me," she says. "A little self-dedication. A little song-medication. You okay with that?"

"Anything you want to talk about first? Tie it into the song?"

She's very silent. I just let the air deaden. Kimberly signals me to *talk*, but the dead air is my tiny gift to Gabriel's bodyguard, I know she needs to take a moment. Then Emma does what she does because she's a human stun gun and you never know when she'll strike. She starts to sing the lyrics to her dedication song in a nice alto. The first line is soft, the rest grows in volume.

*"I'm just standing in the shadows of love. You know, I'm getting ready for the heart aches to come. I'm just standing in the shadows of love. Doin' my best to get ready for the heart aches to come..."*

This show thrives on odd turns. So I don't hesitate. Why not? If I can twist the night away, I can stand in the shadows of love. I jump in and join her.

*"I want to run, but there's no place to go..."*

She laughs, completes it, also singing.

*"For heartaches will follow me I know...."*

Heartfelt *a capella* on this impromptu Rick Lang family special. I don't remember ever doing this before, not in ten years behind the mic, not in ten years tied to the mast of loneliness and it feels good. Emma lives in Hollywood, on the fringes of its craziness, she has a cinematic sense of drama and when she's around, no straight line is safe from her natural born urge to swerve. As Emma continues to sing, I lower her volume and address my listeners.

"Why is this song okay for a Desolation Row dedication? Because the singer isn't going to wallow in it. The singer is going to fight back." I signal Kimberly to open all seventy-two lines, automatically letting them bypass Bridget and stampede in our front door.

Emma goes for it, right on cue. Of course she knows the words, what doesn't she know? Her alto is stronger by the line. "*Now wait a minute! Didn't I treat you right, now baby, didn't I! Didn't I do the best I could, now didn't I?*"

I stoke it. "Everybody out there? Loosen up and listen up!"

And so Emma sings to one nation, indivisible. "*Don't you see me standing in the shadows of love! I'm getting ready for the heart aches to come!*"

It's so nonsensical, it works.

Owen, whom I had almost forgotten, and Kimberly join the party, no doubt Kimberly's idea. I see her flipping on all six of the studio microphones. Bridget, hanging onto her vow of silence by a thread, has also flipped her mic so she can beat-box non-verbally, skillfully banging and rap-a-tapping with lightning speed on our lousy 1940s galvanized steel piping with her palms. Who am I to upgrade our sub-standard plumbing when our *success mojo* has been on a ten-year roll?

Owen is a baritone, Kimberly is a soprano. I signal them, flick a switch so their voices will pop. They sing: "*Can't you see me standing in the shadows of love! Doin' my best to get ready for the heart aches to come!*"

I slide the volume back to Emma, who keeps on keeping on: "*All alone I'm destined to be, with misery my only company! It may come today, or it may come tomorrow. But it's for sure I've got nothing but sorrow.*"

I hit the conference button. For the first time ever, I prepare to put all seventy-two waiting phone lines on the air simultaneously!

Emma sings on. "*I thought your conscience would kinda bother you! How can you watch me cry after all I've done for you! Hold on a minute! I gave you all*" *the love I had, now didn't I? When you needed me I was always there, now wasn't I!"*

I've timed this right, oh yeah. "Everybody on the phone lines, SING!"

The studio speakers shake until it seems like they'll explode as my waiting callers let rip!

*"STANDING IN THE SHADOWS OF LOVE, I'M GETTING READY FOR THE HEART ACHES TO COME!"*

Whatever my listeners are suffering from tonight, it's got to be gone for at least this preposterous moment. It's a split-second, *augenblick* triumph of joy and connection over anguish; it shows me the range of courage in the back alleys of affliction.

"One last time, Emma from the city of lost angels!" My Sennheiser is crackling, very un-pro, but it does this when I'm out of control, out of control, happily out of control! I slide Emma up to full throttle again, tamp down all other voices. She now holds the solo. *"I'm trying not to cry out loud, cause all this crying, it ain't, it ain't gonna help me none!"*

Emma wraps it up with a flourish. *"Standing in the Shadows of Love, I'm getting ready for the heart aches to come. Can't you see me standing in the shadows of looooooove!"* She holds the final note with admirable skill.

*Yes!* I unhook the conference line. "Okay, Riders, let's ask Emma if she got the self-dedication, self-medication she asked for…"

Suddenly the ears of late night America are on line thirty-two.

"Thanks, Rick. I'll be able to sleep now. "

And just like that, with a *click*, she's gone.

I put warm colors in my voice. "Midnight riders, one and all, it is three minutes to midnight. I'm going to keep the ball rolling by spinning the original *Standing In The Shadows Of Love* and then we're going to call it an early night and play some lyrically awesome music until Righteous Ray rolls in at two. In the meantime, the KHEL chat room is open. Work with each other, work for each other, be good to each other. This is Rick Lang, the Midnight Rider saying goodnight."

I fade myself out. Kimberly looks at me. "What's up with that?"

"I thought you told me you have classes to sign up for tomorrow?" Mills College waits for *no* man. Especially given its undergraduate classes are all female.

"I do."

"Then off you go." I call to Bridget. "You get the rest of the night off, too. Mind closing up shop?"

Bridget pinches her earlobe, a Brazilian gesture for victory, and circles her nose with her fingers, a French hand gesture meaning she's off to get drunk. I tap two of my fingers together, as Egyptians do, to ask her jokingly if she's going to get laid…and she rewards me with a thumb stuck between the fingers of her fist, a very rude Costa Rican gesture indeed. Bridget, being of Anglo-Irish descent, then punctuates the non-verbal exchange with two fingers rotated in a reverse victory sign which in this case means: sure I'll close up you for you, you dickhead. I blow her a kiss, which is universally understood, although not always culturally acceptable, and then I wave at Owen, using a genuine American gesture, to follow me. He gives me a thumbs up, which in Lebanon and other middle east countries is extremely rude, but works for me here in Oakland, crossroads of my world.

Owen follows me to Studio A which is unoccupied tonight; I grab the universal remote control from its perch near the door and, with a press of a button, bring Disneyland to life.

Studio A is the opposite of Studio B. Twice as big, lit brightly and to perfection, its technology is state-of-the-art and there is a lot of it. It resembles your basic football stadium corporate suite. The furniture is plush, televisions on each wall, gaming screens and other entertainment paraphernalia, a full kitchen and bar with monogrammed mugs and plates and glassware and actual silverware instead of the pink and blue plastic we favor in my cave. Bright and cheerful original art on the walls, signed photographs of every luminary imaginable, the beat goes on and on.

We move to Studio A's two-ton marble conference table with 'KHEL, a Cloud Channel' chiseled in gold at one end beneath our Conglomerate logo. I take one pimped out captain's chair, he takes another. Each chair has two cup holders and one mobile phone holder. It definitely makes up for the fact that my studio chair, upon which the fate of the free world sits every night, doesn't even have an armrest.

"Here's something we forgot." Owen extracts a Three Musketeers candy bar from a pocket, cuts it in half with his Swiss army knife, fishes a book of matches and candles from another pocket, sticks one candle in each half of the chocolate bar. Strikes a match and lights both. He carefully slides my half over to me.

"You're right," I note. "We never got our birthday cake."

"Never too late," he replies. "And here's your gift." He reaches into another pocket, pulls out a small gift-wrapped box. "I'll open it for you since it's my birthday too." Out of the box come two shot glasses. They each show a San Francisco cable car. One bears the name 'Rick' and the other is labeled 'Oliver.'

I give him a look. "Oliver?"

He shrugs. "They were out of Owens..." He slides the 'Rick' shot glass to me and places the 'Oliver' in front of him.

"You shouldn't have."

"Chinatown. A buck fifty." He adds. "For both!"

"What are we going to drink?"

Owen, a man of many pockets, now extracts a hip flask. "Jack Daniels." He then extracts a deck of cards. "And Jack's fifty-two closest partners in crime."

"We're going to cut cards, aren't we?"

"That's how we've done it for years. Why stop now?"

"Let me guess.' I say. "First we're going to make a wish?"

"Rick Lang, the Psychic Rider! You ready?"

"Say when."

"Go for it."

I blow out my candle. He blows out his. We look at the makeshift birthday cakes.

"I hope wax and chocolate mix."

"Sure they do."

Candles fly, chocolate down the hatch.

"What did you wish for?"

"Global Harmony. You?"

"World Peace."

"You're so predictable." Owen begins to skillfully shuffle the cards.

"What are we cutting for?"

"If I'm high card, you open my envelope for me and tell me what you think." He slides his blue envelope to the center of the table.

"And if I'm high card?"

"You won't be."

"Why is that?"

"It's a trick magic deck. Don't you recognize it?"

"Oh, yeah. I do. I gave it to you."

"How about a shot?"

"One shot.' I reply. "That's it."

He pours us a pair of shots. "Not me. I'm going to have more than one." He looks around Studio A. "You mind if I crash here? Because I've got a little more asocial drinking to do and this place has got the most comfortable couch in the East Bay."

"Be my guest, it's not my studio."

He downs his shot. "It should be. Your show paid for it."

"Me and Righteous Ray, we're fundamentalists. We keep it simple."

"You keep your studio dark and damp and cold as hell. That's fundamentally weird." He lifts his glass. "Here's to the birthday boys."

We clink glasses, shoot our shots. Owen finishes his card shuffle, offers the deck to me. I cut the cards, pull the Jack of hearts.

"Doesn't matter, does it?" I ask him.

"You should know."

He cuts the cards after I shuffle them. It's the Ace of Spades.

Owen slides the blue envelope to my side of the table.

"Okay..." I open it and glance at its contents for a few moments, give him a shrug. "Congratulations, Professor Brucker. It's a girl."

"What else?"

I look more closely. "Impressive. It's got pictures. It's got statistics. It's got tables and graphs. It's got a mission statement. It's got a résumé…"

"What do you think?"

"Depends. Still planning to go for the gold?"

Owen locks eyes with me. "I thought we'd cut cards for that too…" He pours himself another drink. I cover my glass.

"I'll stop while I'm ahead."

Owen, the son of alcoholics, is the farthest thing from a heavy drinker. But it is a barometer of his anxiety level. "You and Leah had dinner together. What did you two decide to do?"

I involuntarily smile. "You'd be surprised."

"Meaning?"

"Meaning she and I will return to Montgomery Street tomorrow and we'll all have yet another Secret Society not-secret vote."

"But which way are you leaning?"

"I'm not avoiding your question. I just want to wait until we're all in the room. Then we'll decide."

"I went looking for Shannon. Like you suggested. But she's not answering her phone. So I got worried and drove to Tiburon, she's not at home." He shakes his head. "You think she'll show up?"

"What do you think?"

"She's mixed up, she got hurt. But she'll show up."

"What would've happened if Shannon had been at home? What would you have said to her?"

"I don't know. You're the one who always knows how to talk to her. She and I just hang out together."

"Everybody seems to think I'm the only one who can handle her when she's upset."

"Oh, I can handle her just fine. We never fight. We have a lot of fun. I guess it's not really fair. She and I go to concerts together. All you guys do is discuss her boyfriend problems. She and I go to the movies together. All you guys do is discuss her hopes and dreams and goals and failures and thoughts and feelings until you're both sick to your stomachs." Owen is smiling now. "Shannon worked with me at my booth at the Machine Age Radio exhibit last year at the Moscone, you remember? She had 'em rolling in the aisles and pulling out their wallets; of course she was the best looking woman in the building and ninety percent of vintage radio collectors are older male geeks. Say no more."

"Guess I don't see that side of her too often, do I?"

"You got to look at it this way. Me and Shannon both came from the worst kind of broken homes, the kind that you either run from or take a shotgun to. Our expectations are low."

"But you think she can handle this marriage bet thing."

"She's a whole lot more resilient than she lets on with you. I think she likes to play you a bit, in a nice way I mean. She loves you and all that. But as women go, Anjuli and Leah have much better boundaries. They both can tell when you're depressed and need to be alone. Shannon, she's not so good at that…" Owen sighs. "…she also doesn't really understand *at all* this thing about how the dead talk to you…"

"She doesn't understand *what*?"

"Leah explained it to us one time. It actually made me sort of cry. Because I hadn't thought of it before…"

This is startling stuff. I've never seen Owen show all that much emotion. In this way, he and Shannon are absolutely alike. They can tolerate a lot of pain without either losing it or letting on. He offers me another shot of Jack. What the hell. My night is starting to take a downturn, might as well. I nod. He fills my glass.

He continues. "Leah says that when people you love die in a…in a sudden *violent* way…before it's their time….they *call* to you. Like from beyond the grave. They're never really dead in a *final* way…because you're always imagining it… the moment of their death, I mean…over and over again…in your mind…"

"Leah said that? She explained that?"

"Yeah, long time ago. She set us all straight. Happy as Leah can be, she's seen a lot of people die…she doesn't talk about it much… in emergency rooms…

that kind of thing. She understands stuff like this. She says it never goes away…your Mom and Dad, for example…they're always going to be *calling* you…because you'll always wonder what they were thinking just before they died…"

It's true. I re-imagine their deaths over and over again. Over and over.

He continues. "…that's why I don't feel sorry for myself. I have no right…my parents were monsters, I hated them, they're dead, and they sure are silent now." He stops himself. "Puts that blue envelope in perspective, doesn't it?"

"Leah's amazing." I add.

"Yeah. She is."

Owen screws the top back on his hip flask, gets up and takes the two shot glasses to Studio A's gourmet sink, starts to wash them. "To hell with it. We'll all meet up tomorrow like you said. We'll talk about the money, we'll talk some more about the downside. We'll take a vote. There's no point in forcing it. We either all agree to do it. Or not."

"Sounds like a plan."

"It's the only fair way."

"Glad you agree."

We share a nod. He finishes drying the shot glasses, hands them both to me. "We should keep these handy. We might need them tomorrow."

I take the shot glasses; I pocket the one marked 'Rick' but hang on to the one marked 'Oliver.'

Owen scoops up his deck of cards. Does a very impressive bit of flashy card play before tucking them in his coat pocket.

"At least God left me with a brother." I say.

"Amen."

We're quiet for a moment.

Then I hand him his shot glass so he can see his misspelled name. "Although who'd want a brother named *Oliver*."

He quickly grabs his cable-car shot glass from my hand, tucks it and his cards in the same side pocket where he's rolled his blue envelope. "Give me a break. What do you expect from Chinatown?"

# CHAPTER THIRTEEN

ALKING WITH OWEN, SINGING WITH MY RADIO NATION, KNOWING TOMORROW'S MEETING WILL be bye-bye so long to the Marriage Game, it's been a fantastic night. Leah's sudden revelation this evening, clan McLaren, wearing plaid like some bonnie lassie from mythical Brigadoon, that Scottish town which appears out of a foggy mist once a century, has me thinking. Can love, which appears for me about once a century as well, finally emerge out of my foggy haze?

As I drive through Mill Valley, now only a few minutes from my home, my fat companion also known as the thick green envelope on the seat beside me has transformed into a defused grenade, a harmless war souvenir. Now it even seems to have a kind of poetry to it, the one peculiar touch that makes it seem inconsonant with all the other chicanery:

*Love me, I am her secret*

Further, as I approach the house on Cascade drive which Paige's ancestors had built when four-story houses made from redwood were imaginable, it suddenly brings to mind that it was here, on Cascade Drive's half-acre front lawn, that I first met Leah, the day of my wedding to Paige.

Owen had brought her as his last-minute date, the girl who had just rented the apartment next to his in the Berkeley Hills, stunning Leah who was twenty-three and newly arrived from Boston. As the jolly groom, I was in just the right mood to admire her stylish walk-and-talk, the classy, sassy little cherry red dress which let the sun shine through it showing off a pair of long romantic legs. I remember noting without judgment, upon our being introduced, that my new bride couldn't buy (despite her inheritance) Leah's kind of liveliness and charm.

What did Leah think of me that day? Did Owen tell her the story of how this nice, ordinary young guy had just won the lottery of love? Could she herself see through me, see that this new groom who was being so attentive to her had really lucked out by managing to find such an extraordinary, competent and confident, sophisticated bride.

Leah was all feminine and fun that evening when I danced with her at my own wedding reception. I recall being somehow mature enough to absorb that this woman in my arms was a *third* kind of woman, not a Shannon or a Paige, but a woman with a deeper, sweeter attractiveness... something I had never known was an option. I was so fascinated with Leah that Owen was forced to tactfully suggest that I not continue neglecting my wife of three hours. But I remember Paige simply blissing out in her fabulous handmade royal wedding dress, meeting and greeting and hobnobbing, not needing to worry about me because I was the very definition of faithful and loyal.

Cascade Drive is geologically lower than the rest of the village, lined and circled by redwoods, and the Phillips mansion, as it is known in the neighborhood, sprawls on a hillside beside a deep but narrow stream, a cold gully which is shored up by irregular rock fences. There is a short but unpleasantly steep sloping drive up to the entrance. I negotiate it tonight as all nights, with my heart numb but perhaps less numb than usual. If I pay penance in my working cave, it is nothing compared to the iron mask which usually snaps shut as I approach my Museum of Hurt. When Owen moved in with me after the crash, he installed driveway lights which had motion detectors, not pleased that I had driven into the same tree, and twice, late at night. Yes, my vision has often been faulty here on my museum driveway. But tonight I clearly see something upsetting, something I have never seen before.

There is a brand new black Lexus LS 430 parked next to Paige's rusting Mercedes, a car I cannot believe is here, a car I desperately don't want to be here. This is an immediate crisis, one with timing so horrendous as to make my stomach churn.

I move to the double entry doors underneath the redwood portico which has grown wild with Paige's night-blooming jasmine, the scent of which eventually became so intense that it evolved into Paige's forever scent, her actual scent now long forgotten. The alarm system has been turned off and not by me, but I am not surprised, as many people know the code. Just punch in the birthday of a pair of dead twins and *open sesame*.

Tonight there is a lamp lit in the downstairs study, a light which is never turned on. I take the green envelope because now it may be needed as a supernatural shield, an enchanted armor to hide behind. I walk toward my unexpected and unwanted appointment with a mystery which will not be a mystery.

I pass the living room, still overcrowded with antiques original to the building of the house. I pass through the downstairs hall and the entrance to the kitchen where I can see that the children's little clip-on seats are still in their positions at the kitchen table. And that their porcelain Peter Rabbit tableware is still stacked, kept clean and bright, by the side of the sink. And as I enter the study, with its Tiffany lamp and Morris chairs and massive two-sided oak partner's desk, my focus is entirely upon the wraparound window seat in its bay window, where she is sitting, waiting for me.

Shannon is always terribly needy when she is upset or agitated. But she also can be, and almost always is, excruciatingly seductive at these times. Despite her obsessive need for independence, her refusal to be tamed or captured or changed, when she is nakedly needy she is without any coy shyness.

*Leah, right hand on the truth. Leah, left foot on the facts. This is the real life Twister game I am twisted in.*

Tonight, as I enter the room, Shannon slips to her feet. I see in her green gaze the heavy agitation she feels; it must be so for her to come unbidden to my ghost house for this purpose, for the first time ever. And how her heavy agitation turns her erotic loneliness into my palpable lust. I grow rapidly erect for her, just like that, I have no control. This arousal, this explosive knee-jerk sexual spasm caused just by the sight of Shannon's raw longing, has been bred into me over the last five years. It started in her office building's elevator one dark night when she emotionally pushed all my buttons to unbutton the sexual me, exhorting how it was what I needed to restore that aspect of my life. But it was also because *she* needed mending and saving because only *my* physical love can soothe Shannon who can't self-soothe. It is different from the sex she has shared and enjoyed with her many other lovers. And not in a good way.

For me, that is.

*Leah, men hide in sex, you know that. It is a place where a man can feel every-thing and feel nothing. You're a woman. I don't expect you to understand. You're a woman; I don't expect you to forgive.*

Shannon is wearing tight black leggings with high-heeled black boots and a long black turtleneck. Within seconds she is pressed against the length of me. "I'm sorry. I know this isn't okay here, not here in your house."

"Shannon, stop it…"

But she can sense my erection and, because her boots add height, Shannon is able to wrap-hug me in such a way that her sweet spot, so easily available through her thin leggings, is at just the right angle to literally suck onto the fabric of my pants and latch onto my stone hard and pointing-toward-perdition tip, which she squeezes once and again. Her sexual hunger is potent and enflaming. It sends spasms of unwanted pleasure shooting up and down my spinal cord.

But tonight I will find that credible way not to give her what she craves and needs and has always gotten at desperate times like these. The question is *how.* I try to pull free. But this unexpected strong movement to detach myself only causes her to react with greater excitement, molding herself against me even more forcefully; her wet frontal assault continues to squeeze my tip and her body shudders and the moans begin.

"You saw what they did to me today." She is breathing hard.

"So let's *talk* about it"

"I don't want to talk."

"This isn't the way to deal with it."

"Of course it is. It always is." Her cadenced gyrations are small and subtle but she has tremendous control of her sweet spot and she's working me so I can think only in waves of monosyllabic thought. She continues. "I'll take you with me. We'll go to that place. I'll take you to that place. Do *not* push me away."

"It's been *seven months*. It's not okay for you to just show up after seven months."

"You've never made me beg. Do *not* make me beg!"

Of course, I can shove her away. I can raise my voice, demand that she stop, force her from this room, drive her from my house. But what explanation can I give? And what right do I have? For five years, whenever her East Tennessee blackness threatened to smother her with its pillow, I have always, without exception, helped her through it with my body and my acceptance. It's been a contract I break at the expense of her trust and friendship and besides *I can't think*, she's about to bring me to orgasm and that is one thing I *can* control.

*Leah, this isn't what it looks like.*

*No, I'm not being truthful. It is what it looks like.*

*But I can explain, I can explain!*

In desperation, I slip my right hand down the back of Shannon's leggings, under the wisp of her panties, and gently slide my middle finger back and forth along the soft erotic inner fold. She gasps. And with a last stupendous squeeze of my erection through the fabric of our clothes, she suddenly comes, loudly and completely, sagging in my arms.

I count to five, as tenderly as I can manage. Then subtly I create space between us. I step back and prop myself against the edge of the oak desk, willing my erection to calm down.

"Feel better?"

"Yes."

"Are you okay to drive home?"

"Rick, I need more."

"Shannon...you're tired...I'm tired....and you're right...you shouldn't be here..."

Shannon's eyes cloud briefly. She has a powerful intuition which guards her, that keeps her alive in a world which has shown her evil at far too young an age. Something has changed in her universe; something has left its orbit.

"It's been seven months." I repeat.

Now she knows. She knows because we share a private set of tarot cards which she has thumbed over and over again.

"Not like this. Not this way."

"We *will* talk about this. But not tonight."

Shannon approaches the partner's desk against which I have taken refuge, pushes close to me once again, a girl who knows how to work the room. A strand of hair is caught in the corner of her mouth, her face is slack from release but her eyes have not come yet, they glow green hot. Her top clings to her as if it were part of her skin, her leggings too, she is skin tight and, although she is not now touching my body, my erection begins to throb again. She continues. "I've never told you this. But every time we make love, I always tell myself it's going to be the last time. That's why I'm so crazy with you and bad with you and so hungry for you. That's why our sex is what it is. Because every time is always the last time." She hesitates. "So is this going to be our last time, Rick? Because that's okay."

She sees I am thinking too hard, trying to come up with the right words to say. So she continues. "I'm prepared. Don't doubt that. It's always been your decision when to end it. Is it tonight? Is it now?"

The house on Cascade Drive has four staircases, four flights of fifteen stairs apiece. Upon the bottom stair in the entrance hall, just adjacent to the wall, there is a heart which Paige carved into the wood when she was a child.

Inside the heart, she scratched '*I Love You*' and '*Paige*' and '*Age 9*'. After the crash, I used to meditate on that step for hours on end. Now I make sure Shannon does not step on that step as we go upstairs.

*Leah, there is no avoiding this. Please close your eyes. Please turn away.*

In Paige's house, the home of her parents and grandparents, I have a room that belongs only to me. The attic had never been inhabited until I turned it into a room of my own. I slept there when Paige needed to be alone at night or wanted to work late in the master bedroom. I sleep there now because it is not haunted, because Paige refused to climb those last fifteen steepest steps to the attic; she had a thing about Cascade Drive's most dangerous set of stairs; she wouldn't let Cally and Cassie be carried up them either. She was afraid that once they learned to walk, they would fall. Cruel irony, they never learned to walk but they *did* learn to fall, if only from the sky. But the one positive note to our beyond-negative tragedy is that here, in this blank place no one ever visited, my thoughts of them can, most nights, stop at the attic room's threshold and allow me the occasional dreamless sleep.

Shannon has never been inside this room and, as she enters, I see she is aroused just being here. She steps onto the hardwood floors which have no carpet to muffle their cracking sound as we walk. She glances at the built in shelves, the antique wardrobes, and chests, and chairs, and long tables. A long row of old beveled half-windows with their original warped glass, have no curtains. The one full sized window, facing east and through which I can step onto the shingled roof, features my old brass telescope, that spyglass which once hitched my wagon to the stars but now appropriately points only to the ground.

The one object in the room that has the most fascination for Shannon is my single, narrow, 1920s hospital/asylum bed with its narrow wrought iron bed frame, at one time left in the attic by some invalided Phillips relative. I have always, perhaps perversely, liked its Spartan bed-of-nails quality and Shannon apparently likes it too. Within seconds I am on my back, stripped bare by Shannon's excited hands, my black boxers of mourning given none of Leah's love and laughter, here they are lost in an avalanche of lust and clothes-shred.

Shannon retains only her turtleneck and her panties; the latter are nearly transparent and soaking wet. Shannon's mouth begins to suck me with such intense mouth-watering vigor that every thought in my head turns to a single musical tone. With delicate, accomplished delight, she takes every inch of me in rhythmic bliss. She can feel me thicken too soon, so she stops.

She pushes aside her panties and climbs astride me, keeping her turtleneck on. She lowers herself with a controlled elevator motion as Shannon has a thing about elevators. Naturally pale and neatly trimmed, she goes down, down, down ever so slowly until she is impaled on me. She starts rotating in small circles, her eyes glazed and half-lidded.

And I feel myself going to that place she *does* always take me. It's a lifeboat which floats somewhere near San Diego, a lifeboat lit up with sunlight too bright to bear. And Shannon is with me. And we're safe and alone and we'll live and survive and somehow it'll all come right in the end. I can't see because the light is so bright but I can hear her voice. "I'm sorry I'm sorry I'm sorry I'm sorry..." She is whispering now. "I'm sorry, I'm sorry I'm sorry I'm sorry..."

I've made love to her only twenty or so times in five years, always when she is flooded and fearful, and each time I've had to endure this mantra which somehow makes it worse, worse, worse, worse.

Shannon is now riding me to please herself, as usual, riding hard and slow and stopping and twisting and deep dropping. This slowly accelerates in speed until she is up and off me and urging me to my feet. She goes to the foot of my bed, grabs the unfamiliar iron lattice with eager hands, spreads her legs and angles herself forward, her hair draping her face, her heart-shaped *derrière* presented to me. I finally recognize this as the last kiss so I slam her from behind, as if trying to slam her out of my system, which I am, but that's what she wants too because she says so over and over, slam me, do me, finish me hard and fast and hard and fast and now when she begins to come, I know to slow down and rotate my hips counter-clockwise as if unscrewing her, unwinding her last orgasm so it lasts as long as I can make it last for her, one long almost silent cry which goes on and on and on until she pulls herself off me and sinks to her knees, breathing fast, dizzy fast, curling almost into a ball on the floor, soothed and smoothed so that there is nothing inside her, she once told me, but a spotless kitchen with bright chrome and lustrous tile and burnished wood and everything brand new, untouched and unspoiled, perfect and pure.

In my wardrobe, I find two bathrobes. When she is ready, I help Shannon to her feet and she kisses me. We usually don't kiss but this time we kiss because it's a goodbye kiss.

I wrap my bathrobe around her. "It's a little big on you."

"You deserve so much better," she says to me. "Are you hurting?"

"I'm fine."

"I can finish you off. You look so sore."

"It's okay. This is how I want it." I slip into the second bathrobe, one I've never worn. Paige insisted I have a robe with a crowned "R" on it. But I wasn't born to royalty.

"You deserve so much better," she repeats. "Some fantastic Cinderella who will make you come like a cannon inside her."

"Do *not* go there."

This is a taboo subject which hasn't been discussed for eons.

"I've just made it worse for you. I kept you from looking for her."

"I didn't want to look. That was the point, wasn't it?"

"I know. And I took advantage of that." She finds her purse, finds a brush, and starts to untangle her hair, to put herself back together. "I want you to find her, Rick. It's time you tried again. This last year you've been stronger, lots stronger than you've been."

"Even if I find her…" I begin disingenuously.

Shannon interrupts me. "This is the last time I'll ever mention it so let me give you some advice…"

"I'm sure any advice you have to give would sound more professional if you closed your robe."

She smiles wryly, closes her robe; she then takes one of my pillow cases, begins to stuff it full of all the components which earlier on comprised her outfit. "It hurts me too, you know," she says.

"I *do* know. But it's been my problem; it's *always* been my problem, not yours."

"But I've seen the whole arc of it. Back when we were at Cal. And now here and now, always the same. Paige and I talked about it, you know that. We kept your secret but we both felt your pain." Shannon's robe slips open again as she pulls on her boots.

"I especially don't want to talk about Paige right now." I say this softly.

Shannon gets to her point. "You can't come inside me now because I've developed into a world-class taker, I'm not a giver. And you know I hate myself for that. You couldn't come inside Paige because she was too strong for you, she intimidated you, and you were the first to admit it. I'm not saying I'm a shrink but since some experts say the best advice comes from women who know how to strut the bathrobe-and-boots look...."

She's trying to lighten the mood so I gift her a small smile. She *is* going to be driving home in only my bathrobe and high-heeled boots, clutching a pillow case full of disheveled clothing. On any other night, it would've made for a bit of comedy.

She continues. "...all those doctors you went to. It was a waste of time. You haven't met her yet. That's the bottom line."

Shannon throws her brush back into her handbag. Digs. Finds some lipstick.

*Leah, are your eyes still closed? Are you still looking away? It's almost over.*

Shannon continues. "I've had the following speech planned for years. And now the time has come, so here you go." She finishes with her lipstick, tosses it back in her bag. "As long as you were gentle and sweet and kind and loving enough to leave your door open for me, I was going take full advantage. It was always up to you to kick my ass out of bed. And now you've done it. It's the right thing for both of us." She pauses in wry self-understanding. "Don't worry. I can't wait to find some new guys to use and abuse until they figure out I can't be owned."

With that, Shannon gives my hand a squeeze. Clutching her bag and pillow case, wearing only her leather boots and my silk bathrobe, she begins to step out the attic door onto the landing but suddenly stops as she remembers.

"What about tomorrow? Any way I can avoid that meeting?"

"We all have to be there to vote it down." I respond. "Tell me you're in."

"Since you always accuse me of being Scarlett O'Hara…" She accentuates her slight southern accent until it is Gone With The Wind broad. "…I'll think about it tomorrow."

With that, she's off and running and out the door and down the hatch, gone.

A logical, medically-minded, psychologically-savvy man might be able to accept that one's inability to come inside a woman doesn't make him a freak. That same man might label it 'inhibited orgasm' which certainly sounds somewhat normal. But my reality: freak.

I certainly filled Shannon up to the brim again and again when I was the age when juices were more plentiful and life was simpler. But as an adult, my sly and shifty sperm began to know a psychological barrier when they saw one and halfway through college they began to misbehave. Paige never saw it as a misfortune, Paige protected my shame, Paige helped me feel normal. But we didn't have children for six years because of me. And when heirs were needed, the twins had to be conceived in Paige's private hush-hush clinic via my artificially induced sperm troopers. This was helped by the fact that Paige's own sexuality was also enigmatic. Our lovemaking was never a priority for her, she enjoyed it two or three times a year, anniversaries and birthdays and holidays involving fireworks (of which Paige was strangely fond). Ours was a marriage without much of a climax but it was a marriage which saved a young man's sanity. Paige accepted my problem and kept mortification and humiliation at bay. And when Shannon, needier than ever, again became my lover, unfortunately the pattern of inhibited orgasm remained. And so my problem continued without respite and Shannon was always left high on the outside and dry on the inside; there is no delicate way to put it.

*Leah, I know that won't be our problem. I'm sure of it. I can feel it down below. But when and how can I tell you about Shannon?*

Realizing I need to stop thinking as I am about to start thinking very bad things, things that will spiral and go viral until I hit bottom, I walk the sixty steps downstairs to clear my mind.

There I find the green envelope on the floor of the study where I had let it drop. I take it and sit down on the bottom step of the stairs next to nine-year-old Paige's carved I LOVE YOU, wanting to be someplace where I can feel calm. I look at the words...

*Love me, I am her secret*

...and I hope that maybe there's a chance for some light entertainment and some mediocre laughs inside to stop the spiral.

The best thing, I think to myself as I open the fat green envelope, is that whatever is inside here can't possibly make my life any worse. But when I begin to read the first page, the I LOVE YOU stair-step starts to wobble and I'm forced to rush back upstairs to my attic sanctuary.

The devil has thrown his pitchfork.

# CHAPTER FOURTEEN

Dear Rick,

Your envelope is very much unlike the others. We believe we have found the woman you were born to meet. She has a rarity of spirit which we will begin to describe in the ten numbered files you are now holding. Please open them in numerical order. Unlike your friends, there is a mystery to be solved before you can fully embrace her. We apologize in advance for all the discomfort you are about to feel. It is the only way for us to lure you into full participation in our bet. Unlike your compatriots for whom we have, to the best of our ability, tried to create a positive milieu to conquer their issues and promote teamwork, our selection for you achieved transcendence not usually found in the artifice of our games. She is a one in a million woman, not an 'easy capture' as with the others, but well worth your every effort. Her last name, which is not her true name for reasons which will be immediately evident, will only be made available to you if the contract is signed by one and all. We assure you that you will not get to her without our help, despite your certain desire to do so. So without further fanfare, here is Vicki. Have a laptop ready, you'll need it for full effect. We admire you, Rick. We count on the fact that you will set an *example to the others. As you open the ten sealed files, please remember that no matter how agitated you may become upon reading and listening, no matter how often you remind yourself that we are just in it for the money, we have nevertheless provided you with Vicki, the only woman in existence who knows those many secrets which will help you finally let go of the grief you feel for your dead wife.*

The letter is signed by Roger Brock as CFO of New Helicon Corporation, self-styled "Team Leader, San Francisco." I immediately open the sealed file labeled #1. It's a color head shot of my intended paramour Vicki, photographed with a long lens, as seen through the window of a house. A date in grease pencil at the bottom of the photo notes this shot as only three days old. Her thick, plaited, platinum blonde hair is again disheveled. Her eyes seem sad, even depressed, but oddly alert and vigilant. She is neither attractive, nor unattractive. What does compel is that she somehow conveys a hungering ferocity with her body language. Like John Fowles' fictional *French Lieutenant's Woman*, left to stare out her window, left to scheme inwardly about other lives she doesn't live, waiting for someone or something. I put it aside.

I open sealed file #2. And my recoil is immediate. A color photograph of Paige's funeral. Grease pencil circles a mourner at the edge of the large crowd. A further close-up enhances the image. It's a much younger Vicki, appearing stricken and ill, holding a stem of orchids as she watches Paige being buried beside my twins. Ten years ago. What is she doing there? Who *is* she?

I tear open sealed file #3. A third color photo shows a smiling Vicki wearing a bicycle helmet, a sports bra and black bicycle shorts. Her body ripples young and firm and roughly twenty-one years old and she is posing outside *my* house with *my* wife and each woman is holding one of *my* children. Paige is also dressed for cycling, odd in that I didn't know she owned a bicycle; she often expressed a dislike of those cyclists along Camino Alto whom she occasionally attempted to side-swipe. Paige's premature graying hair and thin face, Vicki's hair in silver cornrows and thinner face. Mirror images. The photo looks like a tripod and timer production. Clearly, Vicki is more than a casual acquaintance. She seems every bit a part of Paige's life.

Paige's life. But not my life.

Sealed file #4. Photo number four. Black and white. Candid. Slightly askew. Paige is kissing a handsome, squarely-built young man. On the lips. Firmly and fully. He is not tall, maybe an inch or two taller than Dylan. Black wavy hair, cut short and tight against his scalp. She has her left hand on this man's collar. She wears my wedding ring. Vicki is in the background of the shot, staring at them, her eyes vigilant and wary. They seem to be in an expensive luxury downtown office with the San Francisco skyline in the background. There is a huge, bizarre display of gigantic fencing trophies encircling the entire room, many large cups but mostly tall gold figural trophies with little gold men pointing little gold swords, creating a prickly and glittering diorama of athletic ego.

The jealousy in my gut is like an icicle, sharp and wet. I find myself idiotically trying to see if Paige's tongue is in this man's mouth. Is this an affair? Paige had never placed much emphasis on affection, much less sexual escapade, once we were officially engaged on that shamefully black Thursday when her father gave me, not only his blessing, but a fat dowry check for fifty thousand dollars to augment the fourteen hundred I already had in the bank. Paige had swept me off my feet and loved me *despite* my sexual embarrassment. She never once complained when I expressed concern for her needs and her happiness.

*Why didn't infidelity ever occur to me?*

Sealed file #5 contains a CD released by Island Records. "Vicki Phillips" playing the piano, "Vicki Phillips" singing. She chose Phillips, Paige's maiden name as her professional name. It makes me feel squeamish. I slip the CD into my laptop; I listen to a few tracks. The CD is dedicated to Paige; one song is even called "Torn Pages." It is about two women involved with the same man. I can guess at the two women but certainly not this man. The CD was released five years after Paige's death.

Sealed file #6 is a suite of small high quality nude art photos of Vicki at her youngest, maybe seventeen. All she wears are inappropriate six-inch fetish red stilettos and odd props, satin gloves, scarves. Still, it seems obvious that these stylized shots are not intended to arouse. She is in a room filled with antiques and oil paintings. The lights of the City behind her show me the bay, a beautiful night view with Lombard Street at the bottom of a hill. The location is high atop Steiner or Pierce as far as I can tell, in one of the old money Pacific Heights mansions. It is the last photo of this suite which I am meant to react to; it's the only candid as opposed to a posed shot. It shows Vicki slipping on a sweater as a group of women, all ages, surround her. In the foreground, the most prominent figure is Paige, looking about as beautiful as I have ever seen her, time-frozen in the act of kissing Vicki's cheek while all the others clap. It seems to be an initiation of sorts as Vicki is still not fully clothed while Paige and the dozen other women are designer-dressed to kill.

Sealed file #7 is the out-of-the-blue plate special. It is an engraved invitation for a party thrown at Tavern On The Green by a woman who is not named but seems to be a famous socialite looking much like Ivana Trump. What is particularly unusual is that it comes with a printed insert, in black ink and gold leaf, listing the invited guests, but using only one hundred female *first* names with surnames designated only by an initial.

One of the names has been circled in red ink.

It is not Paige P. which is circled. Although Paige's name is at the bottom of the list.

It is *Emma E.* which is circled.

Emma Earnshaw? It must be. Gabriel's Emma? Who just sang for us? Who else could they mean? What had she said when she called me on air earlier tonight? *Someone left a strange message for her?*

When I turn the list of women over, I get confirmation in the form of a bold handwritten exhortation and it's just bizarre:

*"Emma can smooth the way to true love. Don't waste her expertise."*

Inside file #8 is a clipped recently-published feature article from Billboard Magazine giving the sparse details of singer-songwriter Vicki Phillips' career, the "tortured and tormented" recording artist whose piano "drips with blue blood and melancholy bile" and who, despite several recordings which have received excellent critical review, "remains an enigma" in that she has never toured and lives as "a recluse who rarely leaves her mansion" which overlooks San Francisco Bay.

I pick up sealed file #9. It is a file copy of a handwritten letter from Paige to her family's law firm dated just before her death. Despite the fact that the letter has some blacked out redactions, there is more than enough information for full laceration.

*"Derek, your suggestions don't go far enough, I'm sorry to say. I want to crush any potential defiance on Rick's part. I suggest the following approach. Given he won't be motivated by money, let's attack a different front where he will be vulnerable. I'd like you to file suit in Superior Court, file as many causes of action against his father and his sister as possible. Their law firms may be utterly honest as you have pointed out, however no one is immune to bad facts so create as many as needed to make a plausible case for disbarment. Fraud may be the best route. I'm sure we can whip up some believable offshore banking irregularities without actually having to deposit funds. Rick knows I always get what I want and it will take no imagination for him to understand that we can cause his family serious pain and financial hardship. But as there is no reason to add insult to injury, I also suggest we front-load a half million then set up regular payments for him. But make this very clear. I do NOT want him to see the children again. I do NOT want him to contest the divorce. I want him out of sight and out of mind. I know you are cautious about such things but I am aware you have people in your employ who know how to physically intimidate. If Rick is unwilling to move out-of-state, do what is necessary. I want the papers served next week in person by you and you alone. He's a coward and he'll fold if you just lean hard*

*enough. Do not accept any hysterics on his part. This is a business deal and we will all approach it as such. My parents may not be pleased, as you know they place a ridiculous premium on traditional family values. But I will break the news at their anniversary party in such a way that they will have no leverage. The children will be flying with me to Zurich immediately after the weekend. I do NOT like to ski, so get this done immediately if not sooner. Kindest regards, Paige.*

This note is attached to a copy of the proposed divorce petition, signed in Paige's decisive hand, with Richard Austen Lang listed as the Respondent.

I don't move for a very long time. Eventually, after a long period of nothingness during which I'm unable to make sense of my emotions, my mind being scorched earth, I focus on my brass telescope, a long brazen finger pointing downwards, seeming to indicate the general direction of hell. I take the laptop and the last sealed file and stagger out my turreted attic window onto the sloping roof.

It feels as if I had been trapped underwater inside the house. Now I break through the surface of the cold night chill to see an unfamiliar sky as if from the surface of an unfamiliar planet.

There is a sunrise just now limping above the redwood-lined street from which I was to be banished, a sunrise which has virtually no light or heat to offer. And now I begin to think.

Yes, documents and photographs can be manipulated to perfection. Perhaps that is why I cannot rage or cry with any certainty, despite my gut feeling that there are no lies here, only brutal truths.

They are clever, Matthew Moss and Roger Brock. Vicki becomes the bride I cannot jilt, the garter I cannot drop, the bouquet whose scent I must smell and whose petals I must pluck to see if she loves me, loves me not.

*She has answers.*

And sealed File #10 proves it, raising the stakes in the most dramatic fashion imaginable.

For it turns out I already have an intimate relationship with Vicki.

I play their CD which has been burned with a long series of phone calls to the Rick Lang show. For all along, it seems, I have been Vicki's favorite radio show host. I recognize her speaking voice immediately.

For ten years she has been calling herself Kelli with an "i" at the end.

As a favored regular, Kelli always got the green light from Bridget as she did from all prior call screeners. Kelli is a special Rider, one of the very few Rick Lang "darlings" because I resonated so powerfully with the coincidence that she had lost her sister on the exact day I lost my sister. Also in a plane crash. Also with two children involved. Yes, Kelli and I shed many tears together and America shed tears for both of us. And now the coincidence turns out to be no coincidence. Over the years I have held Vicki/Kelli together, bonded with her, made her one of my family. I have more than just cared about her. I have been half in love with our matching grief, both of us trapped in the same cradle of grief, ourselves twins sharing the same bed of loss.

No wonder this is the Marriage Game's perfect match.

We have both been grieving the same woman for ten years.

It feels like I have been hit by a bullet.

*Yet it is that Civil War bullet to the heart... which hits the bible in a soldier's coat... which absorbs the shot... and saves the man...*

Because instead of collapsing in a jumble of nerves, jumping off the roof in a fit of disbelief or losing my mind in a great paroxysm of confusion, instead of any or all these things...

...I am incredulously witness to a mighty and potent torrential gush of life which abruptly spills out of my wound, soaking me in the very green freedom that once splashed wild-river over me as a youth.

I inexplicably feel *alive.*

And I don't understand why.

But I do know what I must do. I will find Kelli. Because she *is* Paige's secret and nothing matters to me anymore except finding out why, why, why, why, *WHY!*

# CHAPTER FIFTEEN

THE CONTRACT IS WAITING AT THE END OF THE
TABLE. IT SITS UNDERNEATH ITS OWN SPECIAL
desk light which illuminates it, no doubt intentionally, to great dramatic effect.
As I approach, I further note that it is already folded open to the signature
page. Without hesitation, with my only thought being that of finding Kelli *née*
Vicki and forcing the truth from her, I initial each page and sign on the sixth
line. Then I wait a long hour for the others.

The law offices of Matthew Moss are deserted today, Moss allegedly having been forced to take a meeting on some tropical golf course and thus is
unable to watch the signing of our fiendish pact in person. I am not so naïve as
to neglect to search for hidden cameras. However none can be found during
a cursory search as I am not expert in the newest invasive 21$^{st}$ century surveillance techniques whereby the average San Franciscan is caught on camera,
let's say perhaps a dozen times per diem, bad hair day or not.

Upon my arrival, I had occasion to check in with the only employee in
evidence, a beefy attorney who obviously doubles as a North Beach bouncer.
His job is to man the floor-to-ceiling safe within which Kelli's true and complete identity waits. Despite subtle but graphic threats most unbecoming a
nurturing celebrity, I cannot coerce him to open it and prove to me that the

information does indeed exist. But I'm assured that there is most definitely something inside for Number Six and upon receipt of the completed contract, Moss' three-piece-suited bouncer has been told to open Pandora's Box and let slip the dogs of love.

In due course, Dylan is the first to join me at the conference room. He sees me, does a double take. "Whoa, I thought once you wore black, you never went back."

I actually have to look down to see that I am wearing tight faded blue jeans and a red sweater, both as old as the hills. I don't even remember putting them on.

"Don't be coy, this is major news! The Midnight Rider wears red!" He eyes me with a crooked grin. "I hardly recognize you, you look so gosh darn pretty." He continues to further appraise. "Although the stubble on your chin and that familiar sleepless look tell me that you haven't changed all *that* much!"

"Ready to sign?" I hand him my official KHEL pen, a black Mont-Blanc with "No Sympathy For The Devil" in red and gold lettering down its side.

Dylan walks over to the contract, signs with John Hancock gusto on the first line.

"Don't forget to initial each page." I add.

Dylan initials, sighs in satisfaction, pulls out a cigar case and tosses a cigar to me. I try to hand it back but he makes me pocket it. "Then save it for it Anjuli's Tuesday night strategy session." He lights his cigar and puffs with enthusiasm. "Bet you didn't know how good Curly-Locks is at marriage planning. It's all her sales background. She's got a list of fifty ways to meet your lover. She's got pie charts, histograms, practice exercises, flow charts, projections, you name it. She's a genius when it comes to hooking up with the opposite sex." Dylan is reeking of fanaticism. "The way she sees it, we'll stagger the first meets. You know, like those English prison camp tunnel movies? Two out of the tunnel per week, all six in the first three weeks, Shannon kept in the loop with constant updates…"

Dylan breaks off as he sees Gary enter. Gary immediately spots me, reacts pleased. "Looking good, looking *good!*" He walks right up to the contract, signs on the fourth line. As he initials, he frowns. "What am I gonna do? Can't remember the last time I made a move on anybody over twenty-five years old…"

Dylan is growing more cheerful by the minute. "Older women are better in bed, Big Kahuna. Trust me. You don't have to teach them what goes where."

Gary reacts. "I thought I just had to get her to the altar. Who says I have to play spin the bottle with her?"

Dylan snorts. "You're a hunk-o-matic, dude. She'll be all over your boogie board in ten seconds. Don't try to finesse it. You're number four. You have your duty to the group to fake what it takes until the money is out of escrow and in our mitts. Right?"

Gary sighs. "I'll just close my eyes and think of you, Dylan."

Dylan laughs, hands Gary a cigar. "Your ancestors were kamikaze pilots, Gary. You can do it!"

"Isn't it against the law to smoke here?" I ask him.

"You bet!" He puffs away. "Breaking the law in a lawyer's office. Sweet!"

Gary also pockets his cigar, looks at me. "I just *gotta* hear what you found in your envelope. Were they straight with you? Are they really giving you something major as a reward? I'll bet it's huge."

"True enough."

"Tell me!"

"Not going to happen. Not yet anyway."

"Aw, come on. They said she'd be just the ticket. Is she?"

"Just the ticket."

"Then where's the thrill factor?" prods Gary. "You're not looking thrilled enough."

"I was the first to sign."

"So you were! At least tell me the plan? How soon will you meet her? Do you need any help? This could really be fun."

Gary's thirst for details reinforces my decision to hide my feelings. I have only one goal. Get the contract signed. Get the identity of Paige's secret keeper. And go find her. Everything else is pushed from my mind.

Abruptly Shannon and Owen appear together, arm in arm. They look surprisingly merry.

"Fashionably late, as usual." Gary's smile widens.

"Have you two been celebrating in advance?" Dylan queries. "Because how come I didn't get the memo?"

"Happy hour. Just a quick pit stop," replies Owen. "You know the pub around the corner? Where me and Shannon play darts?"

"Yeah, I've heard of that place." Gary replies. "That's where Leah threw, like, a half-dozen of those darts at Anjuli."

"*Urban myth*, man!" Owen retorts. "Anjuli made that up. If Leah really wanted to hit Anjuli with a bunch of darts, Anjuli would be an instant pin cushion." He looks around. "And where *are* both of them? When is the meeting going to come to order?"

"What meeting, dude?" Gary points to the tantalizing illuminated glow at the end of the table showcasing the contract. "It's sign up and shut up."

"What?" Shannon looks taken aback. She swivels and stares at me, happy hour unexpectedly less happy.

"I signed." I say. "I'd like you to sign too."

"I thought we were all going to talk about this. Isn't that what you said?"

"Moss was right. They do have someone I want to meet."

Shannon reacts, usually expert at hiding her shock, but not so expert now.

Before she can speak, Gary interrupts on my behalf. "He read up on his bride-to-be. And just like the legal eagle promised, Rick's world has been *rocked*." Gary turns to me. "Isn't that right?"

"To say the least..." I reply.

"FAN-FREAKIN'-TASTIC," shouts Owen, bolting over and hugging me. "So it's okay to dash for the cash! I didn't see this coming!"

Shannon snags me by the arm. "You mind if I talk to you in private?"

"Let's go," I reply.

"Who's got a pen?" Owen glances around. Dylan hands him my KHEL Mont-Blanc. "Cool!" Owen enthuses. "Owen Brucker, come on down!" With that, Owen swaggers over to the contract and, without hesitation, signs. "Line three, initial, initial, initial, I'm done!"

"Have a cigar!" Dylan throws him a Cuban special.

"I'll smoke it when the money's in the bank." He turns to one and all. "Goodbye to driving on four mismatched tires and adios to a muffler that sounds like a Chinese New Year parade!"

Shannon drags me out of the conference room and into the adjacent anteroom, and then sharply asks. "What are you doing?"

"I want you to sign the contract. I know you weren't expecting this. But I need you to do this and trust me."

"I'll sign it, I'll do it. Because this is never going to pay off, we both know that. And the rest of them will figure that out soon enough. But what's up with you? You are acting, for lack of a better word, creepy. And why are you going to meet that woman?"

"Can't talk about it."

"You are *kidding.*"

"Look at me, Shannon. Not kidding."

"There really is something they have that you want? How is that possible?"

"Sign it, Shannon, please."

"No. Not until you tell *me.* Of all people..."

"I can't."

She gives me a dirty look. "It this because of last night..."

"*Not* about last night. *Not* about you."

Both of us swivel to make sure we are unheard.

Shannon whispers fiercely. "I figured you and I would be okay. Smooth transition. Good for both of us, right? Where's the soft landing?" She is getting angrier by the moment. "Push me away. *Check.* Act strange. *Check.* Hide something. *Check.*"

"I'm sorry."

"I'll sign your contract. I won't ask questions. I'm not getting married for money. I'm not getting married, period. Who the hell gets married these days anyway? I don't care what's up, you know what you're asking me to do is wrong. You know that sending Owen and the others off on this scavenger hunt is wrong. You better have damn good reasons..."

Shannon stalks back into the conference room, stalks over to the contract, angrily signs and initials. Ignoring the cheers from Gary, Dylan, and Owen, she does her Tennessee Walker full tilt trot out the door and I'm not going to chase her.

"Why is she upset?" Owen is confused. "Happy hour was happy. That girl can swallow olives like you wouldn't believe."

"So she swallows! I knew it!" Dylan interjects.

Owen cuffs Dylan around the ear. "You take that back. She just signed on with us. Show some damn respect."

"Okay, okay, okay." Dylan backs away from Owen. "I sexualize women when I get nervous or excited. It's a bad habit."

"You're lucky Leah didn't hear you…"says Owen, "…because she'd take your tongue and lop it off."

"If she wants to give me some tongue, I'm down with that."

Owen tries to smack Dylan again but he dances away.

It's a full five minutes before Leah enters. The entire room looks, the entire room hushes. Leah laughs.

"What are you staring at? I'm here. As requested."

Atop her black jeans and sandals, Leah is wearing a tight green ribbed top with "Nirvana" across the front. She's had her hair cut and colored since last night's twisting dinner. Her sandy blonde hair has been lightened back to her once natural straw blonde color and she's opted to reprise her youthful mid-20s-style unruly swept bangs. With her freckles and lanky walk, she's all girl-next-door alluring but with the addition of maturity and self-confidence in her bearing. She takes my breath away.

But she also causes Paige's divorce letter to burst into flame inside my jacket where I have stashed it. I have spent most of today replaying my entire seven years of marriage. I have strained to recall every memory that I can. I focused on small details, looking for anything that would lead Paige to write a note like that, to want her children to grow up without a father, to yearn for dissolution of a marriage which had no conflict to speak of, no major issue remotely visible. But I have found absolutely nothing behind the white-washed fences and manicured lawns of my mind except a growing sensitivity to the possibility that I was sleepwalking all those years. What didn't I see? What did I miss?

Kelli/Vicki will know, she will explain.

"Is it only my dirty mind, Doctor," asks Dylan, eyeing Leah's Nirvana top, "...or has something been pushed up for better visibility?"

"You look real nice, Leah." Owen smiles at her. "I was going to dress up to sign the contract too. It's a big moment for all of us, isn't it?"

"Come on," she replies. "I just came by to make sure you all weren't dumb enough to sign the thing." Abruptly she realizes. She looks at us in dismay. At our collective and unified affect. "Jaysus, you *didn't*!"

Leah looks at me. I have no breath, she has taken it away. I am in pain; Paige's note has burned its harsh image into my skin. Leah wears a questioning expression which makes no attempt to shield me from her new found love light. I feel tears starting to well up and I don't know why. I have been holding it together, hiding all the rage of this betrayal where it couldn't be seen so I could get through the signing, get them all to sign, get to Vicki/Kelli, get some answers, some truth. But when Leah looks at me, it feels as if I'm trying to hide behind a one-way police mirror, but she can see through that mirror, I fear she can see through me.

"Leah, we've all signed." Owen says. "Except for Anjuli. But she's in and she'll be here soon."

"So there's been no discussion?"

"Shannon signed." Gary adds. "And Rick took one look inside his envelope and he was the *first* to sign. I've got to meet that piano chick. She must be amazing."

Leah takes another close look at me. Yes, she's sees I'm hiding something. What will she do? I don't want to have to plead my case. *Just do it, Leah. Please.*

And so she does. Shrugging, Leah moves on to the end of the table and immediately becomes the only one of our intelligent band of sophisticates to actually thoroughly review the contract itself, eventually initialing all its pages, and signing line five. Gary, Dylan, and Owen muster a hurrah although the adrenaline is starting to wear off.

As Leah finalizes her approval of the contract, a breathless Anjuli arrives in the room. She's carrying a huge glass jar of chocolates wrapped in ornate ribbons.

"Let's celebrate with chocolate, the food of love!" Anjuli has very recently showered in a hurry, her ringlets have gone haywire. She moves to the contract, stands right beside Leah, runs her eyes down the list.

"*Yes!*" She bursts out. "We are the start-up company of *awesomeness!* In one year our shares will be worth solid *gold*!

She hugs Leah and starts to bounce and dance around. "Party at my house!" she announces to all. "Eight o'clock, Tuesday! Tactics, love potions, and pot luck!"

"Sorry," I step between Leah and Anjuli without actually looking at either of them. "I need this for a second." With that, I exit as quickly as I can, clutching the contract. Astonished eyes follow me.

Within a short minute, I find the attorney who guards the safe, which is now ajar and open for business.

"Here it is." I say, handing him the contract. "Let's have it."

He sees the signatures, brusquely hands me what I've been waiting for.

"*Another* envelope?" I mutter. "You've got to be kidding…"

It has my name on it. He double-checks it against my driver's license for some self-serving reason (retaining his job, perhaps) and makes me sign for it.

Then it is mine.

Without a goodbye to my friends, without a clear thought in my head, I take the stairs to the street level. Careening out the building's front door, I immediately start walking toward Geary Street, my fingernails prepped to rip open this envelope which is a scab, rip it open, scratch it open, claw it open until it bleeds and reveals.

# CHAPTER SIXTEEN

KELLANE VICTORIA CABOT-WHITNEY SWIFT. THAT'S ALL THEY'VE GIVEN ME. HER NAME IS fancy-familiar but it is not someone I know. Of course, with the Internet, more information can immediately be had. But instead I walk alone through the City: forty-five minutes of circles and alley-cutting and aimless double-backs. With Kelli's name exposed, I have been given the green light, yet I stop and start and stop again on these streets of San Francisco, unable to think on my feet, needing a dark, very dark, place in which to reflect. And realizing this, my first decisive move is to enter the Clift Hotel, more specifically its Redwood Room, a spot I often go more to think than drink. It is an authentic Art Deco piano lounge built in the 1930s, an atmospheric room which has elegant wall panels made of redwood and a long bar said to have been carved from the wood of a single tree. Art Deco lamps are placed strategically between Art Deco paintings and along the walls can be found plush leather-and-velvet couches so bathed in mellow shadow that human faces cannot be seen clearly. For seven decades this has been a room built for secret rendezvous.

The center of the room showcases a grand piano and I hear Cole Porter and George Gershwin as I walk smack into the monthly meeting of the Art Deco Society, four dozen men and women of all ages dressed in 1930s costume, a conscious revalidation of the spirit of that high society crowd which made this bar their posh watering hole once prohibition in the Depression era had been repealed.

I am well enough known here by the hostess that she doesn't shoo me to the table where nametags await the Deco-denizens. However, scanning the benches, I see no place to sit. Forced to head to the crowded bar, gently pushing my way past the glittery Art Deco crowd, I hear my name called, barely audible above the music being skillfully played by the pianist and the excited chatter which always accompanies San Franciscans when they dress up for fun.

Leah McLaren has not only anticipated my arrival, she has acquired the best (darkest) table in the best (farthest) corner, and now sits on its brass-studded leather bench in the warm dark of the Redwood Room's most coveted nook. She stands and plants a kiss which lands half on my cheek and half on my lips, its mixed message of restrained sensuality somehow the ideal message at this equally mixed moment of emotional confusion. Before I can speak, our drinks appear. A Greyhound for her, an Anchor Steam for me. The shorthand of long friendships makes for easy drink orders.

Her hair is still windblown. She must have just arrived.

"Clever move." I say and chug half my beer in one gulp to Leah's amusement.

Leah sips her drink, smiles. "When I was a kid I could tail anybody from one end of Boston to the other. You weren't much of a challenge. When you started to come down Mason, I knew where you were going to land."

"*And* the best table…"

"My Scottish father taught me the art of frugality." She mimics a Scottish accent. "Ne'er forgit, ma loove, a fifty dollar bribe works just as guid as a hundred dollar bribe."

"Nice work."

"Born to please."

The "Nirvana" lettered across her breasts subtly rises and falls like a flickering green neon sign, with her every breath. Then her hand neatly grabs the little glass bowl from the table and dumps a pile of mixed nuts and pretzels in my lap.

"What the … *what*?"

She feigns surprise. "Aren't you hungry? All that walking in circles…"

I gaze at her. The early evening has been summer cold. Her cheeks have natural blush, her eyes are playful. "Thanks." I say. "It helps."

"The kiss? Or the peanuts?"

"You." I say. "I'm glad you're here. I'm a bit … lost … messed up … you know…"

"Duh." She starts to pluck some of the fallen tidbits from my lap. I jump in surprise but her free arm wraps around my shoulder to calm me down. "Stop wiggling…" she continues to scoop up more of her salty invaders. "I'm trying to pick out the cashews…"

I *really* laugh but snatch her hand from my lap, the booth isn't *that* dark. My tension continues to reduce to a more tolerable level.

Leah continues. "What was in the envelope? What have they done to you?"

"It's okay. I'm going to deal with it."

"By yourself?"

"Yes."

Leah makes a face. "What about us, what about twenty-four hours ago..?" She says this gently but there's iron there too. "We had dinner, we had fun, we made memories, we actually, nearly, almost, *got it on* …" Here she smacks my shoulder. "… we showered, we made plans…"

"Right after I left you…"

"… it all went to hell, I get that. Just explain it to me."

"It's not your problem. It doesn't involve you."

"What are you talking about?! If it involves you, it involves me. Then there's the fact you just made me sign that nauseating contract."

"I'm sorry about that."

"Gary tells me you've got a new girlfriend. Someone you met in your green envelope?"

"They do have something I want."

"Tell me more."

Suddenly a *roar* rises up from the Art Deco Society, a society which has to be far saner than our own. The pianist is now playing Cole Porter's "Anything Goes" which must be their club anthem because they are all singing along.

"It's complicated."

Leah reacts, upset. She finishes her drink, signals *two more* to our waitress who nods. Then she fiercely grabs a few more cashews from my lap. "You've sent Owen, Anjuli, Dylan, and Gary on a wild goose chase. From all accounts, you caused Shannon to boil over into a royal rage. That leaves me by your side to help out. What's wrong with that?"

"Leah..."

Leah gives me a look and then launches, speaking quickly but quietly. "Last night, you said we had to go slow. Last night you said we had to take our time. Last night you said we needed to grow our relationship. Do you want me or not? Do you trust me or not? Do you want us to *grow* or do you want me to *go*?"

I smile despite myself. "Damn, girl. You talk faster than I can think."

"I can try to be more cryptic and clueless. I can work on blunt and boring."

"I'll take you as you are. Will you take me as I am?"

Leah laughs. "Strung out on a crazy man...you bet..."

"This isn't a join forces project; this is a bad stuff from the past thing."

"Put me in coach, I'm ready to play."

"I'm going to get hurt. If you get involved, you'll get hurt."

"I'm like totally scared. What's her name?"

"Kellane Victoria Cabot-Whitney Swift..."

"*Eleven* syllables. That's a whole lot of woman for a two-syllable guy named Rick Lang."

"So you've never heard of her either?"

Leah shakes her head. "Yet she's important to you."

"She was Paige's friend. A friend I didn't know about."

Leah reacts, stunned. "This is about *Paige*? Jaysus, Rick, why is it always about her?"

"I'm sorry. I warned you."

"Fine. You warned me. But you can't get rid of me."

"I'm trying to keep you safe. I want to keep us safe."

Leah's exasperation with me knows no bounds. "You're alone in this right now. By process of elimination, you have no Secret Society members left at your side. That leaves *me* as your most trusted babe *and* your sidekick babe. Given the kids have three more weeks of summer camp…we can go to the mattresses together, as they say in the mob…or even *share* a mattress if need be, fully clothed of course…sidekick babes are good to go…"

Just then, the waitress drops two more drinks at our table. Notes our empty glass dish. "More nuts?"

"You bet," answers Leah. "Heavy on the cashews…"

As our server disappears into the throng of Deco wannabes, Leah continues. "Rick, I've spent a whole lot of my time in an emergency room. I have to be ready for whatever comes through my door. So whatever door you're about to go through, wherever you find yourself, you may need a quick-thinking, fast action back-up who can keep her head in a crisis. I won't let you down. If nothing else, if this is about Paige, you might need my objectivity."

"Okay." I say. "Sidekick babes are good to go."

"You won't regret it. I might grow on you even more." She smiles and touches her green neon top. "Nirvana has that effect on people. So I'm hired."

"You're hired."

"Okay. Straight to work but give me a second. We're a team. We need theme music."

Leah sweeps out of her seat, parts the sea of colorful and laughing people, and goes to the pianist. She sits on his bench just as he finishes a melody, whispers in his ear. He laughs, shakes his head as if she's out of her mind. Money appears in her hand like magic. I see a twenty dollar bill being popped in his tips glass.

As Leah returns to me, she's pleased. "Ne'er forgit, ma loove…" She reprises her Scottish accent. "…why pay forty when twenty will do?"

With that, she cues the pianist. Unexpectedly I hear "White Room" by Cream being played on a grand piano to the mystification of the Art Deco devotees.

We have theme music.

"Oh, one other thing…" Leah opens her purse. She extracts my wedding ring, puts it in my palm. "I found it just after you left. But I didn't want to chase after you…"

I don't hesitate. I place it, not back on my left ring finger where it has belonged throughout ten years of hard grieving, but in my pocket.

Then I *do* hesitate. I wait a moment to collect myself before I pull Paige's handwritten time bomb divorce decree from my pocket. It has creased and crumpled its way into a little ball. So I straighten out the crinkles and place it face down on the table for the moment. "There are a lot of things to discuss. But it all starts with *this*." I tap the paper.

Leah is tired of all these hesitations. Leah picks up Paige's letter and the current love of my life begins speed-reading the handwritten divorce request from the former love of my life.

Within moments, her face is wet with tears.

The pianist finishes his version of Cream's *White Room* to indifferent, scattered applause. The crowd begins to shuffle and stir.

It looks like the party is over.

# PART II

# CHAPTER SEVENTEEN

EAH AND I MEET EMMA EARNSHAW IN OAKLAND AIRPORT'S BAGGAGE CLAIM AREA AS INSTRUCTED, although she has brought only a small carry-on, a backpack slung over one shoulder. Los Angeles must have been summer-hot as her medium-length natural anglo-saxon, very-flaxen blonde hair is pony-tailed and she wears lightweight cargo pants, sneakers with no socks, and a thin baby-tee short enough to show her pierced navel. The golden fox inked on the inside of her left forearm is easily seen as she approaches, arms outstretched, for a hug of greeting. Emma's walk is cobra-cool and her chin resolute-square. She is deceptively ordinary in build and height but her coiled athleticism provides a clue to her nature. When I faxed her some of the lowlights provided by the green envelope, she didn't hesitate to jump the next available flight north with the kind of aggressive alacrity usually reserved for no-nonsense mercenaries, locked and loaded.

"I'm ready to smooth the way to true love." Emma announces with dry amusement as we hug. Leah, whom she knows only by listening to the Midnight Rider show, is given a much firmer handshake than Leah is used to. "So what say we kick some ass?"

For over a week, Leah and I had tried and failed to contact Kelli Swift. Visiting her house on Steiner, despite constant tries, proved a waste of time and energy. Search engine queries revealed little despite Kelli's family having been very newsworthy over the years. And details about Kelli herself were shockingly scarce. We did learn some essentials such as the fact that the Swift family holdings... built from astonishingly profitable early oil pipeline and mining ventures... are estimated by Forbes at four billion, split between Kelli and her brother. Kelli, at twenty-nine years old, isn't your ordinary Midnight Rider regular listener. She is one of only twelve women (eleven heiresses plus self-made marvel Oprah Winfrey) who have a place on the Forbes 400 census of richest Americans. Furthermore, she is the only woman on the list under the age of forty-five. Paige had herself quite a gal-pal.

As we walk to my car, Emma, not one to waste time, thrusts upon us a stamped postcard. "Rick, the night we sang together on your show? I'd gotten this in the mail that morning ..."

Leah and I look at the postcard addressed to Emma with its San Francisco postmark. It features a photo of the Golden Gate Bridge, a shot angled north toward Marin County. It is unsigned and no sender is indicated. It reads:

"Dear Emma. Tell Rick what he needs to know so he can find his path. Show him that good will and trust matter."

Leah reacts. "Really?"

"Reads just like a fortune cookie." I add. "That's how they are."

"Then a mysterious stranger from a far-off city will soon provide you with answers," replies Emma. With that Emma tosses her backpack into my trunk and we're off.

Leah's lovely blue-and-white 1888 Victorian, complete with carriage house, sits less than a block from Magnolia Avenue, the road which connects Leah's Larkspur to my Mill Valley, a straight shot as the crow flies but a road which actually winds and meanders with plenty of signs warning of dangerous curves, signs which Leah insists (to Secret Society jeers) were erected in her honor. Unlike Cascade Drive where my mausoleum of a home dominates an entire lonely hillside, Leah's jewel box is adroitly set in a small crescent of like Victorians, a situation which offers her boys a place to boisterously skateboard, bike, and rabble-rouse with other young neighborhood teens. But it was also chosen for its ornate historical grace of detail and its potential for entertaining outdoors as it possesses a magnificent wraparound front porch complete with a pair of oak rockers, a porch swing, and a foursome of large white wicker fan-shaped chairs.

By the time the three of us finally settle on the atmospherically-lit veranda, the late evening summer sky is just beginning to change to a darker hue. Emma spent the drive from the airport carefully sorting out the actual physical documents and photographs, making the occasional fearsome groan. It was a silent, intense drive. But now, Emma is ready to discuss all and everything she knows. Leah has been kind enough to provide us with refreshments. Emma is equally kind in her pretense of enjoying the thick paste of displeasure otherwise known as Leah's famously-avoided homemade guacamole. It sits beside Leah's so far untouched, notoriously too-tart, lemonade, on the porch swing.

"Just a quick question before we get going," offers Leah. "Could she be out of the country?"

Emma shakes her head. "Not likely. I don't think she would risk it."

Leah and I exchange a look. *That's* an enigmatic beginning.

"Well, she's not home." I point out. "We've been spending roughly two hours a day parked right across the street in plain sight. One hour in the early morning. Another in the late afternoon." I rattle it off: "No sign of life. No deliveries. No mail. No visitors. The blinds stay down, the lights stay off…"

Emma interjects. "There's a second entrance around the corner on Pierce; but it's only accessible through the garage of another house, one which hardly anyone is aware she owns. In fact she commands a whole lot of Pacific Heights real estate under a variety of different names."

"How can you know all this?"

"That'll be part of my explanation."

"Do you think she's aware we're trying to contact her?"

"Absolutely. That appears to be the whole point of this three-way game you're mixed up in. The gamblers want you and Kelli to hook up. You want to hook up with Kelli. Kelli wants you to hook up with her. Everybody on the same page, cool, huh?" Emma's irony is less than subtle.

"Then why is she avoiding us?" Leah asks.

"She's waiting."

"For what?"

"Rick, the message, *love me I am your secret*, was intended for you, yes, but it was also a signal to me."

I look at Leah. "Seriously?" I ask. "How do you know?"

"I just know. I'll explain. But let's get to this stuff they've dumped on you."

Leah jumps on it: "First of all, is it *all* real? The pictures? Everything?"

"They're real. Nothing's been faked. Not that I can tell." Emma answers. She has another taste of Leah's guacamole, pushes it out of reach. "I'm sorry. Don't mean to be rude. Mind ordering me some dinner so I can think a little better? Steak, rare. Glass or two of wine? I'm going to be doing a lot of talking as I go over these documents."

"I can make us some hamburgers," offers Leah.

Emma responds with a smile. "No offense, Leah. But I think I'd rather trust my red meat to the professionals."

I stifle a chuckle. "Lark Creek Inn. They deliver."

As I pick up my cell phone to order food, Leah gives me a glare for disparaging her cordon black cooking. At the same time, fidgety in her big wicker chair, she crosses her legs and in the process hikes her taut-but-stretchy white summer dress halfway up her thighs. I like what I see, she catches my eye, and we share a meaningful look.

True to her promise, Leah has this past week used her position as most trusted babe to keep me from sinking low, doing her best to minimize my Paige-pain with her endlessly inventive distractions. Two days ago, knowing I was starting to have a getting-nowhere meltdown, she arrived at our stake-out location wearing what she termed her "Casual Wednesday" outfit, a little black backless cocktail dress. It was eleven in the morning and all the more entertaining as she was clutching a starting-to-stain sack of fast food.

The phone order made, a short break taken by Emma to freshen up, we get back to business. Emma picks up the green envelope. "Okay, let's get ready to slice and dice!"

She empties the contents of the green envelope sitting before her onto a small wicker table and begins pointing as needed. "This recent picture of Kelli doesn't look much like the Kelli I used to know. But it's definitely her. And the photo of her at Paige's funeral is no surprise. She wouldn't miss it, although it must have broken her heart to watch from a distance." She pauses to look up at me. "Yes, it does seem that she met your kids, Rick. But the photo with the bicycles is a bit deceptive; I'm guessing this was a one-time thing. Paige would've taken great care to keep Kelli far away from you and your children."

"Good to know," I say. It's not good to know.

"The man who Paige is kissing in the photo is the one and only Matt Swift Junior, Kelli's half-brother. As far as I'm concerned, this photo was used to arouse your jealousy or curiosity. Paige hated him almost as much as Kelli did and does. There is affection suggested here in the photo, but it's false." Emma peers more intently, reacts. "I *love* the fencing trophies in the photo. He was a champion collegiate fencer at Harvard. All those trophies awarded for stabbing people, so appropriate."

Emma digs out the compact disc. "This CD is just to show you how enmeshed the two women's lives were." Then she holds up the now very crumpled handwritten letter, winces. "The divorce petition is brutal, Rick. I don't know the full story here. But I'm sorry."

I glance at Leah. I can see she wants to comfort me but can't figure out how. Continuing to fidget, Leah yanks down the hem of her dress, her nervous habit striking again, stretching it so she can slip her knees underneath making her look a bit like a little girl lost.

Emma on the other hand is starting to hit her "all business" stride. I can see why Gabriel used to call her his combination nurse and hatchet man. Pretty, mid-thirties, feminine, face like an angel. But what woman examines documents using a potentially lethal Swiss army knife as her pointer? "As for the clippings showing what a recluse she is," continues Emma, "Kelli's a recluse for a good reason. I'll explain that, too, in a moment. By the way, the people who circled my name on this invitation know that I'll paint a portrait of Kelli which you will find very sympathetic and, if you respond with a Midnight Rider urge to rescue her, maybe even irresistible."

Leah doesn't like this. "Right now, she looks like a train wreck. How irresistible is that?"

"Actually, she's had to become adept at changing her appearance."

Abruptly, we hear a *honk!* Dinner is delivered; dinner is laid out on the same porch swing. Leah and I have little appetite, but Emma, apologetic for being so ravenous, eats her nearly raw slice of prime rib with masterful military efficiency. By now, when Emma decides to cut her meat with another, longer blade of her Swiss Army knife, we hardly register surprise. Better edge, explains Emma. There is no point to small talk so we are quiet for a time. Finally Emma finishes, then continues her debrief.

"First of all," begins Emma, "the reason I know both Kelli Swift and Paige Phillips is that Kelli, Paige and I all spent time at regular intervals with an organization called Widows of Inherited Wealth. It is still active and still head-quartered in New York City. The name is misleading because only a fraction of our membership consists of actual widows. But all of us inherited extensive wealth, from a minimum of twenty million on up. And that in effect widowed us from the possibility of normal lives. Kelli was eighteen at the time I met her and by far our richest member..."

Emma pauses when she sees my expression, knowing what I'm going to say. "Rick, I'll get to Paige in a second." She widens her gaze to include

Leah. "And I'm not going to discuss my own personal financial circumstances. Understood?"

"Yes." I say.

"Absolutely." Leah seconds the motion.

"Good."

Leah and I exchange a quick puzzled glance though. When I first met Emma at her wedding to my older cousin Alec, Gabriel's big brother, it seemed obvious to one and all that she was broke and was most likely marrying Alec for his money. Even after her marriage, Emma showed working class habits: still drove a battered Camaro in desperate need of a paint job, bought clothes off the rack, flew coach, eschewed fanciful make-up and pricey jewelry. Not your Beverly Hills princess. But now we learn an undisclosed truth that perhaps even Gabriel wasn't aware of. Emma has revealed herself to be wealthy to some extraordinary extent. And we are also being told, with restrained forcefulness, to keep this fact to ourselves.

Emma continues. "The Widows are secret for good reason. The organization was created *by* rich women *for* rich women, created in order to protect women of inherited wealth from the endless predators who sought to seize our fortunes, to use and abuse us. I was recruited when I was twenty-two. The stronger and wiser women among us are charged with helping the more vulnerable, a counter-measure which has proven to be extremely effective time after time. There will always be too-persuasive lawyers and so-called trusted advisors, manipulative lovers or dominating male siblings, treasure hunters or white collar criminals with a taste for easy prey, the list is long, an endless gravy train of bastards whose sole ambition in life is to strip the Poor Little Rich Girl of as much of her cash and self-esteem as possible."

Suddenly Emma spots the unforeseen dessert, crème caramel. She attacks it with gusto as she continues her disquieting tale. "To be fair, many of our Widows can more than handle themselves, direct their own family offices, handle the minutiae of wealth management. The stronger members of our organization are called Black Widows, but this is a term of affection, as the number one responsibility of a Black Widow is to take care of what we call the Poor Little Rich Girls. Often, unfortunately, they were terribly exploited before we could get to them. Kelli was lucky. She was only fifteen when her father died and because she was so sensationally wealthy, we brought her in right away. It was rough for her, a terrible age to have so much to deal with. We always paired a Black Widow with a Poor Little Rich Girl and Paige asked for Kelli. She was the one who really was there for Kelli during some of the worst times after her father's death."

It's like listening to a well-told Grimm Brothers' fairy tale and halfway through it realizing that the main character in the story is the wife you loved and lived with for seven years. "Emma, I'm familiar with Paige's estate, it wasn't that complicated. She wasn't worth twenty million, she wasn't worth two million; she worked for her parents, they paid her bills, gave her a free ride, gave us a house..."

"Brace yourself. You won't like what I'm about to say."

"Haven't liked much of anything so far."

Emma grimaces. "We still talk about Paige from time to time usually in the context of fact-checking when we recruit a new member. Paige falsified real estate holdings. She hired hackers to create false bank accounts. It was such an unexpected thing... to find out about us and contrive to join us... that nobody saw through it. In fact, we didn't find out until Kelli herself informed us. And that was after Paige's death."

I look at Leah helplessly. But she has nothing to offer, it's all so overwhelming, just keeps pulling her stretchy white dress tighter over her knees. Who can blame her for her agitation? Her quaint wraparound porch has become Marin County's very own Twilight Zone.

Then Emma startles us. "Oh, crap! Read me the postcard again."

I extract the postcard Emma received from the betting cartel from my pocket and hold it up to the nearby lamp so I can accurately re-read it to her: "*Tell Rick what he needs to know so he can find his path... show him that good will and trust matter.*"

Emma reacts angrily. "That is so crazy *stupid*!"

"What?" Leah asks sharply.

"Your gamblers want me to cut to the chase and tell you about Kelli's father, Mathew Swift Senior's, financial legacy and the distressing, at least to Kelli, details of his trust. I can't believe they know about it! The curse of the patriarch Mathew Swift has never, ever been public knowledge!"

"Good will and trust matters…in the lawful sense…" Leah snorts with lady-like derision. "Clever-ish…"

Emma stands and begins pacing. Like General Patton with a pierced navel. "Okay, fair enough. They know something they shouldn't know. Guess it's time to go ahead and tell you what only a few people are aware of, with reference to Kelli's family and her father's legacy."

Emma shakes her head in disgust and at the same moment gracefully kicks one of the oak rockers out of her way with a ballet dancer's *allegro* in order to lengthen the area of her porch-pace. She continues without breaking stride. "Matthew Swift, the father, had any number of mistresses. But he was married only twice, both to wealthy socialites who had no need for his money and could never have been considered gold diggers. Each marriage brought him a legal heir, but each marriage fell apart because of his endless rages and first-class hands-on sadism."

Emma pauses to gather her narrative. By now, given I have ceased to breathe whatsoever, I indicate for Leah to join me, she nods, and somehow she folds her frame into my lap so we can sit in the same wicker chair together.

Emma continues: "Matt Junior's mother was a well-bred Philadelphia blue-blood and nobody's fool. She saw that Matt Junior was going to be a chip off the old block and so she left young Matt with old Matt and took a hike to the Arab Emirates with the man who became her next husband." Now Emma is softer in tone. "Kelli's mother was the last of the Cabot-Whitney family, it was a scandal, they covered it up, made it a natural death because it sure would've been front page news…anyway, Kelli's mother hung herself…. yeah, I know, just awful… Kelli was nine years old…"

"Oh. *God...*" I blink stupidly, stunned.

Leah shudders and I hold her tighter as a wave of nausea washes over both of us. I continue, flustered: "No, not possible! Kelli called me virtually every week for years and years and emotionally we dug deep and *how could I not know any of this*?!"

"Kelli was nine years old when her mother killed herself, Rick. Oddly enough, her father *did* teach her some important skills. To survive, she instinctively knew to be careful about revealing too much of herself. And by nature, she's secretive, a loner, very hard to get to know. Didn't you find it hard to draw her out? Didn't you ever sense she was being evasive?"

"Not that I could tell. Nobody's *that* good at hiding themselves."

Emma's shrugs continue to remind me that all I know is nothing. She continues: "In the weeks before his death, but with complete lucidity, meaning he had several psychiatrists confirm his sane state of mind, Matthew Swift Senior divided his fortune equally between Kelli and Matt Junior. But neither was to be allowed full control of their half-share until they reached the age of forty. And neither would be allowed to marry until that age unless they wished to be disinherited in favor of their half-sibling."

I interrupt. "If Kelli inherits at forty, then Kelli has a huge financial disincentive to marry at twenty-nine." I say. "Moss and his betting cartel must know this. So what the hell are they thinking?"

"Don't know. But let me finish this before you try to put it all together." She takes a deep breath, then: "Matthew Swift Senior's hatred for both his wives is clearly shown in the very specific and unconventional design of his trust. He had raised his kids to be warriors, he gave them the mind-set of soldiers. So when the time came, he wanted them to go at it tooth and claw like two rats in a bag."

"Why would they fight each other? Isn't two billion apiece good enough? It would work for me." Leah shakes her head.

Emma, still pacing, stretches her dancing muscles like a cat. "Matthew Swift, Senior had other conditions which Junior and Kelli still have to deal with today. They also would have to abstain from sexual intercourse until the age of forty. Or else forfeit all shares to his or her sibling."

Leah is startled. "He put *'no sex'* in his will?! That's just... twisted and sick...and *ridiculous*. Nobody is that perverse!"

"The original intention, according to Kelli, was to ensure that his family tree maintain its strength. Only the strong survive, only the strong are allowed to procreate. He figured that by the age of forty, one of his kids would have destroyed the other. Leaving the bloodline free of weak genes."

"Seriously?" I react. "Because what you're saying sounds like he was psychotic. And besides, how can abstinence possibly be enforced?"

"Given the stakes, I expect both Matt Junior and Kelli police each other very thoroughly. They are also motivated by the fact that each has been bred to hate the other. Matt Junior inherited the sadistic gene, throws famously vicious wild parties at his family compound in Sea Cliff. Kelli inherited the clandestine gene, does her best to keep on top of things while staying away from him and everyone else. She stopped coming east to our New York meetings years ago. If you can imagine a billionaire-in-waiting completely flying under radar, living life off the grid, that's Kelli."

"Just to clarify...you mean they've both been celibate all or most of their adult lives?" Leah is aghast.

Emma treads more carefully. "It was suspected that Matt found a way to get his needs met in the early days. Now he's older and content to bide his time, endlessly plotting Kelli's fall."

"And Kelli is a virgin?" I ask. "Unlikely. She always talks on air about men she's involved with, men she's attracted to but can't have. She has married man issues, gets involved with them."

Emma takes a deep breath, sighs. "And so she does."

"You don't mean Rick?" Leah exclaims. "She's never even met Rick!"

Emma comes over to me, crouches by my chair, and takes my clammy hand with her cool one. "I'm now 100% sure why Kelli is hesitating to meet you despite the fact she obviously urgently wants to. I should have realized that she doesn't want to be the one to tell you this, Rick."

"Tell me what?" I ask in a voice suspiciously akin to a whisper.

"It's in her message. *Love me, I am her secret."* Emma pauses, then: "Once she knew that I was going to be involved, Kelli realized that I would be willing to explain the circumstances...and that I could ask for forgiveness on her behalf...so that you would not stop caring for her. Because she deeply, deeply cares for you."

"Forgive her for what?! I don't get it..."

Emma plunges in. "Kelli did have a regular lover for years. Definitely not the lover she wanted, but one of convenience." She pauses, truly uncomfortable for the first time tonight. "After all, she was seventeen, eighteen, nineteen years old. She was completely alone in the world; she would have lost her mind without a lot of affection." Emma pauses to make sure I've kept up with her, then: "But after Paige died in the crash, there hasn't been anyone else."

"What? No! That's impossible." Leah is disbelieving. "Paige and Kelli were lovers?!"

"Try to put yourself in poor little Kelli's shoes." Emma replies. "I might have done the same had I been faced with the same choices."

Silence.

"So Paige was bisexual?" I finally say.

"No, Rick. Paige was whatever she needed to become in order to get what she wanted."

"And Kelli? She has to be heterosexual...from everything we've ever talked about on air over the years..."

"Kelli is straight, you have that right, she's attracted only to men. But given her father's will and last testament, plus her fear of her brother, well she had no outlet and she needed so much."

"And what did Paige need?"

Kelli shrugs. "Money, power, nobody knows for sure. All the Widows knew what Paige was doing although no one was happy about it. And so Kelli had our blessing to begin her affair with Paige. Of course Kelli's brother quickly found out. He tried to contest Kelli's relationship with Paige through the courts. But Kelli's loophole was legitimate."

"And somehow you never told me." I note.

"Paige was dead and gone seven years when I married into your family. You were creating miracles on your radio show, Rick." Emma softens her voice. "You were needed."

"Did Paige love me?" I demand. "Did she *ever* love me?"

"I don't know. Kelli will know."

"Okay, enough." I say to Emma. "I want you to come to the station with me. I'm going to put you on air, you're gonna DJ tonight. Find a way to tell Kelli in whatever the hell code you have that I know about her and Paige and that she's forgiven or whatever she needs to hear but she and I have to meet and we have to do it soon."

I turn to Leah to ask her what she thinks, but Leah is already clambering off my lap, pulling strands of her newly straw-colored hair from the buttons of my shirt. "This is great," she begins. "I don't like the idea that Kelli may be in love with you. But I know you won't fall for her. And actually I'm happy in one sense, because I want the whole of you, Rick, and you'll never be whole until you know why Paige did what she did. Until you get the answers you have to have." She manages a wry smile. "Hey, get to the truth and you and I might live happier ever after…"

With that, Leah hugs me so hard I feel my ribs bend.

Emma smiles at both of us and taps her golden fox tattoo with two fingers. "If I'm going to DJ tonight, I'm calling myself the Quick Blonde Fox. Not only will we get the job done, your Midnight Riders won't know what hit 'em!"

# CHAPTER EIGHTEEN

The quick blonde fox is instantly a hit on the Rick Lang, Midnight Rider show where generally the further I fly off-format the happier everyone is. Studio B is lit by its usual floor candles, the San Francisco skyline has the moon behind it, and on this night of Kelli-quest our world is a little bit brighter than usual. During Desolation Row and the Temple Of Loss, Ten-One-One and No Sympathy For The Devil, Emma has intentionally been providing spin and taking calls which focus on the issue of fathers who betray their children. She also promotes debate as to whether a painful relationship is better than no relationship at all. The Quick Blonde Fox even plays far-too-many deep cuts from the "Vicki Phillips" CD because, despite all the ways we successfully cloak it as a national program, this show is entirely customized to appeal to a very specific fan base of one.

Bridget and Kimberly have been enlisted into supporting our format without having been given too many details. Their nosy queries are easily aborted by my threats to bring Howard Stern back yet again as a featured guest on the show; his last appearance was a disaster, both Bridget and Kimberly indignantly refusing to lie on the floor to test for artificial breast implants, and Bridget inappropriately chasing him from the studio with the aluminum baseball bat she keeps on hand in her booth. However, since some explanation of Emma's Quick Blonde Fox agenda is required, I do let slip the news that our frequent caller Kelli is secretly the mysterious "Vicki Phillips" and we have an urgent need to connect with her. This is no big deal for them... but what *is* a big deal is their firsthand experience of the "Rick and Leah" show.

Their comments have been few but their faces say it all. They can see that their ten-year mourning man is exhibiting sudden easy physical affection for long time friend Leah who is listening in on the guest headphones while sitting on the Oakland Stroke wearing a tight black skirt, sexy jewelry, smoky club make-up, and a look of more-than-friendly intent. Every time Leah crosses and uncrosses her legs, Kimberly gives Bridget a conspiratorial wink. Although I didn't have the same opportunity to change clothes, I did find an old shirt of mine in Leah's closet, left at her house at some point during the Reagan years or earlier. So I am wearing a bright blue shirt with white stripes as I announce that, starting next month, all studio personnel will adhere to a new dress code which eliminates the color black. Bridget's scowl is not unexpected.

It isn't just the staff-members who are feeling continental drift. During this past week while my days had been focused on staking out Kelli's residence, my nights on air have been aimed at helping my midnight riders make an adjustment to our longstanding action algorithm. No longer will we use our set protocol when emergencies arise. Certainly riders are still being sent to pinpoint locations as needed, but now I call for them to create local chapters and elect local dispatchers, to be free to ride to the emotional rescue, nightly and daily all over the country in the manner and spirit which they learned through experience over the years.

I have even gone so far as to climb up on my teetering soapbox and declare war on our ever-glowing screen-culture, inciting all Midnight Riders to question whether it's part of being with God, pick a God, to push past distraction together, to evolve a new and more aggressive science to defeat the temptations of isolation, to bypass the niche-marketing of shallow pastime, and to get the important stuff done *face to face*. In short, I am guilty of preaching to *my* congregation; I try to inspire them to define for themselves what physical and moral actions they might take to embody the lyrics of Mahalia Jackson, the great gospel legend of yesteryear when she sang: *I'm going to live the life I sing about in my song.*

It is now a little past 1 A.M. but Emma's confidence remains unshakeable despite the fact she, like all the other Widows Of Inherited Wealth, lost contact with Kelli years ago; she has faith Kelli is poised to call and she'll continue to say and play what is needed. I take a break, approach Leah on our Oakland Stroke where she removes the house headphones and gives me one of her ever-increasing eye-locks. "How are you holding up?"

"You don't want to know."

"Yeah, waiting is hard."

"Depends on what you're waiting for."

I move to join her on the sofa but halfway in the act of sitting, I find myself pushed off-balance by Leah who yanks me down beside her on the Oakland Stroke, causing its cushions to twirl and whirl and my pocket change to waterfall and jingle out of my pants pockets.

"It's driving me crazy…" she continues, with a touch of accusation. "… being into you, you being into me…" With that, she jams me against the back of the Stroke, the same pin-against-the-wall trick she pulled on me at the hospital. Leah glares, finishes it. "… and *still* not being able to sleep with you…" She practically growls but with smiling eyes. "You flipped my switch. I don't care anymore, just try to stop me. I'll do you *right here…*"

Before I can answer, not that I have an answer, all my cannons below deck primed and so ready to fire when the time is right, we hear a CLANG resonate from Studio B's galvanized steel pipes. It's Bridget raising her fist of solidarity in the air.

Leah self-consciously tugs down her skirt, tilts her head toward Bridget. "What's she saying?"

Bridget's furious hand signals are clear as a bell to me. I signal back just as furiously to stay out of it. Bridget persists by circling both her eyes with her fingers, miming a pair of voyeuristic binoculars.

"You really don't want to know." I reply.

Leah laughs and slips her hand up the back of my shirt. Her fingers rove along my ribs and across my stomach. She calls to Bridget. "How's this for a start?"

Bridget gleefully gives Leah a thumbs-up.

"She's got one of her ankle boots tangled in the Stroke, Boss." Kimberly joins the fun, pointing out that Leah's heels have indeed broken through one of the many frayed holes in our famously scruffy couch. "So she's all yours."

Emma calls over, also getting into the spirit. "The Quick Blonde Fox has it under control…at least give your long-suffering lady a kiss…"

It's been a tough night and it's not over yet so *why the hell not?*

I kiss Leah full on. Her hands are inside my shirt, my arm circles her waist. She slides one of her legs so slowly over my jeans that I can actually feel the pattern of her hosiery trace itself over my thigh. Four of my fingertips are now pinioned underneath her skirt. My shirt, once buttoned, is now half-buttoned with a few deft twists of Dr. McLaren's surgical expertise. And the kiss goes on and on and on, submarine deep.

My eyes are closed yet somehow I sense to open them.

And there is Shannon standing in the studio doorway, watching us wide-eyed.

Next to her is Owen, blank with astonishment.

And behind them are Dylan, Gary, and Anjuli, frozen in total amazement.

We're the not-so-secret society once again.

To make matters more excruciating Leah continues to lie in my embrace, her eyes still closed, one hand now encircled behind my head so she can bring the kiss more deeply to her, her tongue now gently probing and playing, her breasts pressed warmly against my chest, her face unguarded and full of pleasure. As subtly as I can, I shift my weight and slide my leg from under her leg. She opens her eyes to see that I'm not gazing at her but instead off to her left.

Her eyes slide, following my stare, and sees the (only briefly) silent group of bodies filling the small studio like a huge Mormon Tabernacle Choir of disharmony. The joy in her face fades. I slide over to the other side in order to make the Stroke look less guilty. But it proves a waste of time.

"Whoa, baby! Always wanted a little action on that couch," chirps Anjuli. "After all, it does have those cute little wheels that roll…"

Gary is more to the point. "Hey! Whatever happened to our Society by-laws against incest?"

"Who cares about that?! Incest is best! Anybody mind if I'm on the bottom?!" Dylan looks like a kid whose Christmas has come early.

But I really only have eyes for Shannon and Owen. Yet Shannon remains perfectly poised, back in unreadable cipher mode. Owen, on the other hand, looks totally confused.

Then it strikes me. I note that this motley crew, all five of them, are wearing matching bowling shirts and jeans.

"Welcome to the Quick Blonde Fox show where anything is possible!" Emma waves from my listening post, pulling her headphones off, obviously trying to help the awkwardness. The Secret Society, having known Emma only by reputation, throws her a variety of introductions and greetings.

This gives me a further chance to create a little more physical distance between Leah and myself. I also have a tough job calming myself down. Like the famous Spinal Tap amplifier which could be turned up to eleven, I had actually gone straight to my eleventh level of arousal, unable to act on my urges in actuality given we were in the middle of a radio studio watched by impressionable if enthusiastic employees. But in my mind's eye I am already softly *on* her and slotted *behind* her and deeply *in* her, imagining her surrender.

"We've all been listening to the show!" Dylan announces, his eyes still drinking in the Scarlet Duo.

"Sounds like Vicki's gonna bite!" adds Anjuli, eyes only for arch-nemesis Leah.

"And here I was, thinking Rick was doing his best. And here you are, Leah. Getting in the way of progress. This is no time to screw around with the plan," notes Dylan, sarcastically.

"Maybe screwing is the right word," adds Anjuli, innocently put to Leah.

Leah sits up sharply. "Lose it, Anjuli. I still haven't gotten any in years. So if you're concerned about your reputation, don't be. You'll always be the local ten-toes-up champion."

"Couple minutes later, we could've seen some really hot midnight riding!" Dylan chortles.

"So incest is suddenly part of our bill of rights. Fine. Cool." Gary is sounding increasingly irritated. "Okay, next time maybe I *will* let Anjuli cuff me to her roll bar."

Dylan's ire fires up. "Wait a second! What's this?! How come *I* wasn't offered handcuffs and a roll bar?!"

"Get in line. Take a number." Anjuli retorts.

Dylan turns back to Leah. "What's your game, Doctor Freckles? You're messing with the strategy."

"Hey..." Emma calls out, bringing a little General Patton back into play. "You're all on a need to know basis. And you don't need to know. If you've been listening to us then you know Rick is doing his best to make contact. This is a covert op not a bowling tournament."

Gary speaks up. "We're here to support Rick, we haven't seen him for more than a week, and he needs to know we're behind him. That's why we're here." He looks accusingly at Leah. "I don't think it's going to do any of us any good if Leah distracts him just as he's about to score."

"About to score with Doctor Foxy, you mean." Dylan persists with his surgical strikes, the better to enflame Leah.

"Hey, you like the bowling shirts? The bowling shirts are my idea," interjects Anjuli. She spins around to show us all that her bowling shirt has the number '2' on it.

"Check these out!" Dylan takes Owen's arm and swivels with him. Owen is wearing number '3'. Dylan has got a '1' on his back.

Gary, wearing number '4' on his back, cocks an eyebrow at me and holds up a shirt still wrapped in a transparent plastic bag. Clearly intended to be my shirt, it has a '6' on its back. And Shannon also holds up a similar wrapped bowling shirt with Leah's '5' on it and hands it to Leah. "I brought this over, in case you were here….and here you are."

Shannon's face is completely neutral. Owen, on the other hand, is starting to facially indicate his growing cognitive grasp on the possibility that Leah and Rick are involved in something unimaginable even for a guy who can imagine Centaurs roaming the forest.

"Look," asks Gary. "What ever happened to the plan we all agreed on?"

"Since you're here…" I begin, "let me explain what's going on between me and Leah."

"Dude, a picture is worth a thousand words. I'm not liking this."

"It's none of your business, Gary," snaps Leah, who is trying and failing to extract the heel of one of her ankle boots from the frayed threads of the Stroke's ripped lining.

Dylan's turn. "Okay. Let's put aside the obvious for a second. You two have missed every strategy meeting so far. You also haven't been picking up our phone messages," Dylan turns to the others. "I vote we have a roll call and show them why we're upset. Anjuli, why don't you show off first?"

"I picked up Target Two in the supermarket. Made my move in the produce section. First date is tomorrow night…" says Anjuli smugly. "He'll be chopped salad as soon as I can get his hands out of the lettuce patch and onto my tomatoes."

Dylan points to Gary. Gary steps up to the metaphorical plate.

"I've also made first contact. It was primo, no doubt. It may take a few months, but Target Four is the kind of chick who is into holy padlock." Gary shrugs with understated confidence.

Dylan points to Shannon. She reports matter-of-factly, but without any readable affect. "I've promised to call Chuck. He was my first fiancé, remember him? The investment banker with Goldman Sachs? Would rather make money than eat? He's always been turned on by my balance sheet so if I actually had to shaft somebody because I love my friends, then he's Target Seven."

Dylan preens. "I've had two dates with Target One. You should have seen her face when she saw my hot tub. Splash dunk!" He points to Owen. "But Owen's the real winner. You won't believe what a stud he is."

Owen laughs self-consciously. "Well, I started out by hiring this girl Justine, um, Target Three, to give me singing lessons. In exchange for this portable Bendix I'm working up in green and gold bakelite. She's real nice."

Dylan sighs impatiently. "Owen. Details. Come on."

Owen hesitates. "You all know I've got a terrible voice but she *still* wants me to play a role in her dinner theater musical. Oh, and I think she wants to go to bed with me like right away. But I kinda lied and told her I only just got my Buddhist Noble Path Merit Badge for being all celibate ..." He looks at Dylan, who sighs with exasperation. "... well I had to make something up so I could say I'm, you know, saving it for marriage ... I don't think she believed me but she's still real interested ..."

"Give the man an Oscar!" Dylan cries out. "Now who's the big winner after our first skirmish in the battle of love?! Not *moi*, not crowd-pleasing Anjuli, not cover girl Shannon, not surfer boy Gary, but the man of the hour, Owen Brucker, our beer-swilling, talks-like-a-truck-driver, eccentric lecturer in Medieval Studies: *he's* the true stud captain of the Secret Society millionaire squad!"

Leah, despite still being trapped by her boot heels, nevertheless manages to strain for and reach a sheet of KHEL stationery, which she wads up and throws at the unofficial captain of this bowling team.

"Dylan, stop acting like a circus ringmaster! You're giving me a migraine!"

"Whoa! Come on! Who cares what you think? And how many dates have *you* been on with Target Five, Princess Leah? The answer is a big fat death star zero, isn't it?"

I know it is best for them to let off steam, to adjust to what they've just seen. But I sense the need to protect Leah who normally needs no protecting. "Dylan," I snap. "Lay off her and *shut up!*"

But Dylan is still honed in on Leah, years of old baggage piled high now toppling over into nastiness. "If Vicki bites tonight, then Rick's on his way to Target Six by all accounts. We'll all have made contact!" He takes a beat. "Um, except for our Society's current underachiever. The woman determined to spoil it for everyone because all she cares about is making life a drag for the rest of us. Our resident self-centered *bitch,* Doctor *Selfish…* "

"Dylan" I snap loudly this time. "Enough!"

"She deserves it, Rick."

Leah is suddenly as soft and vulnerable as a velociraptor. Dylan's taunts have achieved their goal. She loses it, launching herself tooth and claw from the couch, aiming for Dylan's throat, forgetting in her moment of fury that her foot is snagged in the frayed cloth weave and metal struts of the Oakland Stroke. And so Leah slams down hard, very hard, onto the studio floor, head first, avoiding sure facial contusion or fracture only by managing to get an arm under her face at the last second.

Horror all around. I can see Bridget and Kimberly wince. They know Studio B. One hundred percent concrete slab under cheap, threadbare Oakland industrial carpet. The ensuing silence is broken only by the cloying sound of the "Vicki Phillips" ballad 'Torn Pages' which emanates from the studio speakers.

I gently untangle Leah's foot from the torn lining and its frayed web. I help Leah up. She holds my shoulder for balance as she checks to see if the ever-more-cherished ankle bracelet I gave her so long ago has survived her fall intact, which it has.

Gary, Owen, Shannon, Dylan, and Anjuli gather around her, concerned.

"Leah," Dylan anxiously says, facing her. "It's not easy always being the Society's Mister Excitement. It's a tough job and I try not to be an ass-a-holic too often. Now I can tell by everyone's faces here that I've crossed the line. So I'll let you hit me once. Not too hard. And not in the balls. But anywhere else. I'll take it like a man."

The offer is sincere, I suppose, but I can tell he's just hoping for verbal forgiveness. So he's not entirely prepared when Leah *slaps* him. And a split second after his recoil, she doubles the ante by backhanding him *hard.*

Dylan yelps, the Society's jaw drops.

Leah pulls plastered strands of her hair from her face, brushes the carpet dust off her black skirt and top, ensures that her earrings haven't been lost, her fingernails aren't broken; there is a red scrape on one elbow which she eyes with displeasure but fortunately that's the extent of the damage.

But now she turns her attention to all those sporting bowling shirts. "Anyone *else* want to tell me how to run my life? Or want to make fun of me for kissing the most extraordinary man any of us know?" Suddenly she explodes into a tirade. "Look around you! Look at yourselves. Look at Rick. Have any of you done as much to help this insane world be less insane? This is a man who makes a difference, I don't care if that sounds like a cliché. You all love him. But I *love* him." Her tirade starts to spiral out-of-control. "I met him *seventeen* years ago and it was hidden love at first sight and it's never gone away and sure as hell I've tried to cover it up and make it something it's not. I married, had kids, tried to push him away except he was like my... my... *underground river* and now he's bubbled to the surface and he's *mine*, I'm pretty sure he's mine, so get out of my way because I *will* be kissing him again." She pauses, out of breath, then looks at each of the group, staring them down. "So grow up and *deal with it!*"

Leah excuses herself from the studio, slips past me so she can squeeze my hand, and then heads for the clean and tidy ladies room known by all to be found only in our refurbished Studio A.

Out of the blue, Emma interrupts at just the right time; what she sometimes lacks in sense of humor, she makes up in pitch perfect instinct. "Rick, I'm going to ramp up my plea for Vicki to put it in higher gear. We've only got forty minutes left....and I've got a plane I'd like to catch but probably won't..." She addresses the others. "If you want your Target Six in the bag, I need you all to get quiet or leave the studio..."

Gary responds. "Rick, we have to know, Leah or no Leah, are you going to meet Vicki and are you still with us?"

"I'm going to meet Vicki ...." I say. "You can count on that. So how about losing the bad attitude for the time being?"

Owen has been quiet. "Rick, I'm sorry. I've never been much good at figuring things out when the paradigm shifts or when there's a ripple in the Force or whatever. But I'm always behind you a thousand percent."

Dylan leaps into action, passes me on his way to the door. "I'm gonna go to Leah. I'm really sorry I said what I said. I deserved what I got. And I want to tell her that too."

Anjuli adds to this, twisting her ringlets fervently. "I think we should all go out tonight and take a break! Since we've outgrown doing the Group Hug thing, I say we get hammered together!"

"Hear, hear." Owen seconds the motion. "*And* it's Friday night. That's Rick Lang night at the Boom Boom Room ..."

"True." I reply. For eight years or so now, following my Friday shift, I've gone to the same after party hangout in the city to chill what usually is my end-of-the-week feverish mind. "If tonight works out, sure, let's do it."

Anjuli, Owen, and Gary happily march off to Studio A. But Shannon hooks my arm and draws me away from the others, pulling me to the darkest corner of Studio B, its utility corridor where it's dark and the sound is muffled. "So it's Leah ..." begins Shannon, whispering. "Of course it would have to be her ... given she and I have always had our issues, it's kind of ironic." She adds. "I felt you were a little different the last time we ... we were together. You must have known then."

"I knew."

"And you haven't slept with her yet."

"You can tell."

"Of course," she whispers even more softly, "Is it because of me? Or because of Paige?"

"Because of you."

Shannon shakes her head, swishing her perfectly-in-place thick French-braid unhappily as she unsuccessfully tries to straighten her bowling shirt to some semblance of shabby chic. "Forget me. Forget what we did...what *I* did... because it really was my fault. I know how to make the most out of vulnerable men and hopefully I won't burn in hell for it. Forget anything happened. I promise I will."

"Shannon, I don't know what to do. I honestly don't know how I can possibly tell her about what happened between you and me. Every which way I imagine trying to explain it to her, I see her not understanding, not forgiving...'

"You're a truth-teller, Rick. But sometimes telling the truth is overrated. If it means losing her, then don't ever tell her..." Shannon sighs, almost annoyed. "I can't believe a smart girl like me didn't see this coming. Well so be it..."

Shannon reaches up to brush her lips against mine... but catches herself, shaking her head with dry self-recrimination. "Sorry. I won't be doing that again..."

Suddenly Emma's voice can be heard. "Rick! Now!"

I rush back to my chair where Emma steps aside and slips off my headphones, hands them to me. I see we're patched into my family and friends warm line and I'm surprised. Kelli shouldn't have my private number. But she does.

I take the phone, take a breath. "Kelli, thanks..."

"Sorry to bypass your screening system. But I have my reasons." Her familiar voice is thinner than usual, more stressed than ever before, but still rich with unmistakable tenderness. "Did you really have to play my CD three times? You're lucky you have any listeners left..."

"I'd like to see you in person. You know why."

"Yes and it's getting to be urgent. Please thank Emma for me."

"Will do." I reply. "So when and where?"

"Very soon. Leave that to me..." A brief pause, then she adds: "...but stay away from my house, it hasn't been helping."

"I've got a right to be impatient. I've got questions... a lot of questions... and you owe me some answers..."

"You'll get what you want. But I'm going to get what I want too."

"And what's that?" I'm trying to be measured, but this is a different Kelli. Her tone is more commanding. "What haven't I told you over the last ten years? We've talked to each other every week. What was that all about? I was being real... what were you being? You could have told me..."

"I didn't have that option."

"And what does that mean?"

"Please, Rick. Don't be difficult. We've needed each other over the years. I can't begin to tell you how important you are to me. And you know that."

"If my show had a best friend, you were it. But that was then and this is now and what the hell is going on?"

"I'll explain when I see you. Be ready."

She disconnects.

It's unsettling. I'm unsettled. But I'm also content. Finally. Answers. I turn to see that all the Secret Society members are present and listening including Leah. What do I say? So many faces, eager, concerned, nervous, curious. So I play to the crowd, always the pro, put on a smile, raise my arms above my head in triumph. "You'll be happy to hear that she's good to go..."

"Three cheers for Target Six!" Dylan is once again his usual self. "Rick, I knew you could pop her in your toaster! She's toast!"

Supportive cheers from Anjuli, Gary, and Owen. Shannon turns away.

Leah doesn't hesitate. She heads right for me. By the time I signal Bridget to start blowing the phone lines clean in preparation for Righteous Ray Jefferson, due any moment, there's Leah by my side wearing her no-nonsense expression.

"I'm coming with you to meet her. Don't fight me on this."

"What good's a most trusted babe if she can't come along?" I reply, hoping this will be possible given the slightly entitled vibe I'm getting from

Kellane Victoria Cabot-Whitney Swift, newly discovered to be far less lost and confused than once believed.

Leah smiles, satisfied. Then looks around. "Where's Emma?"

"She had a cab waiting downstairs." Kimberly calls out. "Gosh, she's so wickedly cool! The minute she saw her plan worked, she just waved bye-bye to me and took off." Kimberly's eyes go all college girl dreamy. "I want to be a quick blonde fox someday…just like her…"

I nod, not really listening, one-of-a-kind Emma is gone. But she got the job done, bless her.

Righteous Ray can be seen through the studio glass, making his way toward Studio B, my cavalry has arrived. Ray catches my eye, salutes me with a shake of his gray head. As always, he's got one strange act to follow.

It is quickly agreed by the almost-forty-year-olds in the studio that it's time for another well-deserved celebration. A late night after-party, a Society pep rally, at Rick Lang's well known favorite all night rhythm and blues hangout. The magical way station of the universe known as The Boom Boom Room where one can always expect the unexpected.

# CHAPTER NINETEEN

THE BOOM BOOM ROOM IS ALWAYS FUN, ALWAYS FILLED WITH UNRULY MUSIC FANS WHO ENJOY their blues and soul hot and true and whose passion for the harmonic seventh causes nightly mobbing and throbbing in the thin aisle between the long, long bar and small round tables. I am always humble at this wholly holy crossroads because its owner, the great John Lee Hooker, took pity on the blue devils in my lost and grieving heart so many years ago and made me his honorary 20th grandchild, gifting me the Midnight Rider Friday night blues-plate special, my very own after-party table up front and dance-floor central.

Tonight, this same special table houses a seven-headed hydra of orange bowling shirts which makes a visual mockery of Marvin Gaye Tribute Night that otherwise might have looked cooler than cool. Currently one of the drop-in vocalists, a handsome young singer from South Chicago, is on the Boom Boom Room's small stage, fronting its extraordinary house band, bringing extra edge to Marvin's *I Heard It Through The Grapevine*, a version already full of menace. He is getting more help than he can handle from his back-up ensemble of older black musicians, many of whom were in the recording studio for Motown and Tamla, Stax and Volt, King and Atlantic and Chess. The Bass player channels James Jamerson, the Funk Brother who syncopated and improvised in obscurity until Marvin put him in the public eye. And the horns tonight remind me of the Memphis Horns, with a mix of brashness and subtlety. But there is a little bit of pale here as a perky white girl barely out of her teens plays keyboards with hands that blur and a bit of Latin flavor as an ancient bearded Latino clones Carlos Santana or *is* Carlos Santana in disguise because, at the Boom Boom Room, one never knows. The two back-up singers are both black women in their late-sixties who sang behind Aretha and Dionne and Dusty, later Diana, Donna and Gloria, and still work here and there with Mariah and Janet and Christina.

Leah has been antsy since we arrived, fidgeting more and more as each guest vocalist has outdone the next. She was calm at first, tapping her foot as she listened to a singer from the Big Apple do some outstanding early Marvin, *Hitch-Hike* and *Too Busy Thinking About My Baby*. But the next singer stamped a groove on *Let's Get It On* that caused her to start twitching restlessly. And this agitation grew as a budding superstar from New Orleans came up from the crowd and sat in with the band, adding some extra sweetness to a smooth *What's Going On* and giving surefire heat to *Got To Give It Up*. But now one of the Boom Boom drop-in regulars is laying a mind-blowing *Sexual Healing* on the room and Leah has had enough.

"Why isn't there one woman up there?!" Leah whispers. "It's just been one hot black guy after another!"

"And that's a bad thing?"

"You know what I mean."

"Then go up there and sit in! I'll let Brother Duke know you have the pipes."

"I can't. You know that. I don't." Leah is consistent in her refusal to sing in public but there is something new in her voice which seems to offer a clue.

"So you always say." Then something occurs to me that had never occurred before. "Is this another thing to do with your Dad?"

Leah shrugs, admits. "In church, he'd let me practice every day and sing my heart out but otherwise ...." Leah's Scottish accent once again burrs in an imitation of her father: "... singin' is fur fowk wi' nae brains!"

"And he actually meant it."

"Och, aye indeed!" Leah shrugs again. "I was offered not one, not two, but *three* professional contracts when I was in high school…."

"You never said…"

Leah interrupts me. "*And* Berklee College of Music recruited me like crazy. *And* the college was located right next to his precious Fenway Park! But Dad threatened to throw me down a well, disown me, and make my life miserable. He wanted me to have a profession." Leah's tone softens. "And he was so proud when we moved here and I got into med school…I'll never forget how happy that made him…"

"But in truth you wanted to be a high school dropout pop diva?"

"Doesn't *everyone* want to be a high school dropout pop diva?"

I indicate the stage. "It's never too late."

"I'm too *old* to get up there. Every one of those hot guys is under twenty-five…" She adds. "…besides, I'm wearing an orange bowling shirt…"

"What if I offered some kind of reward?" My hand reaches under the table. Okay, shoot me. I want to hear her sing. So I run one finger down her inner thigh.

Leah abruptly bolts to her feet "Oh, Oh, Oh!" She points a finger at me. "If that's all it takes, bubba, to get your motor running, then stay here, don't move, hang tight!"

Leah whirls and I watch her trot to the back of the club where she begins to chat with Duke Jackson, the Boom Boom Room house engineer who handles its high-quality sound booth. He's been a good friend over the years. But who wouldn't get on well with a six-foot-six giant, with dyed-gold Don King hair and several gold front teeth? And now I see a mouthful of gold as Duke is grinning big at what Leah has, no doubt, proposed.

I decide not to tell the others although Owen and Shannon do look quizzical as Leah follows Duke backstage. Shannon, who always used to routinely check in with me via subtle glances when we went out as a group, hasn't looked at me once all evening. This is a good thing, a healthy and long-needed change-of-habit. Owen does throw me a few looks. I can see that the new reconfiguration of Rick and Leah is starting to seem less odd to him as his beers arrive in a sane but steady progression.

As *Sexual Healing* becomes *My Love Is Waiting*, I find myself turning my attention to Dylan and Anjuli who are on the dance floor together. Anjuli keeps slapping Dylan's joking hands away from her body but now she's got it so well synchronized that she can bat away his attempts to cop a feel precisely on each downbeat which is impressive. Dylan's jerky, white-men-can't-dance moves have always been amusing because he names them. Tonight he is rocking the Saturday Night Fever gyration he calls "the suck-it-up" which, as he'd be the first to admit, does suck. Gary, on the other hand, is a natural on the dance floor and he has been doing his thing, dancing with one soul sister after another with his Asian-American swirl on.

As the applause for this last vocalist is still going strong, I can see Leah upstage, as orange as she can be in her #5 bowling shirt. Her introduction to the band consists of one or two handshakes, some general nods, what looks like a brief discussion of song and key.

The dance floor has almost cleared and the members of the Secret Society gather back at my table, one by one spotting Leah, one by one realizing what's about to happen. We've heard some of her old cassette tapes of course, although Leah would never allow them to be put on CD. We've heard Leah absolutely kill the Star Spangled Banner whenever we go to sports events en masse, we've seen her deliver an awesome Happy Birthday To You and a brilliant For He's A Jolly Good Fellow. It's true that one of us has recently earned a medley of Twist tunes in the shower. But none of us know for certain what to expect.

The stage darkens, and in the dark I hear Leah do a quick, nervous sound check with Duke Jackson. And when the follow spot hits her downstage, although she holds the mic like an old friend, she looks awkward and gawky and straw-haired and ever so Caucasian as she blinks out at the crowd in the darkness. The lights also make her orange shirt look even more orange. It's not a pretty sight although *she* is a pretty sight; I expect her to sing but instead she speaks.

"My Irish Catholic mother and my Scottish Presbyterian father let their white daughter attend Twelfth Baptist Church in Roxbury from the age of ten because she loved gospel music, it made her feel and cry, and she wanted to understand why..."

The audience is murmuring and responding to her so, although she continues to blink into the darkness, it's with a hint of a smile. "I loved Marvin Gaye for a lot of reasons, who doesn't, but I especially loved him because he had stage fright all his life. I know this for a fact because *I've* had stage fright all my life....." She pauses. "....so I'm going to keep my bowling shirt on until I'm not quite so scared..."

This elicits quite a few laughs during which Leah nods and the young girl on keyboards calls up a Hammond B3 patch on her Kurzweil. The ensuing urban gospel blues riff is a good one and, with only the organ to accompany her, Leah begins to sing her take on Marvin Gaye's version of *His Eye Is On The Sparrow* and I can feel the room get chills from the very first note. Leah has the gift of instant emotional energy, it's immediate and powerful, especially so because her voice is so deep and expressive. Although they are not doing traditional gospel call-and-response, the back-up singers begin to fill the gaps in Leah's sustained phrasing and, as she delivers the song, the pitch rises and falls and rises dramatically until the song begins to soar.

*I sing because I'm happy, I sing because I'm free, for His eye is on the sparrow, and I know He watches me.*

I only know one true thing about gospel singers. An audience can always tell if the performance is heartfelt and honest and here Leah shines, tugging heartstrings until they break then mending them with joy and I'm trying to wrap my mind around the knowledge that I thought I knew what she was capable of when, in actual fact, I had no idea, not a clue; she is glorious beyond measure.

Then, with a neat segue, the house lights slowly come up full on the band, and *His Eye Is On The Sparrow* becomes a bluesy vamp and Leah starts to sway her body side-to-side. "Guess it's good-bye to stage fright..." She starts unbuttoning bowling shirt #5 and the wolf-whistles and cheers start. Underneath, she is still wearing the same clothes she wore in my studio but now her jewelry sparkles, her short skirt seems shorter, her top seems tighter, her ankle boots seem more kick-ass cute, her hazel eyes pop from their smoke-daubed setting and she is one fine forty-year old prime time Most Trusted Babe.

Another nod to the band and, *POW*, it's an explosive full-horn romp into Marvin's dynamic rap-with-the-audience Copa version of *Pride and Joy* and the dance floor packs within seconds. Maybe it's the gospel training but she brings the song up and down and soft and loud until the crescendo tears the roof off the room.

It's such a roll-camera moment, and I'm so increasingly distracted by the Secret Society members beside me gleefully going berserk, that I don't notice Duke until he places a standing microphone smack in front of my chair. Duke cues, and suddenly I, too, have a follow spot on me. Duke jams the mic into my hand and that's when I realize Leah, in *her* spotlight, is going to sing to me, in *my* spotlight.

"Ladies and Gentlemen, for those few of you who don't know him here at the Boom Boom Room, Rick Lang, the Midnight Rider!" I get some of the spill off the residual excitement she has generated and thus get a good round of applause. Leah continues. "Rick knows the words to every song on the planet so I'd like to honor Marvin Gaye one more time with something he did better than anyone else. The duet…"

The Boom Boom Room hushes. And as her now very smooth skating-on-water voice flows to me, I recognize *Ain't Nothing Like The Real Thing* and unfortunately for those with ear drums, I am required to sing along with her incarnation of Tammi Terrell, and I sort of half-speak Marvin's lines and half-sing them and feel incredibly embarrassed and yet she sings to me… and soon that's all that matters…

*I got your picture*
*Hanging on the wall*
*But it can't see*
*Or come to me*
*When I call your name*
*I realize it's just*
*A picture in a frame*

And I sing and speak and my eyes never leave her:

*I read your letters*
*When you're not here*
*They don't move me*
*They don't groove me*
*Like when I hear*
*Your sweet voice*
*Whispering in my ear*


And then, we do it together, as I hope we'll always do it together:

*Ain't nothing like the real thing, baby*
*Ain't nothing like the real thing*
*No other sound is quite the same as your name*
*No touch can do half as much*
*To make me feel better...*

And as we finish to sustained crazy applause, once again the house band fades and suddenly all we have left is the keyboard player once again, and the simple sound of a church organ and Leah reprises *His Eye Is On The Sparrow* as she small-waves to me, blows me a kiss, and the stage fades to black as she finishes in complete darkness with:

*I sing because I'm happy, I sing because I'm free, for His eye is on the sparrow,* *and I know He watches me.*

All I can see now is a kind of smoky after image, probably just a trick of the eyes, the vague red-filtered outline of where she stood, legs slightly apart, singing her bliss, showing her proof, that she is the real thing, my real thing.

The house lights come up, Leah has disappeared backstage and the Secret Society is not going to wait. They rush off to find her, everyone without exception, wanting to climb all over her in an orange bowling shirt society love fest.

And I let them go on alone. Because I just want to stand here and milk this deeply defining moment for as long as I possibly can.

House music returns to fill the room and Duke Jackson gives me a grin as he comes back to retrieve my microphone. I congratulate him on his skillful spontaneous sound-and-light improvisation for which he takes ample credit. And people, sober and stoned and sideways, continue pounding me on the back with their congratulations and appreciation. But as that throng begins to disperse, I see someone nimbly dart and juke their way through the horde of bodies, and this someone takes me by the arm. It's the house band's keyboard player and, close-up, she has a sweet all-American wholesomeness to her.

"I'm Kelli." Even in the clamor and din of the Boom Boom Room, her familiar voice can be clearly heard because her words are spoken with urgency and authority and speed. "You were great, Rick. And Leah was just *awesome*. But there's the possibility that I was followed which means we have only a little time to get out of here ..." She indicates the nightclub's far exit and begins to pull my arm in order to get me to follow her. "So we have to go *now*!"

# CHAPTER TWENTY

**I**N THE GLITTERY DARK OF THE CROWDED BOOM
BOOM ROOM, KELLI IS NOTHING LIKE I IMAGINED
her, nor is she as described in the green envelope. On the radio, her voice
has always been low, mature, but in the flesh she looks not much older than a
college student and an ordinary girl-geek version at that. Her plain tee-shirt is
now covered by a heavier hooded sweatshirt. Her black jeans are tight enough
to show how very thin she is. Her high top sneakers I note are pink with stars
on the toe-tops. Her diminutive John Lennon round glasses have a slight tint
to them making it hard to see her eyes.

"You knew I'd be here."

"It *is* Friday night. And this *is* where you usually spend it."

I indicate the stage. "And how...?"

"You turned your listeners onto this place ages ago and of course I came
to check it out. I ask to sit in from time to time. Tonight I made sure. They
don't ask names here."

"Then this is great. Great to finally meet you. But there's no privacy..."

"Follow me... I know a quiet place..."

I glance back at the stage, still blown away by Leah, the duet, still soaked
in the vibe, wanting to catch her eye, willing her to come back out so she can

join us. But as Kelli leads me by the arm through the crowd's hubbub, Leah doesn't appear and quickly I find myself in a toothpaste-tube of a corridor, surrounded by pipes on both sides, the emergency fire exit lit by a single film noir light bulb with a chain pull. Kelli continues to lead me out the fire exit toward the alley which I know to be directly behind the Boom Boom Room. I gently tap her shoulder and stop her.

"This is good... we're alone..."

She swivels to face me but her body language clearly indicates that she wants us to continue out the alley door which is only a few feet away. "Rick, it would be great to hang out, I've waited *so* long to meet you for real. But I've got to get you out of here and keep myself safe, and that means no one can see us leave."

I try a joke. "Why rush things? Maybe we could start with dinner and a movie."

Kelli grins. Briefly. But then she glances back down the corridor from where house music is blaring. "Emma told you how things stand."

"She did. I'm not interested in judging, I just want to understand. Just want answers. And now I know you've got them.

"I do. But much of what I have to tell you, I also have to show you. You have to see things for yourself."

"I'm ready."

"That's why I need you to come home with me. And it may take a few weeks. My brother will *not* be cool if he finds out... it would be a serious disaster..."

I react, startled. "A few *weeks*?!"

"It's urgent."

"Leah..."

Kelli looks over my shoulder. We both hear the sound of someone coming toward us from the direction of the club, a wristwatch clanging against a pipe, a change in the shadows. Kelli continues, more quickly. "I was on stage next to Leah as she sang to you, I get it, I saw it, and I felt it. But she's going to get in our way." She must be seeing my expression harden because her tone intensifies. "I know you trust me, Rick. Right now you have to trust me completely."

"I do trust you. But I can't leave right now."

Suddenly I realize Kelli has back-up. The presence behind us turns out to be a large solidly built military type, in his 30's. I'd seen him in the club, figured him an odd ball, Blues Brother Suit and thin tie, no eyes for the ladies on the dance floor, untouched beer, a sharp eye on the band, and now revealed to have been there for Kelli's safety. He blocks my way so I can't retreat into the club. He holds a Taser, not pointed at me, but pointedly by his side.

"No...*really?*"

"Rick...just come..."

"Then we'll all come!"

"Your friends need to keep playing his game...my brother has to see that..."

I'm not following. "What's your brother got to do with the Game?"

"More than you realize. And wherever he goes, trouble follows. And in this case I'm sorry but your friends are in the line of fire..."

"That's crazy! That makes no sense at all. Are you saying that they're genuinely in *danger?* Of physical harm?"

"We're all in danger. Of physical harm, yes. You most of all, I *will* explain. I *will* show you why. Just come. Please."

She nods to the man behind me. He bodies up against me.

"Leah..."

"No."

"Let me say at least goodbye."

Kelli shakes her head. "Once we step out the door, you keep your head down and get into the car. Don't look left, don't look right. Just go."

This is too abrupt. I need to stall. "What about my work?"

"The Midnight Rider is on vacation."

"Tell that to my General Manager."

Kelli sighs. "I own your radio station, Rick. I've owned it for years. Your radio station, the entire Cloud Channel conglomerate, and I've protected the Midnight Rider show, all the good you've done…but we're reaching the point where everything you've spent ten years building is also at risk."

"I don't get it…I don't get any of it…"

*But she's not kidding. I feel it.*

With surprising strength, pale and slight and waif-like Kelli kicks open the Club's rusted back door. Her Taser-companion continues to body me forward toward the back alley. There's a smoked-glass modified stretch Lincoln, engine running, waiting for her, for us. The chauffeur steps out, an even bigger man, a very alert man, he's armed or at least there's something dark in his shoulder holster. As he opens the back door, he signals to a similarly smoked-glass SUV which has blocked the end of the alley which abuts Geary Street, keeping the Lincoln isolated. Its engine is also rumbling, ready to roll.

We pause on the threshold.

The City night is chilly, a typical San Francisco August, no stars, just fog. In the lights mounted outside The Boom Boom Room, I grab a quick but better look at the real Kelli. Short brown hair, turned-up nose, not much of an upper lip, and with dark blue eyes almost too big for her face and which match the enormous sapphires, suspiciously genuine, set into her clip-on earrings. Her frame is boyish yet feminine. Her hands are small, her fingernails bitten and, as she brushes her wispy bangs back with one hand, I see she wears a 'Supergirl' cartoon watch. She is slight yet her posture is somehow impressively regal, her affect poised, self-confident, and patrician. Her bearing is that of a woman who gives orders and doesn't take them.

"You look so different," I find myself muttering.

"Make-up, wigs, deliberately planned unattractive photo ops for the paparazzi. What kind of eccentric recluse would I be if I didn't look like an unhealthy mess?"

"Leah is probably freaking out. Have a heart. Thirty seconds, max. I'll be back." I turn back toward the Boom Boom Room, with half an idea that I can delay this situation so I can think, perhaps even summon my cavalry.

To her discredit, Kelli lets me turn and take two strides back toward the corridor before she lobs her grenade, albeit in a compassionate voice.

"They weren't your children, Rick. You didn't make them. Paige used another man's sperm."

It's so sharply dissonant, that I spin around violently. I can't help myself. "*What!*"

Kelli rattles it off quickly. "I have copies of Paige's lab reports, her contract with the donor, her bank wires to the fertility clinic, the clinic's files. I have copies, they're the real deal, I can prove this and I can prove everything else..."

I stare at her. Her bodyguard, blocking my way, also has a compassionate expression. But his Taser is now slightly elevated in my direction.

Kelli steps directly in front of me, intimately close without presuming intimacy. She stands on her tip-toes, and puts her eyes more fully and directly in front of me, a few bare inches away so I can look right through her. "I'm telling the truth."

*She is telling the truth. She is telling me the truth.*

I tremble. I tremble and stagger and her bodyguard catches me from behind by the armpits. He walk-drags me across the short ten-foot gap into the vehicle and I tumble and collapse onto the Lincoln's plush rear seats.

*Two babies in the same coffin. It was my idea. Together forever.*

Kelli gets in and straps herself directly across from me, facing backwards. She's energized and talks with quick vehemence. Her words are faster now, a fusillade. "My brother has tried to have me killed so many times it's like a running joke. Frankly he's lucky I'm more like my mother and not like our sick, sick father. Because if *I* wanted *him* dead, he'd be long gone."

*Leah. Where are you?*

Kelli continues, still overheated. "I'm a Midnight Rider, too, Rick. You've inspired me. My goal is to become your billionaire rider once I come into my full inheritance. We can work together. Your agenda, my cash. Wouldn't that be something? Imagine all the good we could do. But that can't happen unless we deal with my brother once and for all. Besides I've had enough of him, I'm sick of him, he's going *down.*"

I'm still thinking about my twins, Leah, my friends; I'm badly confused.

Kelli continues, unstoppable. "You've got half a million people behind you, more people join you every day, and many are willing to get out into the streets and *act*. This is 2001, the first year of a new millennium and this world is headed for another monster age of hurt and greed. Exponential changes, technology, whatever, can either go north or south depending on who controls the information age. I am *not* letting my brother stop you, mess with you, mess with your vision and your motivation. This game of his is the final straw; I'm going to kick his petty ass from coast to coast. But to do that… and I hoped it wouldn't come to this… I will *need your help*."

She is so articulate and passionate. I am so tongue-tied. Still it's easy enough to choke out: "This game of *his*?"

With us both safely sequestered in the back seat behind smoked glass and a thick glass partition between the front seat and back, the chauffer and his shotgun/Taser sidekick slam their doors and take their seats. But the car engine idles. We don't move. We wait.

As if reading my mind, Kelli continues. "Your friends are extremely important to me too. Although I've never met any of them, I feel like I know them pretty well. In a few minutes Leah is going to come out that door looking for you. That's why we're waiting."

"We're waiting for her? But you said she's not coming…"

"You don't always think things through, Rick. That's why I'm doing it for you…" Kelli interrupts. "Leah moves me. She's genuinely kind and caring, not a phony bone in her body. She knows how to love. She's authentic. She's the kind of person I would have liked to have been had I not been born my father's daughter. But she's in our way. If she tries to follow you, she tips my brother that you and I are already working together. Which would put her directly in his gun sight."

"So take her along with us…" I say, still failing to find composure. "Take her along. I need her. She'll help."

206

"This is about you and me and Paige. It's not about Leah. Besides you're in trouble with her. But, worry not, I'm going to help!"

I don't know what Kelli's talking about. This isn't the measured, soft woman I know so well from our on-air discussions, she is in Midnight Rider mode. We fall into two very long minutes of silence. Then Leah exits the club, looking for me. Because the windows of the limousine are smoked, Leah can't see me, but I can see her and the confusion in her unhappy expression. I can also see her shuddering from the cold, underdressed for the chilling fog. My heart begins to tear open as if being roughly unzipped.

*This is out of my control. I control nothing.*

The chauffer looks back through the glass at Kelli and Kelli nods. I can see him take a pink manila envelope from an attaché and lower his window.

"Dr. McLaren," the chauffeur calls out, surprising her. "I've been asked to give this to you." Despite his menacing appearance, his voice is unexpectedly kind, his manner that of a well-educated man.

Leah cautiously walks over and takes the large pink folder. As she extends her hand and bends slightly to accept it, she is so close to me that I can see the tear-tracks on her cheeks. The folder has her name written on it in Kelli-calligraphy, this time it is written in Uncials; I recognize the well-known Lord Of The Rings middle-earth-ish hand now used as a font by Wizards and Elves everywhere.

I quickly spring forward to speak. I rap sharply on the glass and loudly bark out Leah's name. She doesn't react.

Kelli puts her hand on my hand. "Soundproof."

A puzzled Leah takes a long look at the folder, a longer look at the limo, an even longer look down the alley, looking for the man who can't be seen. Then, discouraged, she disappears from view.

"What was it? What was in it?" I am abruptly thrown back in my seat as the Lincoln rumbles into gear and then roars forward. The SUV at the end of the alley also begins to roll and slips into a follow position behind us.

Kelli partially turns away from me as we start to drive off. She taps on the partition glass and it rolls down. The Taser-wielding bodyguard is suddenly at the ready. Kelli continues. "I need you with me for as long as it takes. Leah will come after you unless she's stopped." She turns her gaze further away from me. "I've been watching you over the last decade. And by default, I've been watching your friends. I was shocked by the quick lightning shift between you and Leah. I didn't see it coming. But I'm happy for you..." She hesitates, continues. "But Leah will never entirely be yours until she forgives you for the five years you've been sleeping with Shannon."

I feel a ballistic missile start to launch in my throat. How can she know *everything*?!

Kelli continues. "Try not to be too upset although that's probably impossible. I think it's all going to turn out okay." Kelli continues to see all, know all. "That's why the folder I just gave her contains only tame and tasteful pictures of you and Shannon, partially dressed but nothing graphic because I don't want to burn any negative images into her mind. Plus I've provided a detailed letter indicating how infrequent your sex actually was, how Shannon never spent the night, how your participation was merely an effort to comfort her when she was emotionally self-destructive. Leah knows you're vulnerable to that kind of manipulation." Kelli hasn't been able to look at my face during this long confession and it's a good thing too because I must look agitated to the point of lunacy. She adds. "She needs to stay away." A pause, then she continues. "And now I've made sure she will."

Kelli's instinct to have her bodyguard at the ready is a smart one. I half-rise out of my seat, wanting to do damage to her throat. The Taser is in my face. The man with the weapon has sympathy on his face, how weird is that, but I know he's prepared to use whatever force necessary. I guess it is fortunate that my overwhelm is such that I just sink low back into my seat, defeated, ashamed, horrified, enraged, frozen in passivity.

Kelli murmurs. "You never would have told Leah about Shannon, would you?"

I meet her gaze reluctantly. But I say nothing. Kelli nods yet again in the direction of the Taser. Her bodyguard lowers it and turns his gaze forward, although leaving the partition down.

"Rick. Leah was married to a man who nuked her ability to trust. Ask yourself this. What was going to happen down the line, after you and Leah built your life together, when this thing with Shannon came out? Because eventually it would've come out…" Kelli punches it home. "Leah has no tolerance for sins of omission and no ability to protect herself against betrayal. She's an all or nothing girl, I love that about her, and by hiding this Shannon situation, you will eventually pay the price and she will suffer. So don't waste your time getting mad with me. By revealing this now, you have more than a fighting chance to be forgiven. That's my gift to you for being my rock for so many years."

Kelli presses a handle and out slides the limo's mini-bar. I see she has both my favorites, Anchor Steam and Jack Daniels, at the ready. A nice touch but not so nice given I have just been whipped and shamed and violated, albeit in the service of hope and truth and love.

I pour myself a drink with shaking hands, chase it down, and find a tiny wedge at the far end of the long seat to make my home. Might as well enjoy my ride in this nice limousine, because no matter where we're headed I clearly won't be coming home the same man.

Through the window, at this darkest hour before no promised dawn, we pass a corner speakeasy which spews out a half dozen girls-night-out girls. A few of them cheer and wave at our darkened stretch Lincoln windows, perhaps imagining they are viewing a similarly buoyant boy's night out. This sight makes me all the more miserable.

A few steep blocks later, the limousine turns sharply into a covered portico which fronts a massive ivy covered brick mansion. Brick being a rare sight in this land of earthquakes, I realize I know this building. It is one of the many foreign embassies which can be found scattered along the highest streets of Pacific Heights. A typical San Francisco single-car garage door attached to the building smoothly slides open and all of a sudden we are driving underground into a *vast* parking garage. It's like a company parking structure filled with a whole lot of black SUVs just like the one following behind us which now peels off as the deceptive garage door slides closed behind us. Not a foreign embassy at all. But I'm about to enter a foreign world, that seems certain.

Kelli takes off her small, round John Lennon glasses and flashes me what actually, almost, maybe, is some kind of shy smile. "Welcome to your home away from home," she says, indicating. "I'm thinking of giving you my bedroom, what do you say?"

# CHAPTER TWENTY·ONE

KELLI'S UNDERGROUND EMPIRE BEGINS ABOVE GROUND WITH FOUR PACIFIC HEIGHTS MANSIONS, quite a distance apart from each other, which are linked by two levels of underground tunnels. These secret conduits, large enough to drive trucks end to end, date back to the 1920's, having been engineered by an old boy's club of shipping and railroad tycoons who enjoyed dabbling in the forbidden fruits of prohibition: prostitution, gambling, designer opiates, and white slavery. Union Street to the north, Jackson Street to the south, Pierce Street to the east, and the 1776 Spanish garrison known as The Presidio to the west, this is the unfathomably far-ranging map grid, *twenty-five square blocks*, of the elaborate below-ground bunker Kelli calls home. There is no way out for me although it takes two full days of non-stop dazed wandering (which has included the use of handy-dandy electric vehicles) mixed with frustrated raging to determine this. Likewise, I am trapped in a high-tech universe where all computers and other telecommunication devices have clearly been removed so I cannot access them. This subterranean world has also been vacated by an estimated eighty or so regular employees presumably so that I can be left completely alone.

The first night underground is a disoriented emotional catastrophe; I awake a few hours after arrival and find I have been left on a long padded bench in what turns out to be Kelli's main battle station located one level below her "Embassy." Being groggy from the sedative added to the bourbon I downed in her limousine doesn't prevent me from immediately tormenting myself as I imagine how Leah's heart must have snapped in two. It is a rare specimen of man who can disappear into a void seconds after a love relationship's single most defining moment.

Imagining Leah's reaction to Shannon's seductions of me is so distressing that I do my unsteady best, upon waking up, to fist-smash and kick-splinter a few of the battle station's masculine NASA-command-style furnishings, to throw whatever available at its enormous but indestructible floor-to-ceiling digital wraparound maps, to upturn work stations and hammer furiously if unsuccessfully at her shatterproof, steel encased electronics, to not even question (until later) why Kelli's war with her brother requires such comprehensive troop movements and an arsenal of surveillance technology. Kelli lets me vent until, as Kelli has no doubt intended, I find a way to shove my Leah-sorrow to that mysterious space at the back of my brain where fire has not yet been invented, a place where paralyzing self-doubt can ebb into perpetual dark.

This need for me to calm down and focus is why Kelli doesn't appear by my side until my third day underground.

As for the barely bearable notion that my children were not conceived by me, I do a better job of confronting that truth and so I'm prepared when documents I find on my fourth day here do make it a proven fact. But Cally and Cassie were real, I assisted at their birth, I fed them and bathed them, I changed diapers, I sang and read to them. I was there for them every day of their short lives and quickly I'm forced to accept that *it is what it is*, and so what, so what, *so what?* They were mine.

The invitation to sleep in Kelli's bedroom is acceptable to me once I determine that it is the only bedroom to be found in her vast cavernous fiefdom. It is a climate controlled, cleverly illuminated and imaginatively designed windowless suite. Its walls are festooned floor-to-ceiling with boldly colored murals painted by Kelli herself; I later discover similar hand-painted murals in virtually every tunnel underground (inspired I ultimately learn by a self-taught fin de siècle French painter named Henri Rousseau, whose primitive artwork Kelli has emulated) and this privileged Old Boy's netherworld is now adorned with long and intricate panoramas featuring lush jungles brimming with tigers and strange buffalo and gaudy but glorious imaginary tropical birds. The rest of Kelli's bedroom is crowded with delicate antiques including a harpsichord which she no doubt plays as skillfully as anyone. Her gigantic four-poster bed is home to a half-dozen thick silver-colored quilts and is draped with yards and yards of diaphanous shimmering platinum-colored fabric. Behind the bed, there is a faded 17th or 18th Century silver-and-gold tapestry featuring the classic image of a Unicorn being tamed by a Virgin. My first astonished impression of this young-fantasy-feminine sight is so great that the two dark suitcases, filled with clothing taken from my home, and which sit on the bed, appear at first like two sleeping Black Labradors.

Speaking of sleeping, calm restorative sleep is not an easy thing to acquire as my nights in white satin are no antidote to the impact on my psyche made by the eye-popping discoveries and occasional horrors which shortly become my daily fare. And so I force myself, every single night, to close my eyes and conjure up the same bit of guided imagery. I begin by following Leah along a summer boardwalk although I can never quite bring her face into focus, usually the best I can do is a glimpse of sandy hair and long, tanned legs. But once I do fall into dream, it is a dream which recurs night after night. It is always Leah standing atop a massive Salvador Dali-esque 1950s automobile dashboard which is the size of a billboard. She is watching me, I'm inside this dashboard which is transparent, and she is waiting as my long and eerie clocklike hands attempt to turn up the radio's volume, to tune it to the right station, or to make its dark dial suddenly glow green. Some nights I can do one of these things, but never all of these things, and Leah waits and waits as my dream eventually figure-eights like a Möbius strip, going around and around until I wake unrefreshed and drenched in dejection.

Hot gourmet food for which I have no appetite is always to be found in the plush chandeliered dining room adjacent to the bedroom at the beginning, middle, and end of my 'work day' efforts. The bathroom has vintage tiles which form a pattern suggesting dragons in flight, and a Jacuzzi tub which could fit an entire not-so-secret society. I use it to unknot although I never unwind.

On my third sunless morning, I am rewarded by awakening to the sight of a pink boom box sitting in the center of the bedroom on its own rolling room service cart, a compact disc waiting within. Upon hitting the right buttons, to my considerable shock, my introduction to Paige's "other" life begins with a bang. I listen to a recording of the last phone call Paige Phillips made before her death. It is a conversation between Paige and Kelli. I almost don't recognize Paige's voice; her inflections are so different from the ones she used with me.

Paige was never boastful in front of me, just quietly confident. But here she is indeed boastful as she speaks of having *absolute proof* that not only has Matthew Kellane Swift, Junior had a night of repeated sexual intercourse before his fortieth birthday, thus violating the key clause which determines whether he will receive or forfeit his full inheritance, he has done so by the use of a date rape drug, and then, *best of all*, caused demonstrable physical injury impossible to refute. I hear Paige's animated description of this holy grail which in fact she does name the 'Absolute Proof' and it includes irrefutable DNA samples of Matt's carelessness plus sworn affidavits by all the witnesses needed to make his disinheritance a fact. There is even a *fantastic* video log of the injuries inflicted. *Absolute proof!* Upon Paige's return from her parents' big anniversary party in San Diego, Matthew Kellane Swift, Junior, will soon thereafter become the victim of a legal blitzkrieg which, in the state of California, should net him eight or ten years behind bars.

Toward the end of the phone recording, Paige reminds Kelli of their written agreement (later learned to be a 60-40 split of the aggregate spoils) once the full inheritance defaults to Kelli (later calculated by me to give Paige a 1.5 billion dollar payday). Finally the recording ends in lavish endearments for Kelli which have subtextual sexual undertones and motherly-sweet-concern overtones.

My first thought after the CD has run its course is that Emma's description of Paige's devious entry into The Widows of Inherited Wealth now makes sense. Once inside, with access to Kelli, her careful manipulation of these two über-wealthy siblings gave Paige the remarkable opportunity to leap-frog from her own limited means into joining the world's wealthy elite.

Kelli has clearly timed her entrance so that it is in sync with the end of the recording. After a brief knock on the bedroom door, enter Kelli In Wonderland, wearing a little blue dress with matching blue eyewear and slightly blue feet (given she is barefoot). Perhaps this is her version of formal wear; she also sports a strand of thirty or so large black pearls ending in a single dropped black pearl which is nearly as large as Golden Gate Park.

"Nice necklace," I say, as what does one use as an icebreaker when speaking with a woman who has imprisoned you for both your own good and the good of mankind?

"It belonged to my mother."

"I'm sorry."

"So you know."

"Yes."

"She was wearing them when they found her."

"They're beautiful."

"*She* was beautiful." Kelli pauses for emphasis. "And Paige was beautiful too. In her own way. Even though what you just heard sounds harsh, she kept me from ending up like my mother. At least try to love her for that."

Kelli picks up her pink boom box, hands me a folded note. "These are instructions. I've kept files on Paige. There's a lot to look at. I'll be watching and listening although you won't see me. There are call buttons everywhere. If you need me, just press one."

As I take the note from her, our hands brush causing her to blush. "Why aren't you coming with me?"

"I want you to look at everything with fresh eyes. I've been over and over everything you're about to see for the last ten years." Kelli indicates her sheet of instructions. "Everything you need to know about Paige is one level down. Everything you need to know about Matt's marriage plans for you and me. If you find anything, anything at all which might help me locate her Absolute Proof…anything which looks odd…feels dissonant…doesn't ring true…" Kelli breaks off. We stand in silence for a second. Then she repeats, softly. "I've looked absolutely everywhere."

"Where did Paige call from?" I indicate her boom box.

"Your bedroom." Kelli replies. "She had a separate phone she used to call me."

I let that sink in for a bit. "I assume you've searched my house."

"It's always been the most likely place, not just because she was more likely to want to keep it close, but also because she didn't leave the house during the last couple of days before the crash. We've done a full search of your home and grounds seven different times, plus another dozen partial searches. We couldn't have been more thorough. If she'd hidden the Absolute Proof in something metal, a hidden safe or box, our detectors would've found it. Of course we can see through walls and floors and ceilings to some extent but a very small container made of the right materials wouldn't register. DNA samples, a few legal papers, a single tape cassette…just a small package…" She shakes her head.

"At least you cleaned up after yourselves." I joke, though nothing is a joke really.

"It was trickier when we used the sniffer dogs. You know, because they shed and German Shepherd hair is hellishly tough to meticulously remove. But my people are professionals."

"Good to know," I reply.

"Yeah. Sorry."

"Are my friends okay? Everyone?" I ask.

"They're fine. We're watching closely. But my brother's surveillance teams still have them under observation. He also uses helicopters, uh-huh, I know, that's over the top but he does like his toys."

I react, shaking my head. "Leah…"

"She's calm. Not going in to work. She's spending a lot of time in her garden."

*She's still trying to grow things…*

*That's good… I think…*

Kelli squeezes my hand then pads out of the room in her bare feet and pearls, boom box clutched by her side. She gives me one last look before closing the door behind her. "Try to find it, Rick. Do your best. My brother turns forty in only two years. Unless I find the Absolute Proof before then, he'll have access to his full inheritance, a dozen times what we each have now and something *I* won't have for another eleven years. With that, his money will buy him the means and the power to destroy me. Two billion dollars buys a lot. He'll be so above the law that he'll own judges, city hall, police. He'll have some key Feds in his pocket, Wall Street on his side, powerful allies inside the D.C. beltway. On a more personal note, he'll also destroy you because of Paige. And your friends will suffer if only because he's petulant and he'll be enraged when they fail at his game." Kelli reacts to my shocked and slightly incredulous reaction. "He set squirrels on fire when he was a kid… don't give him credit for being rational when it comes to revenge."

With that, Kelli In Wonderland disappears down her rabbit hole. If her aim was to help motivate me, which it was, then I am motivated.

There are twenty-five or so underground file rooms hidden here and there along the length of her underworld empire one further level below, for a second set of tunnels lies beneath the first set. I now finally have a full access pass to Paige's looking-glass life, the other side of the life she led with me. These rooms are filled with the cumulative data Kelli has compiled from ten years of hard research and there is so much of it that my mind begins to numb almost immediately. Much of it is devoted to Kelli's quest for Paige's Absolute Proof which will lead to her brother's downfall. But there is so much more to interest me.

The "Vanilla Ice" room is the first file room I discover. Deep in the bowels of the city, two stories below Kelli's manse on Broderick, I begin my journey to the center of her earth. I quickly open five other easily found file rooms in short order: The "Lynyrd Skynyrd Room"... The "Ted Nugent Room"... The "Britney Spears Room"... The "Air Supply Room"... and the "Abba Room." The names of the rooms are not sign posted, instead they are made obvious upon entering when, triggered by sensor, a panoply of "greatest hits" begins to play. I come to understand this manifestation of Kelli's eccentricity in due course... she has coupled documents and artifacts which she finds either hard to bear or distasteful to music which she loathes. We clearly have different musical tastes as I loiter happily in the inexplicably disliked "Abba Room." But the next day, when I'm in the "Devo Room" listening to the mind-numbing sound of *Whip It* being played over and over while I sift through the pur-loined contents of Paige's city office, I realize Kelli's sound design has some merit.

Each room I visit in the beginning is exactly fifteen feet long and ten feet wide. Each has every tool one could imagine for sifting information. I can see, hear, and touch any of the well-labeled files, original videos, origi-nal recordings, original relics which Kelli has compulsively compiled to a degree of completeness which seems utterly fanatical. My thoughts, should I choose to vocalize them, are automatically recorded for later regurgitation simply by speaking out loud (my voice also blessedly shuts off the music). A large posted flow chart in every chamber ensures I don't miss a single exhibit. Unfortunately there are no flags of warning and my first stumble into a tiger pit is the uncovering of an unedited sex tape made by Paige, very early on, showing a naive and very naked 16-year-old Kelli being bedded gently but with obvious intent by an equally naked but far more cunning manifestation of a Paige I never knew. It is as if a knife were jammed in my eye and yet, soon, there are so many like surprises that they become more like bee stings than knife wounds.

I speed-read endless reports and see hundreds of labeled photos, watch computer reconstructions, examine minute forensic evidence, a lot of which reveal Paige's tireless manipulations of Kelli ...yet even more reveal manipulations *on behalf* of Kelli. I can see a method in Paige's madness as these manipulations viewed on a time line can be seen to have successfully created an unbreakable bond between the two women, a mother-surrogate-Stockholm Syndrome-traumatic bonding interaction which explains why, years after Paige's accidental death, Kelli still accepts and admires and even sees as a kindness, Paige's control of her life. Thus it is not hard for me to grasp the powerful legitimacy of Kelli's grieving over the loss of Paige for these last ten years because their relationship had a primal intensity which dwarfed even that of a loyal and dedicated Midnight Mourner.

Ever the conspiracy theorist, Kelli has devoted the entire "Backstreet Boys Room" to her exhaustive examination of the plane crash and her indisputable substantiation that no foul play was involved. I find this relieving even though the thought of foul play had not once entered my mind in the past decade until I entered this archive of attestation.

Systematically covering three rooms per day, I scrutinize and inspect my way slowly and thoroughly as requested, room after room after room. Yet even as I follow the bouncing ball, I can feel a deadness start to creep inside me. Nothing suggests a hiding place for the Absolute Proof. After awhile, I start speaking out loud almost non-stop, recording even my most unnecessary thoughts because the difficulty of this process begins to deteriorate my morale. My alertness for clues to the location of the Absolute Proof also starts to dull. So much so that I almost miss the only genuinely interesting anomaly of promise found during this first week.

I pocket my discovery without a word. I press no button to summon Kelli. It is not enough on its own.

On the morning of my eighth day underground, just as I am reaching a tipping point after which my exhaustion will render me useless, everything changes.

In one corner of Kelli's quadrant furthest to the west, a branch of tunnel which dead ends two stories under the skeleton of the Letterman Army Medical Center, I begin my second week underground with the exhumation of the "Barry Manilow Room" and there I find myself enlivened out of torpor. It is Kelli's shockingly comprehensive archive of the lives and times of the secret, not-so-secret society itself!

It is a harsh stuff, this discovery which is a mix of fascination and repulsion. And what is immediately and patently obvious is the unmistakable evidence of Kelli's obsessive feelings toward me. Although some of the files are older, much of the material found here seems to have been recently acquired as a reaction to Matt Junior's perhaps not-so-crazy plan for our wedded bliss.

Shannon's section takes up more than her share of the room. Kelli's fascination with her is clear. And her research team has been especially intrusive. Every job. Every man. Photocopies of her appointment books. Photocopies of her diaries. Phone records, media footage, a sophisticated psych profile. A large segment refers to those days when Paige and Shannon were very close friends suggesting a kind of jealousy on Kelli's part toward Shannon, bizarre as it is for me to imagine. There is also a big block devoted to my sexual relationship with Shannon. I feel angry at that part of me which was, and still can be, so emotionally passive in stark contrast to my activist calling as the white knight of radio dispatchers. But who isn't a walking contradiction? So I move on.

Owen's section is far smaller and it raises barely an eyebrow. Very little of Kelli's gentle snooping into Owen's past proves fraught with unsung information. His brutally lonesome years in foster care, his love life full of badly chosen girlfriends whom he had to keep at a distance to avoid the unlikely but frightening possibility of ending up like his parents, his disastrous finances based on a lifetime of poor decisions: all of it I skip through, partially because it hurts, but also as I sense no relevance to the task at hand.

Anjuli's files are also slim but Kelli's profilers clearly like her spunk. I learn that she is far less the opportunistic curly-haired tramp than self-advertised. Her many sexual encounters in her fire engine red Miata are actually nothing near her proudly voiced conquest-rate. Kelli's detectives have identified only "six acts of penetration" in her famous car with a mere two different men over a span of half-a-decade which puts her in a very different class indeed.

Photocopies of her letters to her parents show the power of her Catholic upbringing and the values of her large and close-knit family. She even goes to church on saint days I've never even heard of, which explains many an absence from our Society volleyball games. Her psych profile suggests that Anjuli is not really in the market for a sugar daddy as she so often claims. She is actually in the market for any man who won't hurt her the way she was hurt in her first failed marriages, someone who will take care of her insecurities with his solidity. It is a testimony to Anjuli's size two buttery leather defenses that I could not see the nice girl behind the girl who is afraid to be nice, who is afraid nice is bland, who is afraid that being nice will cause her to end up with a bland life with a bland man who won't really be there for her. By the time I finish the Anjuli section, I realize she is much more deserving of my respect.

Leah's section is substantial, the largest of all those files devoted to my friendships. And, with what wisdom I have left, I leave it alone. I don't want to learn about her this way. I want to learn about her day by day, in small doses of love and revelation. And so, without hesitation, I move on.

Dylan's section is filled with all the little lies and exaggerations he's known for. Too many to mention, a laundry list beginning with his inability to be faithful all the way to those inventive methods which he has found to cheat on his taxes more enthusiastically than most. But on the good side of his ledger, it turns out he keeps in more constant contact with his sons than I realized. And child support is one thing he always gets right. Overall, the materials that Kelli's researchers have gathered paint Dylan in a sympathetic manner. One profiler's comment catches my eye. Dylan is a man who actually courts all the many physical abuses he receives from Leah and Shannon as he believes women should punish him for the punishment he himself has doled out to women. Pretty sophisticated stuff for me to ponder, making me once again second guess my choice to shun the learning opportunities of psychotherapy in favor of radio catharsis.

The only light moment, if one could call it that, was my discovery that Kelli also has files on each of the various employees and executives of KHEL with whom I have worked over the years. Bridget's file is the most enjoyable to read. I discover, without surprise, that my deadly call screener has silently broken her vow of chastity on forty to fifty occasions with at least three different partners over the last year. Bad girl!

At the very end of the "Barry Manilow Room" is an annex, a room-within-a-room. I immediately assume it must be the Rick Lang vault given its size because I have been waiting to unearth an entire unpleasant wing devoted solely to me since Day One. But as I step inside, I see it is nothing of the kind. The room is clearly meant to be a small-scale mock-up of the law offices of Matthew Moss, specifically his conference room. In my immediate line of sight is a jumbo-sized placard which serves as a huge prop wedding invitation. It sits on the child-sized conference table next to a huge prop wedding cake. It bears Kelli's ever-familiar calligraphy:

MATTHEW KELLANE SWIFT, JUNIOR
INVITES YOU TO ATTEND THE WEDDING OF
HIS DEARLY UNLOVED SISTER
KELLANE VICTORIA CABOT-WHITNEY SWIFT
TO RICK LANG, THE MIDNIGHT RIDER

There are four large and impressive photographic portraits lining the far end of the room, all in a neat line, each in a matching gold frame. Draped above the frames is a large unfurled red-white-and-blue banner such as you'd find at a political rally. It reads "Welcome To The Four Matts of the Apocalypse!" I quickly scan the first three photographs because a horrible feeling is beginning to swell in my gut. Each portrait sports an oversized brass plaque. Left to right, underneath their respective frames, the plaques read:

MATTHEW KELLANE SWIFT, PATRIARCH, MAY HE ROT IN HIS GRAVE.

MATTHEW KELLANE SWIFT, JUNIOR, MAY HE ROT IN PRISON.

MATTHEW MOSS, ATTORNEY-AT-LAW, ROTTEN TO THE CORE.

MATTHEW INAGAKI, ROTTEN FRIEND.

I stare at the last portrait, the huge color depiction of the man I know as "Gary" wearing his favorite tropical shirt as he leans against his surfboard.

I stare, I stare. And of course I get it.

Without a wave, there is no surfing. Without a shill, there is no scam.

# CHAPTER TWENTY-TWO

GARY.

*Gary.*

EVEN THOUGH I UNDERSTAND THAT THE MARRIAGE GAME WAS A CON CONCOCTED BY EXPERTS, IT IS still emotionally difficult for me to see in such black-and-white detail just how clearly my family of friends has been used, like the colorful scarves magicians use for misdirection, simply to get to me. So that Rick Lang, and only Rick Lang, can ride down the aisle with Target Six, the only target which matters.

Anjuli, Owen, Shannon, Dylan, Leah. Just collateral damage.

Attached to the frame which features Gary is a key which opens a special cabinet skulking just underneath the portrait. Kelli has chosen this moment for me to devour a comprehensive summary of the lifelong war between brother and sister as it relates to the Secret Society Marriage Game. It is grim stuff.

Initial plans by young Matt to have younger Kelli murdered were anticipated by Paige and several early attempts were foiled although some came disconcertingly close to succeeding. Thus Paige encouraged Kelli to demand a judicial re-definition of the Trust's provisions to make it emphatically clear to lawyers on both sides that the untimely death of either sibling, for whatever reason, would, by default, shatter and break up the Swift inheritance into a thousand diffuse bequests. This annoyed Matt Junior no end but as he was a champion Ivy League fencer, he simply changed foils. He began a long campaign to have Kelli declared legally incompetent; Paige also helped fend off these kind of attacks and in the process taught Kelli numerous lessons about vigilance. Kelli has made it her life's work to stay ahead of Matt Junior's various conspiracies but I can see from her recent penciled marginal notes that she is in some ways actually impressed by the evolution of Junior's conspiratorial prowess as seen in the "Marriage Game." Brother Matt had matured enough to finally seek out ways to push hard on *psychological* buttons. Kelli Swift's love for me being genuine, her attraction to me made obvious by our countless radio interactions, her potential disregard for fortune in favor of happiness as indicated by her character, and a postulated state of exhaustion after nearly fifteen years of non-stop warfare, all these elements made Matt Junior's gambit not as naïve and outside the box as one might think.

Matt Swift Junior's hatred of Paige was justified. Paige protected, advised, and served as Kelli's whip hand when she was a teen and at her most fragile. The two clashed on many occasions, verbally and physically. On one occasion outside a courtroom, she raked his face with her fingernails so deeply that plastic surgery was required. He responded in kind by gutting the Phillips family's pet Airedale (which was explained to me as an attack by especially vicious coyotes). When he further escalated their enmity by putting a warning bullet through her precious daddy's office window, Paige's payback was to have him road-raged, driven into a ditch, and his licensed bodyguards beaten nearly to death in front of him by her more numerous less-licensed mercenaries. Matt, shrewdly gauging Paige's level of sociopathy, decided against further gladiatorial confrontations. I examine a photocopy of Paige's formal typewritten letter to Matt Swift which "with kindest regards" informs him that, should she experience a sudden death of any kind, those same former mercenaries in her employ have been pre-paid to take away his sight "without aid of an anesthetic" as "an eye for two eyes" is, in her opinion, the correct biblical justice for those who break the holy commandment of *thou shall not kill thy sister's keeper.*

Although I have spent a week being bee-stung with one Paige surprise after another, these particular brutal facts cause me to quickly grow very dizzy and soak myself in sweat. I yearn to slam this file shut. I can't take any more. But there is always more.

Matthew Inagaki, the man I know as Gary, the new friend I have cherished for nearly two years, was planted among our group in a form of deep cover by Matt Moss and Matt Swift. Matt Inagaki was easily able to use his brother Gary's name, social security number and life story, because his brother is still in Shanghai on a five-year tour of duty for the United States Foreign Service. This change of identity was key for two reasons. Firstly, despite all the promises of life success suggested by his being captain of his Princeton swimming team and the president of Princeton's Thespian Society, our Hawaiian-born beach boy managed to spend four of his last ten years languishing in Federal Prison for a variety of venture capital investment swindles which extensively showcased his business and acting talents.

But the second reason was even more helpful.

The real Gary Inagaki was born in August 1961, which was, of course, the sole criterion for anyone's acceptance into the August '61 Secret Society. So when "Gary" deftly befriended Dylan, it was only a matter of time before he easily inserted himself among us. A sidebar is that "Gary," in actuality, is only 33 years old not on the cusp of 40. And Princeton's theater program is obviously a good one as he never hit a false note in all the time I was with him.

As his handlers knew via their no-stone-unturned research into Rick Lang, "Gary" as our newest member, was entitled to host the annual Secret Society Game, and that became the crux of the sting. The Marriage Box was devised by Matt Swift's think tank to piggy-back on one of Matthew Moss' well-known betting syndicate wagers. (In fact, Moss was a winner either way. If we all married, including me, he'd collect from Matt Swift. If we failed to marry, including me, his consolation prize was a payoff from Roger Brock and Brock's gambling cartel.) Matt Inagaki memorized and staged the Marriage

Box drawers. But all went terribly wrong when Dylan purchased the #1 position from me for five beer-soaked bucks, landing me in #6. This was a serious error and Matt Inagaki genuinely feared for his life. But there was, as usual, a plan B. Despite greater jeopardy for one and all, the short con was turned into a long con.

Low-level accomplices, all out of work actors with real lives, had been gathered and placed on call to be met, courted, and brought to the altar by the Secret Society, if needed. Matt Inagaki himself had the back-up option of using a real girlfriend, a pick-pocket he had met at rehab in earlier days of wine and roses.

Plan 'B' was more complicated but it was still a go.

*This is so messed up.*

I decide to stop reading. I'm done for the day.

Unable to find any immediate way to process the enormous scope of Gary's betrayal, I put my mind into safe neutral just to keep my brain from exploding. I decide to ascend a level and return to Kelli's central battle station for a break. In her war room, I notice for the first time that Kelli has her own wide captain's chair in an alcove at the very back. It definitely looks like a Star Fleet, Star Trek captain's chair (which would fit Kelli's oddball fan crush mentality I suppose) and, hey, it's a perfect place to collapse and feel ill and so I slot myself in and sleep comes immediately.

*BAM!*

When I sharply jolt awake, I realize my brain's neurotransmitters must have had just enough time to throw their version of my 40th birthday party. During my week and one day underground, my REM sleep has been, as one might expect, a distortion of its usual self. For eight days I have been dual processing, conscious of everything I have been seeing and reading but unconsciously I've felt memories tugging at my conscious mind like small children tugging at my shirt tail. Now as I awake from what must have been a glut of good REM sleep, my brain has clearly done an especially good job of sorting and consolidating memories.

*Because now I have a notion that makes no sense, of which there is no proof, and yet I am sure it is true.*

I begin to run down one tunnel and bolt to the next; my agitation is the good kind, the keyed-up kind, and I careen into Kelli's silver and green and platinum fantasy-jungle-bedroom and pick a spot in the center of the room next to her harpsichord. I have come here because it's the nearest place where one of her listening-post buttons can be found and pressed and pressed and pressed.

"Kelli!" I shout as I hear her questioning reply. "I want you to *show me the plane!*"

# CHAPTER TWENTY-THREE

CROUCHING LOW, I STAGGER THROUGH A CONSTRICTED, TAPERED PASSAGEWAY, A SLENDER and low-ceilinged artery which has to be the narrowest path in Kelli's version of a land down under. Kelli is leading the way and her arm is bent back behind her so her hand can hook mine and lead me. When we come to the very end, everything is blacker than black, but I see a dimly lit panel where Kelli speed-fingers a digital keypad.

Thus, with sudden dazzling illumination, I get a lightning-bolt first view of this enormous subterranean rotunda, three stories high and looking very much like a Capital dome; it comes complete with a 1920s-ish fresco on its broken plaster ceiling featuring sneering cupids and peeling pink clouds. This was once the heart of the Old Boy's Netherworld, where they secretly met for ritualistic Mammon-worship no doubt little different from that practiced by our banking scions in skyscrapers today. But my interest in architectural niceties is very brief because in front of me, hanging like an exhibit at the Smithsonian, is the two-engine, six passenger Phillips family jet. Fuselage cracked, tail half-detached, one engine missing, gaping holes here and there and yet, if this tragic sight could be seen as a fifty-piece jigsaw puzzle made of metal, then forty of the pieces are still intact for the viewing. It has an ominous gravity to it possibly because it is suspended a few feet off the ground in such a vast space otherwise unoccupied.

"I wasn't planning to bring you here until later..." Kelli immediately sits cross-legged on the polished concrete floor as there are no chairs anywhere. "But the fact you *knew*...it's a good sign..." She wears a thick fleece over her tee-shirt and jeans; this is the first really ice cold space I've been in since I arrived. I myself was handed a thick leather bomber jacket by Kelli for warmth, although the aeronautical inspiration for its design seems unfortunate given the circumstances.

A few days earlier, while listening over and over to the musical stylings of her least favorite boy band, I read Kelli's account of the plane's last moments, her description of a pilot who was still hugging the coast and had only just begun his swing around for an east to west night landing, when a component part which powered the flight instrumentation failed with spectacular results. There was no question of pilot error, in fact he was skilled enough to ditch, despite strong Santa Ana wind conditions, just five hundred yards offshore. The attempt at a water landing wasn't a success; the plane hit the ocean surface with just a little too much force, impacting on a side-forward tilt which killed both parents and pilot upon impact. Cally, Cassie, my sister Linda, and Paige drowned. Paige and Linda both had injuries to their hands and fingers consonant with a failed attempt to claw themselves free as the plane sank, a newly understood horror so ghastly that I have not yet let my mind create a picture of it.

Kelli made sure the Coast Guard, along with the NTSB and FAA investigators, gave her both full access to the site and full permission for her salvage team to bring from the bottom of the ocean absolutely anything and everything she needed, including personal effects, so that she could do the reconstruction herself. And Kelli's obsessive nature and organizing genius combined to now at this very moment provide me with an impressive display of photography that lines nearly half the circular walls of the rotunda creating roughly a four-foot high swatch at her eye level.

Although in dreadful awe of the sights before me, I start examining Kelli's wall display at the point where I can see dozens of nine by twelve enlarged photographs, one for each object of interest which had been brought up to the surface, huge nine by twelve blow-ups of everything upsetting one could hope for. From the contents of my mother's purse to my father's college ring, from a baby's blanched and shredded stuffed polar bear to my sister's favorite Converse sneakers.

I pace back and forth, back and forth, in front of this wall of photography for nearly a half-hour. Sometimes I am looking and examining, but often I am just spacing out, my mind trying to back-pedal away from these images made grotesque by their very enlargement. Kelli watches me like a silent hawk waiting for prey to be revealed. Suddenly I find myself in front of several blow-ups of Paige's Cascade Drive key ring and its individual keys.

I must have made some kind of audible grunt or gurgle or gasp because Kelli calls. "What is it?"

"Where did you find her house keys?" I ask.

"In her purse. Where she kept them." She hesitates. "Her purse strap was wrapped around her neck when she was brought up…we couldn't separate it…them…" Kelli trails off, pained.

I hesitate. Not sure this is the time to finally bring it out. But my intuition is kicking in so I reach in my pocket and pull out these very keys and hold them up for Kelli to see. "I took them off the hook where you had them displayed. Don't ask me why."

"I *am* asking you why." Kelli replies. "*Why?*"

I stand and stare and stand and stare at the photographs of the keys, comparing them to the keys in my hand. I continue to put my mind in gear; it continues to slip out of gear. It's the same key chain her father carried when *he* was master of Cascade Drive. Each key has its purpose etched on it.

I look at the key marked *Attic.*

And so I pull out my own set of house keys from my pocket and place them side by side with Paige's keys for Kelli to compare. I slowly let my fingers roll over the blades, the teeth, of my set. "I don't have an attic key."

"I know," Kelli replies matter-of-factly. "But we couldn't find any significance in it. The attic lock was broken even before Paige was born. It doesn't lead outside; nothing of value was ever stored there. Nevertheless we checked. We actually fixed the lock just so we could try the key. And her attic key does, as advertised, open the attic."

"Why would Paige carry a key with no purpose?"

"They're her father's keys. They're the master set. He carried it, she carried it."

"She'd take the key off."

"Why? Just because it's useless?" Kelli looks underwhelmed. "The basement key is useless too. That lock is gone as well. Yet you both carry basement keys."

"I carry the keys I was given. I used only one, the front door key. Paige doesn't carry a larger, heavier key just because her Daddy did. Paige loved her father but she just wasn't that sentimental."

"What about the basement?"

"The basement holds four decades of Phillips family memorabilia. The attic was full of junk. Keeping the basement key makes sense to me on some level. Carrying the attic key does not."

"Like I said. The attic key opens the attic."

*Suddenly I know.*

*Just as I knew about the plane.*

"Kelli," I begin. "Think. Everything Paige did was deliberate. Her life was a streamlined thing of beauty. She does not carry the attic key because of her father. Or because of sentiment. Or because of tradition." I try to keep the drama out of my voice but it's no use, because I know I'm right. "She carried the key marked attic because it also opens *something else.* Which is why it's no coincidence that I don't have it."

Kelli's eyes widen.

I continue. "It's in the house. Your *Absolute* Damn Proof is *absolutely* in the house. And its hiding place must be as old as the attic, probably as old as the house itself. At least it looks that way." I take a breath, then: "Maybe you couldn't find it with all your experts and technology. But I bet I can."

I don't know why I say this last thing. But I say it.

Kelli stands next to me, gauging my words. Not wanting to smile but wanting to smile. Finally she grins. "Okay," she says slowly, "….tomorrow we take you home and we'll see if you're right."

*But my instincts haven't finished today's work; I still feel little children tugging at me in my unconscious, tugging so very hard, nearly ripping the shirt off my back…*

"There's one other thing…" I begin, hesitantly. "I've been thinking about this one other thing for a few days. It relates to how Paige trapped your brother…" I waver again, but now this extra horrorshow must go on. "You seem to have pictures of everything here…"

"Everything." She answers.

"And everybody?"

Kelli gives me a look. "Yes. I have the photos from the morgue. In fact, I was at the morgue. I saw her body. I saw all the bodies." She points to the far end of her wall of photographs. "The autopsy photos are at the far end." She falters. "You don't want to look, Rick. That's one exhibit you don't need to see…"

"Just bring every picture you have of Paige. I'll be over here." I point to the jet.

Kelli nods, unsure of what I'm doing. But unwilling to question me because she knows I'm on a roll. And so she starts to walk over to that part of her wall which in fact I will never look at because, even beautified for their funerals, I could not look at any of the faces.

I walk to the jagged jigsaw puzzle which is the jet. I hoist myself up onto the fully intact starboard wing using the rungs Kelli has welded to the fuselage for that purpose. I balance at the root of the wing and sit down. I do not look inside the body of the jet.

*Not yet.*

Kelli climbs up and joins me a few minutes later. And there we are, the pathetic pair, sitting as if we were having a picnic, with several gruesome pictures recording Paige's autopsy now in my lap. There is only one thing I am looking for. I thumb through the blowups so quickly that when I get to the one I want, I grab it, letting the rest of the photographs fly from my fingers and flutter to the ground below. I force myself to look at the photo carefully and dispassionately and then I show it to Kelli.

"The bruising on her shoulders. The scratching on her neck. Not from the crash. Her shoulders were already bruised when she got on the plane. I remember the scratches on her neck. She covered them with make-up."

"How…?" Kelli trails off. For several long moments, Kelli looks at me while I say nothing. Then suddenly her understanding of what I mean begins to emerge. Her expression starts to change.

I don't want her to suffer in limbo. Because suddenly I'm ninety-nine percent sure I'm right so I rattle it off as fast as I can. "A few days before the crash. Paige came home late, told me she'd had a minor fender-bender. Her dress was torn…there was some blood, not a lot, but she looked shaken-up, she went right to bed. She rested up for a few days…we had a private doctor, you know that …he came by…took tests…more tests…her lawyer came the next morning. He brought papers…took her statement…"

I pause, my brain once again stuck between gears…but this time Kelli isn't patient…she touches a cold finger to my cheek and I snap back to the present.

"Rick, *finish* it…"

"I saw the bruises. I saw the scratches. And this was all *before* she got on the plane…*these* bruises…" I point to this photograph of Paige's battered corpse. Then I let the photo slip from my hand to join the others below, all of which have formed a mosaic of autopsy pictures below us. And down I point to this mosaic. "*Those* bruises…"

Kelli's head suddenly snaps in the direction opposite me. She rapidly adjusts her fleece, tilts back and uses the fleece's surface to slide on along the wing edge and then, with practiced skill, she climbs down, each rung clanging like a church bell in the huge echoing rotunda with each forceful step she takes. I watch her scoop up the pictures of Paige's postmortem and neatly stack them, tuck them under her arm, and place them at the foot of her photography wall. She is trying to calm herself by careful, purposeful movement and so when she speaks it is in a calm voice which only barely hides her rage.

"My brother raped her."

"It could be…"

"No," Kelli replies. "He did it. He raped her."

Revulsion is an emotional rogue wave. I teeter on the wing's edge.

Kelli continues. "Paige sacrificed herself. I don't know how she did it. Maybe it wasn't that difficult. He hated her." Kelli looks me full in the eye, her expression so intense it is almost intolerable. "She did it for me, Rick. She did it to free me."

Abruptly she comes back to the edge of the wing and reaches up to squeeze my ankle, which she does once, before half-walking and half-running toward the small opening which brought us here, no longer willing to share her feelings with me.

"Tomorrow morning…." I call after her. "I know exactly what we need to do."

Kelli's emotions are now starting to explode out of her control; she scurries out of the rotunda intent on not looking back at me. "I'll wake you at dawn! I'll be there at dawn!"

"I won't be in your bedroom. I'll be here…" I slide off the wing to the rungs.

"Here?" Her voice is choked.

"*Here!* Just come get me." I climb down the rungs to the polished floor.

Kelli nods without looking back, pulls her fleece tighter around her then runs and disappears down the narrow artery back into the heart of her lost world.

Just then I hear a new voice, someone is calling for me. So I turn and look. But all I see is the jet's wing, hanging from its wires, still rocking a little from my dismqunt. The plane seems as if it is trembling.

Then I hear the other voices.

They're all calling for me.

It's time.

So I step over to the control panel, the key pad by the rotunda's entrance, and find the single large toggle which switches off the enormous lights. One definitive plunge into black and thus I am left with only the glow of the flashlight I've carried in my belt for the last eight days. I walk to the broken tail of the jet, grab it with two hands and hoist myself inside.

I let the flashlight slowly play over what is left of the passenger seats, the broken interior, and the still intact window on the starboard side which looks out at nothing at all. I am so empty.

And yet the jet is not empty. Everyone is here.

"That's why I'm staying with you tonight." I tell them. "It's okay. I want to be here."

I let the flashlight continue to wander inch by inch through the jet's cabin. Kelli has cleaned out everything, taken everything. And yet she's left behind all that matters.

"Tonight I'm not going to talk…" I say out loud. "But I can only do this once… so tell me everything… I'm here to listen."

With a sharp snap, I turn my flashlight off. It is utterly, indescribably dark inside this black place I've envisioned so often and with such sorrow.

I feel myself sink downwards very slowly into an underwater cave where my tears begin to flow like little fish seeking refuge; they flow into the darkest dark I have ever imagined. I open my ears and I listen and I weep until I'm certain my chest will explode like jets do when they hit water at full speed. But nothing explodes so I let the flashlight slip from my hands and I hear the sound of it as it rattles against the metal, as it falls through a crack in the fuselage, as it softly hits the ocean floor beneath us and rolls far, far away. And I am glad I no longer have my light because they had no light and I want no light and, besides, in the dark we can all cry together as a family.

# PART III

# CHAPTER TWENTY-FOUR

**W**E ARE GATHERED IN A SEMI-CIRCLE FIFTY FEET FROM THE COBBLED ENTRANCE TO THE PHILLIPS Mansion, that house which dwarfs all others on Cascade Drive, which dwarfed me and owned me and served as my Museum of Hurt. Yet on this fog-whispery first day of September, it surely must be trembling in its foundations for we have cut off all its routes of escape and soon the carnage must begin. We are all dressed for dirty work and ready to take possession of various tools of destruction; chainsaws, sledgehammers, pick-axes, and claw hammers lie in neat rows on the highest part of the acreage. Now strewn with metal, this is the grassy clearing where once I danced with Leah during my wedding reception. Slightly further to the east, where Kelli's bright yellow backhoes and bulldozers await, is the softly sloping hillock where once I played with my children, quite near the Centaur fountain which Owen built as balm for my grieving but whose figural four-footed capstone now sits safely out of harm's way in the back of Owen's shabby weather-beaten pick-up.

The Secret Society (minus one most trusted babe and one Society traitor) have been listening dumbstruck for over an hour as Kelli, uptight and understandably so, has been using her best expository shorthand to brief the uninitiated.

"You mean Gary isn't Gary?" Shannon is shocked and upset, as are the others. "His real name is Matt. He works for my half-brother, who is also named Matt."

"But which Matt is Matthew Moss?" Dylan asks, lost.

"He was the middle Matt. You see, Matt Swift, my half-brother, hired Matt Moss, one of his attorneys, to hire Matt Inagaki, an ex-con and a gifted actor to set up your phony Marriage Game."

"Can't tell the players without a bank book," grumbles Owen.

Anjuli interjects, turning to Dylan, Owen, and Shannon. "Come on, guys, it's not *that* hard." Anjuli puffs up with pride at being, on this rare occasion, a step ahead. "Gary called himself Gary because his brother really is a Gary and was born in August '61 like us. And Gary who is really a Matt was planted like a spy into the Society to trick Rick into marrying Kelli! All so she would lose the big bucks left by her evil father…who is *also* named Matt!"

"You've got to be kidding!" Shannon reacts wide-eyed, looking around as if searching for a desperately needed glass of Pinot Noir or a tranquilizer or both.

Owen rolls his eyes. "Four Matts? C'mon!"

But Anjuli is on a roll. "Simple! Because if Rick marries Kelli, Matt Junior gets *all* the cash from Matt Senior's Will. And Matt Moss and Matt Inagaki get a major chunk of change for doing his dirty work." She finishes with a self-satisfied head-swish of her ringlets. Not bad for a woman who drives around in a bright red Mazda Miata with a roll bar and a California customized license plate which reads: "Fly Me."

Kelli nods. "Exactly. The Marriage Game was a scam solely designed to throw Rick at me."

Shannon reacts. "Ridiculous. *And* convoluted. *And* preposterous. *And* delusional."

"What *I'm* hearing is that there never was any two million apiece." Owen mutters.

"Big deal," sighs Dylan. "Easy come, easy go. That's my middle name."

Anjuli guffaws. "Okay, Pool Boy, then I'm calling you 'easy come' from now on."

"Anjuli!" Shannon yells. "Enough!"

Just like old times. It's good to be back with my friends.

*Minus Leah of course.*

Leah has been told I'm alright. But Leah has declined to join us.

"Look, we're wasting our time." I finally say. "Let's get to work."

With nods of enthusiasm, something vaguely like a line takes shape. Kelli moves to the vast pile of tools she has prepared for us and begins handing us each a hard hat, a pair of heavy gloves, and goggles. She uses the toe of her boots to kick and check the toes of each of our boots for fit, regulation construction crew issue. Nobody bothers to wonder aloud how she knows everyone's correct shoe size.

The house on Cascade Drive has perched smugly on its three acres of prime Mill Valley real estate dotted with clumps of magnificent redwoods for over a hundred years and for once its geographical isolation is going to pay the ultimate dividend. It is bordered on the South by the main road, a leaf-covered and very damp two-lane blacktop which is being watched over by Kelli's bodyguards ensconced in Kelli's phalanx of black SUVs. A narrow side street meanders to the West and this has been blocked at both ends by the brave warriors of the Mill Valley Fire Department who have all the correct expedited permits for what is about to happen. The winding brook in its deep stone-reinforced gully toward the East makes that approach impossible and impassable. And a steep hillside covered in pine trees and brush covers the North. Presently there are seven road works vehicles with sixty uniformed workers, all employed by Kelli, blocking the streets and detouring the few cars which attempt to pass. Several picnicking bicyclists armed with peanut butter sandwiches and walkie-talkies keep an eye on the whole scene from the top of the ridge. Yes, we are positioned on a high ground of Kelli's design because one of Matt Swift's helicopters has been shadowing us all afternoon.

My own arrangement with Kelli is simple. My hand-picked five man electrical band of friends will have until midnight to work with my suddenly very effective intuitive inner search sonar. After which, should the Secret Society (minus one most trusted babe and one Society traitor) fail in the first assault, Kelli's equally hand-picked demolition crew with their high tech search toys, will tear the house apart molecule by molecule. This time the Absolute Proof will be found.

"Just documents and tapes and DNA stuff?" Owen eyes a chainsaw. "In that case, the box or whatever it is could be way thinner than we think." It is a tribute to Owen's emotional equilibrium that he is not thinking about his money now, instead he views the house with eyes that have taken apart a thousand bakelite radios.

Anjuli grabs a gigantic fire axe and jams it into Dylan's less-than-callused hands. "Okay, Dylan. Let's see if size matters." She then looks around for an implement of destruction more her speed and it's strangely heartwarming for me to see Anjuli's enthusiasm as, wearing the tightest 501 jeans Levi Strauss ever made, she bends over to grab a claw hammer and nearly splits herself in two.

Shannon and I check out the heavy tools together. Her perfectly-coordinated work outfit of black denim jeans, matching jacket, and matching hair combs, is a fashion statement doomed to disaster given the task at hand. In homage to Peter Gabriel's rock anthem "Sledgehammer," I find the heaviest one I can lift. Shannon gracefully straightens up with a crowbar in each beautifully manicured hand and falls in line with the rest of us.

Owen, a natural leader when it comes to all things physical, hoists the biggest chainsaw in the stack. He flashes a reassuring smile to the assembled rag-tag army.

"Did I not live here for two years after Paige died? I plan to carve out a few more memories!" With that he fires up the chainsaw with a roar. We all wince.

Kelli, satisfied we're ready for action, backs away in order to join her men at the bottom of the drive.

We move into the front hallway, the five of us. "I'll take the downstairs study," says Owen, his chainsaw already making a merciless racket.

"I'll take the kitchen! Absolute Proof here I come!" Anjuli clutches her claw hammer and heads off with determination.

"The entire third floor!" announces Dylan, wielding his axe like a goggle-wearing dwarf from The Fellowship Of The Ring. "I'll start with the third-floor bedrooms."

Shannon pauses at the foot of the first staircase. "I'll take your attic room, Rick. After all, your key does read *'Attic'* so let's get the obvious out of the way." With that, she marches her crowbars upstairs.

Owen with the Chainsaw in the Study.

Dylan with the Axe in the Bedroom.

Shannon with the Crowbar in the Attic.

Anjuli with the Hammer in the Kitchen.

How can we fail to find the clue?

On the second floor, my sledgehammer and I pay an instinctive visit to Paige's bedroom which I realize now was never ever really meant to belong to the two of us. It is the first time I've been inside it since the day the music died thus it's now the "must-see" Museum of Hurt exhibit. And the rush of memory nearly makes me step backwards. The surprisingly small bed, the over-zealous Edwardian yellow wallpaper, the too-dark built-in shelves with some of the dullest business tomes in Christendom. No feminine frills, just many, many closets filled with clothes she never wore as it turned out her favored wardrobe was more conveniently kept at the city condo she owned, the one she neglected to tell me about. And really…truly…totally…I see for the first time with clear eyes the movie set bedroom which was our artificial love nest inside the house that served only as a place to show off the normal children and the normal marriage Paige's parents demanded of her. I note the powerful, recessed lighting on Paige's side of the bed so she could read late into the night perhaps avoiding the possibility that, in a mad fit of normality, I tried to touch her. And most perfectly central to the whole scene is the Amish quilt on our bed, a legacy gift from her parents with its mocking intertwined rings meant for newlyweds.

Locked boxes full of jewelry. A briefcase, locked for over ten years. A locked trunk under the bed. A locked medicine cabinet in the ultra-swanky bathroom. A locked floor safe in her larger walk-in closet. A locked wall safe in her smaller walk-in cedar closet. Did she ever trust me, even for a moment? Probably not. These locks don't excite me. Kelli opened and reopened them several times with her Supergirl X-ray vision.

I put my intuition to work in this room and I come up empty. I sit and hold the 'attic' key in my hand and it doesn't sing to me. But the huge wedding photograph which dominates the wall facing our bed does give off a surprisingly pleasant vibe, airbrushed and color-enhanced and sitting in an elaborate frame. Why do my insides smile? How can that be?

Unexpectedly Owen's head pops into the room behind me. He grins when he sees me sitting on the floor, cradling the sledgehammer. "You'd be proud, man. We're doing it all systematic!"

"Great." I reply. I see his chainsaw is covered in sawdust. There probably isn't much left of the paneling and the floorboards in the study. "Nothing so far, huh?"

"Not yet..." He pauses, then: "Just one question. Who were we dating? The shills they set us up with, I mean. Who were they?"

"Just people who needed money. Like Gary."

Owen sighs. "That Justine chick was a real good actress. I coulda swore she really liked me."

"She probably did."

"'Cause I'm hard to resist, right?"

I smile. "You said it."

"Good thing none of us slept around, huh?" With a wave, Owen disappears back into the upstairs hallway.

It *is* a good thing. The sooner everyone forgets the better.

Cuddling my sledgehammer as if it were a child's comfort object, I rise and slowly move to the enormous wedding picture on the wall, trying to hone in on the vibe. Paige and I are posing hand in hand for the photographer. Her wedding dress was beaded and laced by who-knows-how-many indentured servants from Southeast Asia and cost more than a new Mercedes.

My tuxedo was a gift from my Dad. I can see him in the picture, happy for my happiness. He had this thing for my mother's waist and he had big hands. I can see his hands on her waist as he stands behind her. I can see her face reacting with amusement to his hands. They had a real marriage, the authentic kind. Looking at them, I feel so unlucky and yet so very lucky. They made me, they walked beside me for thirty years, they guided and protected me as they guided and protected each other.

Ain't nothing like the real thing.

And now I see why the picture called to me…because my eye is finally drawn to Leah's image. Leah in the background, Leah at the far side of the cheering, well-wishing crowd. *All* of Leah, from the delicate pair of low red pumps which still left her way-tall and awkward-leggy and gangly-thin, to the tip top of her straw-blonde, wind-ruffled long hair now so much shorter yet no less sexy. And in between *there's* the famous cherry red cocktail dress which lured me like a hummingbird to a feeder. And *there's* the smile, the best smile, the most genuinely beautiful smile in this universe and all those parallel.

Maybe it's just Dylan's fire axe chopping the back beat as he savages the rooms one floor up, but it's his chopping beat which serves to propel me back to the Boom Boom Room where I hear Leah's song lyrics too loudly, too clearly: *I've got your picture hangin' on the wall… but it can't see or come to me when I call your name…it's just a picture in a frame.*

Just a picture in a frame.

So I take down the wedding photo. Remove it from its solid silver rococo-elaborate ultra heavy housing.

And I carefully tear off two sections. The one which features my parents and the one which features Leah alone. They are the only pieces that matter, aren't they? And I put these sections in my shirt pocket as carefully as I can, pausing for one last look at Leah.

*Will you come to me when I call your name?*

I sledgehammer the wall panels in the bedroom and closets as well as the tiling and drywall in the bathroom for an hour to no avail. And then I go on psychic auto-pilot for the next few hours, roaming the house from room to room and from smashing friend to axing friend, failing to understand why I haven't intuited the location of Kelli's Absolute Proof. I hold the key labeled 'attic' tightly as if it were a divining rod. *But nothing.*

Dylan has taken apart the third floor, chopping with unexpectedly disciplined precision, but finding no secret door, secret passage, secret keyhole of any kind. Anjuli, having clawed the kitchen into bite-sized chunks, is now delicately and thoroughly clawing her way through the Nursery, trying to be respectful but effective with her claw hammer. Owen's chainsaw has made mincemeat of four floors of floorboards making walking around somewhat of a trapeze act given the spider web of footing. Shannon has used her crowbars to pry open every panel in my attic room even though I could have told her it wasn't there.

Eventually, I convene the entire gang of five in the ruin and rubble of the front hallway.

"Another coffee break? What a bunch of slackers." Shannon's black ensemble is completely coated with sawdust and her hair is the same fetching color as chimney soot. "Look…" She slides off her work gloves and holds up her hands for inspection with a sarcastic flourish. "I still have two unbroken fingernails. Why are we stopping?"

At the base of the steps, in the front hallway, we have set up a refreshment refugee center with drinks, doughnuts, sandwiches, and a single bottle of *Absolut* Vodka in a bucket of melting ice, the official prize for the winner of the Absolute Proof sweepstakes.

"Gary loves doughnuts." Owen picks one up and stuffs his mouth. "I wonder if we should visit him in jail 'cause he's probably gonna end up there, right? He was a lot of fun when he wasn't setting us up. Kind of a bummer."

"I've got a great idea!" Anjuli, exhausted, perks up. "We have his marriage box bronzed and then it can be the prize at the next Secret Society Annual Game!"

"Like there's ever going to be another Annual Game." Owen snorts in derision.

"There will be lots more Annual Games, Owen," interrupts Shannon. "And you're going to play each and every one."

"Like hell." Owen's scowl deepens.

"Next year is our twentieth anniversary." I say. "You want to miss that?"

He looks at me. "Well, okay, yeah, but no more new members."

"Why not?" Anjuli asks. "Why should any of this change who we are!"

"We're the Secret Society! We stand tall!" Dylan stands tall, as tall as he can anyway.

"C'mon, we've taken a big hit, you all gotta admit that." Owen replies. But abruptly his expression changes. "But then again … it's not how far you fall …"

Anjuli, Dylan, Shannon and I finish it in unison. "…it's how high you bounce!"

We laugh. The Secret Society's not-so-secret motto comes in handy yet again.

And still so very true. We will bounce.

Tools clatter to the ground. We start to pour coffee, grab sandwiches. Every room within eyesight … to the right, to the left, down the hall, up four flights of stairs … has been axed and torn apart and violated beyond any repair. Not that any repair will be coming.

Owen eyes the vodka. "Why don't we open up the grand prize? It's way past happy hour and it's not like we're happy."

Anjuli sulks. "I was hoping we could have a bonfire once we found it. I seriously brought marshmallows …"

Dylan nods. "Cheer up, guys! Owen's got a good idea. Secret Society body shots!"

I shake my head no. "Forget it." Which is followed by pathetic whimpers from those who find this kind of work tough tedium.

I pull out Paige's 'attic' key and eyeball it yet again.

I think of Kelli. Still waiting in her stretch Lincoln at the bottom of the drive, no doubt second guessing her decision to let us go first, surely getting more and more nervous by the hour. I think of her two backhoes and two bulldozers waiting beside the garage should I fail. I think of her crack team of rubble sifters waiting to examine every plank, waiting to bag and tag each bit of sawdust. Maybe I should just let her take over.

"You mind if I sit on Paige's step?" Shannon is eyeing the first step of the staircase where nine-year-old Paige carved her love heart. "I don't feel like having a picnic on the floor."

"Too good for the rest of us?" Dylan asks caustically.

"You should look at yourself in a mirror, Shannon." Anjuli smirks. "You haven't looked this banged up since Leah kicked your sorry butt up and down The Boom Boom Room!"

Owen perks up. "Oh, yeah. I meant to say. Your black eye healed real nice." He gives Shannon an encouraging grin.

"I thought you all were finished with this!" Shannon's eyes flash. Not only is her red-gold hair prematurely gray with dust. Her smeared make-up reminds me of those silent movie actresses who blackened their eyes with kohl for better dramatic effect.

"Rick, you should've seen it." Dylan has already forgotten he has told me about the Leah-Shannon fight in lurid detail.

Anjuli smirks some more at Shannon. "She had that whole hunk of your pretty red hair in her fist. I *wish* she had given it just one big yank! It would've been *awesome*!"

"I'm not going to apologize. To you or anyone. I told you." Shannon snaps, and then adds softly. "And I'm not going to make Leah apologize to me."

"It's nobody's fault." Owen interjects forcefully. "Leah let go of it. We all have. What does it matter, bottom line." He turns to me. "And she doesn't blame you, Rick."

"Yeah, we're all adults!" Anjuli adds.

"And we have a right to do *who* we please!" Dylan's two cents is added.

My face must have fallen because Owen grabs my shoulder and makes me look at him. "I'm gonna tell you again. Leah got over it quick. That's not her problem. Her problem…the thing that made her so sad… has always been about you and Paige."

"It's always been about Paige." Anjuli adds again. "You couldn't let go. How many times did I try to tell you? You just kept telling me to shut up. In a nice way, I mean."

"Shannon, you didn't really mind getting all smacked around, did you?" Owen grins at Shannon. She wryly grins back at him as one old pal to another although the grin fades a little as she pulls a small spider out of her dust-crusted hair and flicks it away.

Shannon turns to me. Her gaze is uncompromising. "Leah still loves you, Rick. And she'll always love you in that way none of us can hope to understand."

"That is totally true," interjects Anjuli.

"Big time." Dylan adds.

Shannon continues: "I was just another impediment in her way. Like Ronny. Like Paige. Like the years you spent mourning. She knows you've never had any serious romantic feelings for me."

"It's true, man." Owen chimes in. "She doesn't give a damn about what you and Shannon did out of loneliness and neediness and stuff. I even get that and what do I know? It's always been about Paige. From like the *very* beginning I sort of knew how you and Leah felt…I mean, it looked like just friendship…but I could see…you know…underneath…"

"Repeat. Leah was angry." Shannon is adamant. "And when Leah's angry, you know how she is. She gets so frustrated, she can't talk it out. That night she couldn't even speak. All she could do was hit and cry, hit and cry."

"It was sad to watch. She just fell apart." Owen adds. "Real heartbreak for all of us."

Dylan jumps in quickly. "And when she hits, she packs a punch. You expect a good left jab or a mean right hook from a gym rat. You don't see it coming from a tall thin drink of water, know what I mean? But *I* know. I've felt her fists of steel and thanks to Leah, when I see freckles on a woman, I *run*."

"Leah loves you so much it makes me sick!" Anjuli confirms. "I wish someone would love me like that. Why can't I catch a break?"

"I've been married five times." Dylan adds. "If even one of my wives looked at me the way Leah looks at you I'd still be married." Dylan pauses, and then adds. "In fact, I'd still have all five wives and, hey, that would be polygamy of the best kind. I could be a cult leader, I could live in Utah. Sweet!"

Shannon interrupts annoyed. "Enough group rehash. Now can I sit down?" She flops down on the bottom step of the staircase. "Love isn't for everyone, troops. As Leah says…" Shannon does a credible Leah imitation. "*Deal with it…*"

Involuntarily, my eyes are drawn to Shannon's feet as they come to rest a few inches away from Paige's age-nine carved heart on the facing stair. And two things happen.

First, it occurs to me in one great gulp of a split-second that Paige never once gave me a valentine. A solid gold tie clip, though I never wear ties. An expensive set of golf clubs, though I don't play golf. I'd write her the occasional love letter, she'd email me back with a single "x" almost grudgingly added as a coda to her no-nonsense messages. Could Paige have been like that as a nine-year old? She wouldn't have liked finger painting. Too messy. She wouldn't have carved a heart. Too sentimental.

And then, only a brief instant later, the idea of Kelli's calligraphy streaks across my thoughts like a spinning, unfolding parchment map. And I have the immediate understanding that if Kelli hadn't been a calligrapher, I might not have noted what I now notice… that the letters in the word "love" actually read as *"LoVe"* with the L and the V sticking up, two nails refusing to be hammered down.

*Las Vegas. Low Voltage.*
No.
*Latvia? Louis Vuitton?*

Oh, come *on*. Don't be dense.

I can feel the 'attic' key in my hand. I can feel its blades, its teeth, so deeply familiar by now.

*L is fifty. V is five. Did she learn that in first grade? Or did Daddy teach her Roman Numerals? LV. Fifty-five.*

I take two long breaths just to let my mouth catch up with my detonating brain. Then I leap to my feet. "Come on, come on, *upstairs!*"

My sudden shout causes Dylan's sandwich to take flight and Shannon's cup of coffee to go all slow-motion-splashy as I charge past them and hurtle up the steps. Owen, ever a slow talker but *always* a fast action hero, is right behind me. Dylan, never one to miss a party, roars up behind Owen. Anjuli shoos Shannon up the staircase and together they bring up the rear, taking steps two at a time, side-by-side.

"Dylan, I need your axe!"

Dylan swiftly whirls to head back down the stairs thus instantly smacking into Shannon and Anjuli. They collide, tangling up like a trio of grade B comedians. Owen grabs the banister and swings around the complaining chaos of the fallen and hip-slides to the bottom where he grabs the axe with one hand and heads back up, hurdling over Anjuli who has landed next to a sprawled Shannon, and hurdling Dylan, who is literally in the lap of both their female luxuries. I can't hear what the two women are yelling at him because I am already chopping at the 55$^{th}$ stair with the axe Owen has handed me. We are only five steps from the attic.

*An attic key which opens the attic…and something near the attic. So obvious!*

I shatter open the stair. But I'm answered only with splinters.

"Not here." Owen grimaces.

"It's here."

"Because…"

"Because Paige carved that heart so she wouldn't forget her Daddy's hiding place." I see Owen's blank face. "Grown-up Paige remembered her secrets, nine-year old Paige couldn't." Owen starts to get it, so I punch it home. "Even at nine years old, Paige was already shrewd enough to put the hidden spot in code... in roman numerals..."

Owen pushes me aside in this enthusiasm. "Wait a second, wait a second! I get it. Obvious, man! In Ohio, they call it the poor man's wall safe!"

He rapidly turns and begins to lift the secret, sliding tongue-in-groove panel from the wall adjacent to the 55$^{th}$ stair, slides it up smoothly, pulls it out, places it to one side. We look inside and react with such excitement that the entire Secret Society bolts up the staircase to join us. Shannon, Dylan, and Anjuli crowd in behind us to see the spacious handmade cavity in the wall.

"It's a *treasure* chest!" Anjuli gasps.

And so it is. A large wooden jewelry box, a hundred year old box made of lacquered oak, has been fitted with the same kind of lock fitted to the attic door. The small metal keyhole in its fitted plate are the only pieces of metal which explains why Kelli's detectors and other search paraphernalia didn't pick it up.

I insert Paige's 'attic' key.

There is a videotape, a sealed glass tube and two manila envelopes sitting inside a sealed, hard-plastic and cold-retentive container. Each item is neatly dated the day of the crash and addressed to Kelli.

We all share looks.

More looks.

"Okay," I finally say. "Now who'd like to tell Kelli the good news?"

So we hammer-scissors-paper it until Dylan wins. And his response is predictable. "Hah, when it comes to any kind of Secret Society Game, *who* always wins? Tell me the truth! Admit it! Who *always* wins?"

With that, Dylan heads off to make Kelli the happiest human being on the planet.

The rest of us collapse on individual steps with our hard hats and filthy clothes and torn gloves and clogged goggles and scraped bodies and scratched-up work boots. I can't take my eyes off the Absolute Proof, just more absolute proof that, in the war between good and evil, evil usually has the better hiding places.

"What next?" Owen jokes with a grin. "Seems too early to call it a night."

Laughs all around. Exhausted but contented laughs.

"You mind taking Leah a note for me?" I ask.

"Hell no." Owen smiles. "Let me have it."

"It needs to get to her tonight."

"You betcha."

From my shirt pocket, I pull out the small patch of wedding photograph which shows Leah in the background. "Anybody got something to write with?" I ask.

"I do!" Anjuli, squirming happily, digs a pencil stub out of her skintight jeans which everyone finds surprising until she explains that you absolutely never know when a guy will ask you for your contact information.

And, on the back of the torn photograph, I write the note which I hope will make everything okay.

Hours later, as Cascade Drive is being deservedly plowed under by Kelli's road gang, we find ourselves staring into a small bonfire jointly made in a far corner of the property. Our cars are already down at the bottom of the drive. Besides Owen's truck which is hauling its gargantuan concrete Centaur, we have two other carloads packed and ready to go in those vehicles belonging to Shannon and Dylan. One is filled with my kids' stuffed animals and their other toys, the small things that have huge meaning because they were once held in little hands. The other holds the monastic contents of my attic room, more wreckage and residue from the life of Rick Lang, the Midnight Rider.

Kelli had years to plan for this magical day... so it is no surprise when I later discover that Matt Swift Junior was arrested and jailed within hours of the Absolute Proof's appearance.

Matt "Gary" Inagaki was also fated for arrest that night. Perhaps Dylan may have tipped him off by canceling their usual Friday night karaoke date with a hurt and curt and not very cryptic message. But in any case, Gary vanished without a trace, taking his Akita dogs with him but thoughtfully leaving behind his ornate Marriage Box upon which a note of apology to the Secret Society was found.

Perhaps I should have been more immediately curious to the fates and fortunes of all those who tried to play us for fools. But helping Kelli was always secondary to what really mattered. And the very second that the Absolute Proof was placed in Kelli's hands, I ceased to think of anything but the only thing.

The real thing.

# CHAPTER TWENTY·FIVE

SEVENTEEN YEARS LATE TO THE FEAST, I AM NOW EAGERLY WAITING FOR HER AT THE EXACT SPOT where we met. I have cordoned off a ten-foot by ten-foot patch of ground with the use of broken shards of flooring as a perimeter. The eight-thousand square foot house which was never a home is now a spectacular site, a jagged plow-under which has left a massive half-acre of broken wood. Some will no doubt consider my actions insane (and possibly litigious, given the neighbors). But my sanity seems not in question for those hundreds of red-winged blackbirds who fly in red-dotted swirls around this sacked and salt-strewn Carthage, alighting in the still-vibrant adjacent foliage and whistling clearly and brightly across today's unrelentingly fresh and sunny breeze.

On the carefully torn photograph which Owen successfully, according to his clandestine intelligence, delivered to Leah sometime after midnight, I had penciled an "X" to mark the exact spot on Cascade Drive's elegant and sloping gradient of a lawn where first we touched and where first we glimpsed the potential of a shared future. And on the photograph's back, I wrote a brief plea for this meeting, implicitly expressing my not-so-secret wish that if I build it (a dance floor of commitment), she will come.

Upon arriving at KHEL's Studio A late last night, I avoided Righteous Ray Jefferson who has been sitting in my time slot at Studio B for weeks now, manning my phone lines and fielding my listeners' calls for action, listening to their revelations and crises. I also hid my presence from my studio team, Kimberly and Bridget, to whom explanations would have become immediately chaotic; it is enough that Dylan informed them I am fine and will return in due course. Instead I showered in Studio A's extravagant bathroom, slept dreamlessly, showered again, and having rescued a suit and tie (if I have the IQ and the EQ, why not the GQ), I am thus dressed old school first-date sharp.

My only visitor last night was Duke Jackson, Maestro of the Boom Boom Room's multi-track digital recorder which preserves every stage performance. My "Ain't Nothing Like The Real Thing" duet with Leah had been recorded on multiple tracks. Now, as an ultimate favor to be paid forward as Duke has requested, he has made magic of that moment by using ProTools at the Boom Boom Room's in house studio to trick out and masterfully re-mix Leah's hot source material. And he has further done the impossible by sweetening my resonant but hardly-tuneful voice so it actually *smokes* underneath Leah's vocals, making me sound a bit like Leonard Cohen crossed with Usher, an unlikely outcome which proves beyond doubt Duke Jackson's brilliance at the wheel.

Leah is not one to be fashionably late when lives are on the line, especially when those lives are our lives. I hear her car angle up the steep drive five minutes before the hour. It pulls into the cobblestone circle and pauses in front of the ruins.

I stand inside my cordoned-off space and wait anxiously. And I'm still nervous as she gets out of her car and I see her head swivel to take in the remains of Cascade Drive.

But then suddenly I'm no longer nervous as I see her walk toward me slowly, crossing the one hundred yards which still keep us apart. It's partially her smile which puts me at ease, a variation so lovely that I feel an adrenalized happiness and exhilaration.

But most of all I am no longer nervous because every question is now answered; she is not just approaching the spot I had marked on the photo with an "X" as asked, she is unexpectedly wearing the very same cherry red dress which also appeared in the photo, the one she wore here seventeen years ago, which for some breathtaking reason she has kept all these years.

Leah grins as she steps carefully over my make-shift border. The sun shines a little through her dress but it shines completely through my body, igniting my soul, I am undone, I am hers.

"You didn't have to tear it down just to make your point..." She indicates the rubble. She is joking but in a way she is not joking. If there was any doubt left in her mind that Paige was still an issue, I have symbolically nuked it to smithereens.

"Yes, I did."

"And this is the exact spot where we met."

"According to my romance-o-meter."

Her eyes twinkle. She moves very close to me. "You look good."

"So do you. You kept the dress..."

"I'm way too nostalgic. It's your fault."

"What's my fault?"

"Whenever I wore it, for years afterwards, I thought of you. So I stopped wearing it." She pauses to correct herself. "Except once or twice... at home... feeling sorry for myself. You know, after a few drinks..." She reacts to my look. "Hey, every woman needs an old favorite to cheer her up, right? I should have given it away long ago."

"And let someone else wear it? You're not very nostalgic after all."

"It's size *seven*. I can hardly breathe..."

"It doesn't look that tight," I say.

"You lie. But you're sweet. It's also too short even for me. I'm forty. It's time to trade hotness for dignity."

"If it's that tight, why don't you just take it off?"

"All in good time, mister."

That said I draw her to me, press her against me, her lips. I taste the warmth of her tongue, I breathe the scent of her, especially the scent of her: it's all perfect. My fingertips glide along the length of her back, I can feel the heat of her bare legs against my skin, her hair begins to move in slowing motion and it brushes against my face gently back and forth like a soft curtain. But the romance-o-meter is still ticking and so I tear myself away.

"Put yourself on pause. Just for a second. Check this out." I take the remote control from my pocket and presto!

Hidden speakers roar to life and Leah hears "Ain't Nothing Like The Real Thing" as reinvented by the Duke. I watch her face, the intense pleasure in her expression as she reacts. Her eyes sparkle and her smile spreads from the corners of her mouth until, as I once remember it being described by some brilliant writer, they are an unimportant distance from her ears.

We start to dance on our square patch, slow dance, slow rocking, slow swaying, slow-turning but the tempo is slightly too upbeat for that so we slow-swing and faster-slide, and whirl right to left and swoop up and down.

It is all joy in this land of not-make-believe. The music ends but Leah wants to hear it again. And so we do.

"Nice work. It appears I *am* one sultry songstress. And you, Rick Lang, are one red hot boyfriend."

I ponder the word. "Boyfriend sounds a little strange... being honest..."

She reaches into her small clutch, pulls out a thin gold ring, puts it in front of one eye and impishly peers through it. "Well, you *could* marry me."

Wherever love never sleeps, alertness should be maintained. Leah, always so unexpected, trustworthy but tricky. I must have involuntarily jumped, startled, and her amusement is all radiance.

"For real?" I say, surely sounding brilliantly clueless.

"Duh." She continues to hold it up in the air, presenting it on her palm like a jewelry pitch model on cable TV. "It can be yours if you say the magic word..."

I am speechless. I suppose I was expecting a lot of talking. And crying. Maybe even some gnashing of teeth. But Leah knew it wouldn't be necessary.

It is what it is.

She continues. "Plus. There's a bonus! The kids gave me their blessing! That is, on condition that you spend some quality time with them and soon! Oh, and bring those free sports tickets. Otherwise I didn't even have to bribe them!"

I clearly am speechless too long for Leah's taste. "Look…" She puts on her Scottish accent. "…dae ye want tae marry me ur nae, laddie?"

"Hang on! Hang on! I've got something for you." I reply.

"Stalling, are we? Caught in a sticky wicket, are we?"

Pretending to ignore her, I walk to the far end of my man-made square of lawn. There I grab a trowel and make a show out of digging up a patch of grass. "Since we're cutting right to the chase…let me unearth *my* absolute proof, here found hidden cleverly in this time capsule of love!" I bend down and pick up the small velvet box I had concealed there. I walk it back to her, place it in her left hand, as her right hand still grasps her gold ring.

"Oh." Leah ponders the box.

"Duuuh." I deliberately draw out the syllable.

"Nicely played."

"Thank you." I reply. "May I open it for you?"

As it rests in Leah's palm, I open it for her. I had purchased a gold ankle bracelet for her on my way here this morning. Nothing fancy, but she eyes it with approval.

"Just as good."

"It's an upgrade over the old one I won for you at the county fair. This one won't turn your skin green."

"No, no, that's *never* coming off. We'll just add this one to the mix."

"May I?" I take it from her and kneel on the lawn beside her.

"Just don't look up my dress…"

"Why would I do that?" I joke.

"Why wouldn't you do that?"

Leah lifts her leg and balances one red shoe on my knee. I fasten the gold ankle bracelet next to the faux-silver county fair bracelet.

I straighten. She straightens.

"My answer is yes." I say as I take the ring from her other hand and peer through it, smiling just as she did. "Yes, please marry me. Yes, from here to heaven."

If I could describe Leah's reaction I would. But I can't.

An hour later we are in the very same company suite in the Pan-Pacific hotel where once upon a time a famous Twister game irrevocably changed our world. This time we are in the bedroom and the afternoon sun has lit up all the tall buildings beside us and we are just a little bathed in a rainbow of bronze and copper and silver and gold as the curtains have not been totally drawn.

I am naked although she is not; she has insisted on wearing her dress for the occasion, although strategically sacrificing her shoes for better flexibility. This Twister move has so far paid big dividends even though I have cleverly countered with my own surprise moves made possible by the fact her dress partially unbuttons down the front. We have been making love for twenty or thirty minutes as slowly as possible, not just because she's a woman who likes a slow hand but because we've turned out to be a perfect fit in every way and it is to be savored.

I have been behind her, beside her, and beneath her. But I have not yet been on top of her as I am saving that for a reason, one she has yet not guessed. Given seventeen years of abstinence from each other, I know our lovemaking will not be able to live up to all the many R & B songs in which the participants do it "all night long" or all week long or whatever. So as I start to feel her breathing quicken as if she can't find enough oxygen in the room and as I distinctly feel her hands grasping for anything, the headboard, my hair, *anything*, I know to flip her over gently and enter her the old fashioned way because when we come, I want to come while looking as deeply into her eyes as I possibly can.

Leah has already located my eyes with hers and just the sight of me and the sense of my intention causes her to thrust her hips up to meet mine with far more urgency. I continue to look into her eyes and she into mine and what we each see must be the biggest aphrodisiac on earth and all other planets combined because we begin to *let go*.

She starts to gasp as oxygen evades her and this time her hands find both my neck and the back of my head and, losing control, her fingers begin to tighten and claw without her being aware of it. Her leg muscles start to tense and, as I'm between her legs and moving in-and-out faster and faster, her legs begin to abrade my sides, squeezing. I am gazing into her soul-windows and what I see is an unconditional release of joy which seems to infuse my being. Leah's return gaze, on the other hand, has lost focus entirely; she looks dizzy and lightheaded and emotionally incoherent. I feel her abdomen tightening beneath me as she begins to come. She gasps and gasps and it feels like a wave to me as her orgasm shudders into full-blown motion, a wave which rolls down through her breasts, contorts her stomach, causing more shudders which convulse her sweet spot yet they don't stop there but seem to proceed down her thighs, her shins; I can feel her anklets jam into my ankles as one of her hands rakes across the back of my thigh pulling me deeper into her.

At the exact point when the wave sweeps past her abdomen, and the shudders begin, I join her orgasm. And I ride her wave, coming and coming inside her. My eyes have never left her eyes and it doesn't occur to me until after her toes have twitched and curled and twitched some more that I have just come like a cannon inside her, the first time I have really trusted a woman enough to do so. And *that* is enough to make me melt, not in a soft way, but in a dazzling way because I am entirely bedazzled by her love for me, my love for her, and the smile she smiles as her eyes finally re-focus on mine, a smile which is both playful yet very, very peaceful.

# EPILOGUE · AUGUST 2011

**W**E ARE STILL A SECRET SOCIETY, BUT EVEN LESS SECRET THESE DAYS, AND THIS YEAR WE HAVE decided to bring our 29th annual birthday party to New York City — where Leah and I have been living for over six years now – in order to celebrate in our usual chaotic signature style. This change of venue is a break in tradition but it's time to shake things up as this year we each turn fifty, one by one, in the same month as always, as noisy as ever in our gleeful sweet-dangerous way. We will not go quietly into that good night despite the fact that we are still tumbling through life like crooked dice. Still single, still divorced, some married, and despite all odds we have managed to gather a little wisdom along the way so some answers have been discovered.

Here at the large circular table in the private dining room which serves the Rider Foundation, everyone seems to be enjoying the novelty of seeing New York's bright lights from the 65th floor. Drinks and dinner glow with warmth and friendship despite the usual barbs and banter which hit hard and go for the throat as is our relentless tradition. This year it is Kelli's daughter Whitney's first opportunity to host the Annual Secret Society Game and given she is only eight years old and the first of a new generation of Secret Society members, we are anticipating disaster and embarrassment and multicolored splatter as paintballs are rumored to be involved (although thankfully not paintball guns). Being a fifty year old may be a slight disadvantage these days, but we all still pack a good punch, especially Leah whose hands are always the steadiest, given her long hours at New York Presbyterian where she is top gun on the East River at the Hospital for Special Surgery.

Dylan is cocky as usual. "Whitney, I don't want to you to be upset when I kick your butt. I've won the last three years in a row."

"Yeah, but Rick says you're an awesome cheater."

"Not true." Dylan grumbles. "I've got the luck of the Irish, that's all."

Leah laughs. "Brace yourself. Whitney's going to win fair and square."

"Yeah," adds Whitney. "I am. Because you're old and slow and I've got killer instinct."

"Brava!" Leah applauds, joined by Anjuli, Shannon, and Owen. Whitney, born in August 2003, is the newest member of our August Whatever Secret Society and our youngest, but she is bright and tough like her mother and I expect Dylan will have a hard time trying to keep his bogus record intact.

Kelli's loss of virginity, made immediately possible after the disinheritance of her brother and the resolution of her father's trust, resulted in a quick pregnancy; but as her first lover was well chosen, marriage and two children followed. She and I spend each working day together as the Rider Foundation always has its hands full. True to her word, her exponentially growing fortune has become a force for good in this world. But neither of us anticipated such inspired widespread greed and global manipulation, not to mention all the other endless obstacles offered to those who dare to attempt enforcement of positive change in a culture which doesn't reward victories for humanity as briskly as it does creators of inventive financial products.

Although I now command more than a dozen major special interest armies which operate as change agents all over the globe, social networking has appropriately absorbed the Midnight Riders. Facebook has been a marvel for better interpersonal connection in the Midnight Rider tradition despite its Big Brother collection of personal info which can't help but make one uneasy. Twitter, despite some self-indulgent excess, is showing greater and greater promise as it functions in real time and a few fantastic and impactful group actions on a major scale have made this graying Midnight Rider proud. Having a foundation isn't quite as fun as operating out of a dilapidated radio station in Oakland but I'm still living the life I sing about in my song.

"Who cares who wins the Annual Game?" Anjuli's ringlets are being twisted furiously by her agitated fingers. "I've got tickets to Yankee Stadium for everyone who wants to come with us tomorrow. Harrison got us into one of the luxury suites." Harrison is Anjuli's husband, patronizing toward the Secret Society as befits someone with admirable seriousness. Anjuli's husband is a dozen years her elder and our retired curly-haired vixen now has grown stepchildren; one of her stepsons now drives her fully pimped-out "Fly Me" red Miata and apparently that young dude is quite the player.

"No can do, Anjuli." Owen is adamant. "Shannon and I are planning to spend the whole week getting culture."

Shannon nods to confirm. "Owen discovered the amazing underground darts culture of Manhattan. We'll finally have some real competition."

"Yeah," interrupts Owen. "But the trade-off is I gotta do an opera and *two* ballets because whatever Shannon wants Shannon gets."

Actually Shannon even now doesn't know what she wants. Still single, happy to have long ago given up dating, she is nearly at her goal of becoming one of the most high profile communications and media specialists in the country. She works with a long list of universities and hospitals; she helps the high-and-mighty of the fashion and entertainment industries. Her experience with the law offices of Matthew Moss (currently serving time in Club Fed for various unrelated-to-us white collar crimes) soured her on most corporate dealings. Although Shannon and I see each other only fitfully, we call often and talk into the night, although our topics now seem so much more positive and emotionally satisfying, the dark days are over.

"Forget ballet!" Whitney intones precociously. "I want you old people to *witness the majesty of my bucket of doom!*" With that, Whitney does indeed unveil her bucket of paint balls and places them with great pomp and circumstance in the center of the table much in the formal manner Gary displayed when revealing his Marriage Box a decade ago. Gary's postcards, I must mention in passing, have become a regular newsy treat for one and all. He is still on the run and, alas, appears to still be plying his trade as con artiste extraordinaire. But he did find time to get married at the Elvis chapel in Las Vegas to Callista, his erstwhile pickpocket girlfriend (that particular post card sent to the entire Society, puckishly reminding us that his Marriage Game continues to weave its magic).

"I'll take any ticket you don't want, Owen." Leah is pleased at the thought.

"My ballet ticket is your ballet ticket," replies Owen, getting a dirty look from Shannon. "Besides, Rick's gonna show me this TV and Radio Museum. I've heard they might have an extra-good comprehensive collection of machine-age radios."

"And I'm making dinner for one and all tomorrow night!" Leah reacts to our dejected faces, annoyed. "And not only that, you will eat what I cook!"

"I'm looking forward to it," replies Owen. "And I promise you that everyone here will pretend to like whatever you serve up..."

Owen married briefly, a woman he met in New Orleans during the months he worked as a volunteer after Hurricane Katrina. It was an unhappy marriage and I had to come to his rescue; he was too naïve to understand what a gold-digger was because he'd been poor most of his life. But the two million dollars which Owen accepted (as did Anjuli, and Dylan) from Kelli as compensation for their manipulation by her half-brother wasn't quite the game-changer he'd anticipated. His divorce was costly. He bought his new Marin County home at the height of the real estate bubble and later had to walk away from foreclosure. His first genuine investment portfolio unfairly suffered from having been administered by one boy genius after another at the failed firms of Bear Stearns and Lehman Brothers. Now he's fifty and unemployed. But he is unfazed. Not everyone gets a happy ending just because they're nice people, he'll be the first to tell you that. He'll find something. Besides, as he says, he has a wealth of friendship.

Dylan eyes the bucket of paintballs and suddenly gets to his feet. "Society vote! I will give Whitney five dollars for the right to throw first!"

"Is that fair?" Whitney's confusion causes the Secret Society to burst into loud and furious debate as, no doubt, Dylan had intended.

Dylan's use of Kelli's bounty was better spent. He is now remarried to his third wife, and was able to put all three of his sons through college. But there are some things money can't buy. Like his ability to turn a whole table of birthday celebrants into a pack of abusive name-callers. Whitney has climbed atop her chair, a paintball in each hand. It is time to escape.

Leah and I find blessed quiet and privacy in my office which is only as large as needed and definitely not a corner office; the urban canyons of New York City are still a daunting distraction to the man who came of age in a small dark radio station in Oakland, California. On one wall I have photographs of my friends when we were less obviously, as Whitney pointed out with the natural swagger of youth, *old people*. On the opposite wall, is a small framed American flag which was unnecessarily awarded to me by the mayor of New York for services rendered. Leah really was the one who deserved it.

Although we didn't know it at the time, Leah and I had only nine days to make love and talk about our future together. We had only nine exquisite days and nights together to hope and dream and plan. I knew all the losses in my life would be part of my inner landscape until the end of my time on earth. But for nine nights and days I felt a new kind of faith. We started talking almost immediately about having a child together. She wanted to have my child, to help raise our child, to love and help protect and care for our child. And I wanted her to be the mother of my child, the co-author of my child's future, and the forever love of my life.

But on our ninth day as a tried-and-true couple, things changed.

September 11th, 2001 was a Tuesday. We flew into New York on that Friday. Leah, thinking her trauma surgeon's skills might be useful at Ground Zero, ended up sifting rubble with the 9/11 first responders. I did mobile broadcasts at our New York affiliate. Her advice as a trauma surgeon proved sadly underutilized as there were so many dead and so few injuries to which she could apply her expertise as a consultant. I did what I could, working on air, but I simply couldn't make enough of a difference because this disaster was too incomprehensible and the situation too helpless for my Midnight Riders. Leah's impulsive decision to volunteer in the initial search for survivors at Ground Zero also made Leah sick for awhile. Thus, although I was proud to help Leah's twins successfully launch into young manhood, we never were able to have a child of our own.

Behind my desk hangs a very large white, red, and green flag. The walking bear, the single star, the words California Republic. It flew above KHEL Oakland during the many years I worked there. I had it sent to me after Leah and I made the decision to permanently move east. I see that Leah is looking at it longingly.

"Are you in the mood for the official ritual?" I ask her.

"Thought you'd never ask." She responds with a grin. "Thought maybe you'd lost your nerve."

"Not hardly. I can still stand and deliver."

"That's something only a wife can judge with complete objectivity."

We married nine years ago. The ceremony was charming, the reception less so. Dylan was the wedding singer; he insisted on performing the song for our first dance. We asked for Marvin Gaye's *It Takes Two*; we got Michael Jackson's *Thriller* with a moon walk. Anjuli, then still unmarried, tried unceasingly to seduce the wedding photographer; strange camera angles dominate our wedding album. Owen got plastered and toasted the bride and groom as if they were Centaurs which was okay, I guess, but Shannon kicked him so he'd shut up and her stiletto heel drew blood, five stitches. Unfortunately Anjuli *didn't* try to distract the videographer; there was a food fight at the reception which really wasn't cool but years later got uploaded as a YouTube video, one of the first to go viral. All and all, though, it was a beautiful and special day. The Secret Society devised a memorable collective wedding gift. A plaid quilt with a "Twister" border. Truly hideous to look at. But later quite perfect for making love on the roof of our converted carriage house in the West Village.

For those who wish to know the final results of the Marriage Game:

#1 Dylan married 3rd in 2003.

#2 Anjuli married 4th in 2004

#3 Owen married 5th in 2006 (since divorced)

#4 Gary married 6th in 2007

#5 Leah married 1st (tie) in 2002

#6 Rick married 1st (tie) in 2002

#7 Shannon remained unmarried.

Not quite perfect. Just like the Secret Society itself.

Leah and I walk behind my desk and stand before the California flag. I turn the lights off so only the ambient light from the adjacent softly-lit hallway illuminates the room.

"Who wants to start?" Leah asks.

"It's a ritual. Don't mess with tradition. *You* always start."

Tall as she is, Leah has to get up on tiptoes to kiss the California Bear. Then, reluctantly, but as required, I kiss the bear. That accomplished, now *we* get to kiss. As much as we like. For as long as we like. Why does she kiss the bear first? Why do I have to kiss the bear at all? True, it's a stupid ritual but it's ours alone. Neither of us can remember who started it.

But sometimes you get homesick. Must have been one of those nights.

### THE END

www.ingramcontent.com/pod-product-compliance
Lightning Source LLC
Chambersburg PA
CBHW070847250626
47159CB00003B/971